DARKEST JOURNEY

Also by HEATHER GRAHAM

HEATHER GRAHAM

DARKEST JOURNEY

MIRA®

ISBN-13: 978-1-68331-223-9

Darkest Journey

For questions and comments about the quality of this book, please contact us at
CustomerService@Harlequin.com.

Printed in U.S.A.

In memory of one of the finest friends I was ever
privileged to know.
Greg Varricchio
Incredible musician, husband and father, Greg
made hard times easier, brought laughter and smiles
to so many so often,
and lived every day with honor and an incredible ethic.
The world is truly a poorer place without him.

CAST OF CHARACTERS

The Main Players

Charlene "Charlie" Moreau, actress
Ethan Delaney, FBI agent, Krewe of Hunters

From the Movie Set

Brad Thornton, writer and director
Mike Thornton, cameraman
Luke Mayfield, sound
Barry Seymour, electric and lighting
Jennie McPherson, makeup artist
Grant Ferguson, actor/extra (responsible for budget and accounting)
George Gonzales, in charge of location, setting and props
Jimmy Smith, actor/extra
Blane Pica, actor
Harry Grayson, actor

Krewe of Hunters

Thor Erikson
Jude McCoy

The Civil War Dead

Anson McKee, Confederate cavalry captain
Ellsworth Derue, Union medical corps

Other Characters

Jonathan Moreau, Charlie's father, historian and tour guide
on the riverboat *Journey*

Emily Watson, café owner

Farrell Hickory, owner of Hickory Plantation
and Civil War reenactor

Albion Corley, professor and Civil War reenactor

Nancy Camp, Charlie's high school friend

Randall "Randy" Laurent, high school friend of Ethan's,
parish detective

Sherry Compton, high school friend

Terese, Ethan's great-grandmother

Chance Morgan, photographer

On the *Journey* (Celtic American Lines Ship)

Timothy Banks, captain

Gerard "Gerry" Amerind, doctor

Haley Howell, nurse

Rebecca Jennings, nurse

Ricky Simpson, entertainment director

DARKEST JOURNEY

Prologue

West Feliciana Parish, Louisiana
High School

"What are we doing?" Charlene—Charlie—Moreau demanded, surprised that both her escorts—senior girls high up in the hierarchy of one of their high school service clubs, the Cherubs—had suddenly taken hold of her arms. "Where are we going?"

She'd started out blindfolded in a car with five of her friends—all of them giggling girls ready to claim the prestige of being a Cherub. They'd been accepted into the club. They'd gone through ridiculous weeks of pledging—running, fetching, even doing homework for the "older sisters" in the club, and now it was their final night. Their great hazing. But the five of them had been split up about twenty minutes earlier; she'd been put in a car with Nancy Deauville and Sherry Compton, who'd gently led her out a little while later.

Now both girls were gripping her arms, nothing gentle about it.

Nancy Deauville laughed softly. "They say your

mama's family has the 'sight.' We're just leaving you where you'll have to ask some of your ghostly friends for help."

"Come on! What are you going to do? Tie me up in the Grace Church graveyard?" Charlie asked, feeling her temper flare.

"Oh, Charlie, no!" Nancy said.

Sherry giggled. "We're tying you up *outside* the graveyard—in the unhallowed section."

"That's ridiculous. And dangerous," Charlie said angrily, a spark of fear entering her. "Three girls have been killed close to here, just north of Baton Rouge!" Her mom had been emphatic about her being careful, about her staying in the company of friends. A serial killer was at work in and around Baton Rouge.

"Don't be alone, Charlie," her mom had warned sternly. "He's preying on young women who are on their own. Make sure you stay with your friends."

Charlie had thought these people *were* her friends. Now she wasn't so sure.

She tried to wrench free, but someone stronger had her arms now, and she heard multiple footsteps nearby.

Nancy and Sherry weren't alone. They'd met up with others.

The two were superrich brats whose dads held great positions with one of the local oil companies—while her dad was a hardworking historian!

She didn't know why she was pledging anyway, except that Cathy Corcoran, her best friend, had insisted that they at least try. The Cherubs were respected at school, plus they had the best parties.

Charlie had managed to handle the weeks of doing what the older girls asked. She'd even shocked Nancy, dropping a pack of cigarettes on her lap after the other girl had demanded that she get them, even if she had to beg, borrow or steal them. Charlie hadn't had to do any of those things; someone on one of her dad's tours had left a pack behind on the dock.

But this…

She didn't tend to be scared of much. Tonight, she was.

She wasn't afraid of the graveyard. She never had been. But girls had been murdered—and not at all far away.

She was angry now, and that anger mixed uneasily with a fear that had nothing to do with the dead.

"You know what? Don't bother. I don't want to be in your club," she said. "This is ridiculous. Where are Cathy and the others?"

"Cathy is taking a little swim," Nancy said, and laughed.

Charlie felt her temper flare another few degrees. Cathy couldn't swim—and she was terrified of water.

"That's it. Let me go," Charlie said. "I'm done with you and your stupid club."

They didn't let her go. She heard a male voice whispering—probably Todd Camp, Nancy's football-star boyfriend. Or maybe it wasn't Todd. At least three other people had joined Nancy and Sherry; she could tell where they were all standing by listening to where their voices came from. All told, there were at least five peo-

ple there, probably including some of Todd's football
goon friends.

"We should just let her go. Come on, Nance."

Todd was there, Charlie was certain. But he wasn't
the one who had just spoken. Todd did anything that
Nancy said. Probably—as Charlie had heard whispered
in the hallways—Nancy only "gave it up" for Todd when
he behaved.

"Listen to whichever of your juvenile delinquent
friends was just speaking. This is criminal. You should
let me go this instant," Charlie said.

"No way, so shut up, you whiny pledge. You'll be
glad when we come back for you. Everyone wants to be
a Cherub, and tomorrow you'll be glad you didn't chicken
out," Nancy said.

Someone approached her and whispered into her ear.
She recognized the voice. It was a friend. Jimmy Smith.
"Charlie," Jimmy said urgently, "it won't be that long.
Tomorrow you really will want to be in the club. I'm
so sorry, but just go with this, okay?"

"I do not want to be a Cherub," she yelled—and meant
it. "I will *never* be a Cherub. You are the most imma-
ture group of brats I've met in my entire life. Let me go!"

"Chicken!" Nancy laughed.

Charlie was strong; she worked out in the dance
troupe and was also on the gymnastics team. She could
have easily taken Nancy and Sherry.

But the two girls weren't alone, and whoever was
holding her now was stronger than she was. Her captor
forced her down to the ground, and someone tied her

wrists and ankles around something cold and hard. A tombstone, she thought.

"Assholes!" she hissed, struggling against the ropes that held her.

"Watch your tongue, pledge," Nancy snapped. "Or you won't get to be a Cherub."

"Don't you get it? I don't want to be in your damn club!" Charlie shot back.

"Maybe we should just let her go," she heard Jimmy plead.

"Shut up! You're ruining my speech," Nancy said. "Oh, pledge. May all cherubs and angels everywhere look over you this night. For you are not in the sacred graveyard of the church but in the unhallowed ground beyond, where criminals—hanged for their sins—lie, where many a Yankee was hidden in the earth, where the most evil among us rest uneasily for all eternity. But you, should you survive the hours ahead, will rise triumphant, a Cherub for all time," Nancy said dramatically.

Charlie's blindfold was slipping; from where she lay she could just see Nancy's arms upstretched to the night sky. She was wearing her cheerleading uniform, which seemed to be a disservice to the entire school at that moment.

Nancy's arms dropped, and she turned, presumably to face the others. "Let's get the hell out of here. This place gives me the creeps."

"Damn you all!" Charlie swore. "Let me up! I don't want to be one of you stupid people."

Her words did no good. Laughing, the group hurriedly left, heading back to Nancy's car and whatever vehicle Todd and the others had come in.

She screamed for a few minutes more—to no avail. Still, it made her feel better, and she realized she was at least ridding herself of the blindfold. It was just a piece of white cotton, probably someone's ripped-up shirt.

She fell silent and worked harder at the blindfold. Eventually she dislodged it by rubbing her head back and forth against the headstone she was bound to. It finally came unknotted and fell down by her side. She laughed bitterly. Nancy and her crew weren't even capable of tying a decent knot.

The boys were, though. She couldn't dislodge the ropes around her wrists and ankles, which were secured tightly against the tombstone.

She let out a sigh, reminding herself that she wasn't afraid of a graveyard. Even an unhallowed one. Her father had brought her here many times and told her of the injustices that had been perpetrated over the years. The townspeople had strung up an innocent slave instead of admitting to the guilt of a rich white man who had raped and strangled a young woman in the 1830s. His grave was unmarked. A horse thief—who was admittedly guilty but hadn't killed anyone—was strung up in 1860. Apparently horse theft had been a major crime back then, since horses were needed for the militia units forming in the lead-up to the Civil War.

Charlie closed her eyes for a minute. She could hear the river—the mighty Mississippi—churning far below the bluff. She could hear tree branches swaying, the leaves rustling. She opened her eyes. Even though this was unhallowed ground, loved ones of those long gone had erected stones and monuments to mark their graves. A broken-winged angel looked mournfully down at her from a pedestal. Tombs and all manner of funerary art graced the area, some of it half-hidden by overgrown grass and shrubbery.

Time passed as she continued to fight with the ropes that bound her. She cursed out loud and then quietly to herself. She prayed that Cathy—who was truly terrified of water—was going to be all right.

Then she heard the sobbing.

"Hey!" she called out.

There was no reply. She inhaled, then let her breath out in a rush.

Yes, her family often saw ghosts or just felt their invisible presence. She'd known that Uncle Jessup had come to his own funeral; she'd seen him stroking her mother's hair, as if trying to assure her that he was all right.

She wasn't at all sure she was ready to see a ghost tonight, though, not while she was tied to a tombstone. Especially not here on unhallowed ground. Some of the people buried had been truly evil. There was even rumor that a vicious voodoo queen—a woman who had poisoned a number of people—had been brought out here, hanged and left to rot, then buried with no marker. It might only be a tale meant to scare away couples who liked to come to the cemetery and drink among the old tombstones, maybe do drugs or have sex…whatever.

She wished she could see her watch. She felt as if she'd already been there for hours.

More likely it had only been thirty minutes or so. Maybe she had imagined the sobbing.

No, she hadn't.

Because the sound came again. She blinked hard. A young woman seemed to be materializing right in front of her, just to the left by the base of an old moss-draped oak tree. The woman's hair was swept up, and she was wearing a pretty blue gown. For a moment Charlie thought that she had come from a different era in history, but then she realized that the blue dress was a beautiful and entirely contemporary formal gown. The woman bent down; she looked like she was trying to pick something up.

But she couldn't. Whatever it was, it slipped through her ethereal fingers.

The woman seemed to sink against the tree and down to the ground.

And then she disappeared.

Charlie watched for a moment, then hung her own head.

Time was passing. Someone would come for her.

She looked up and blinked.

A Confederate soldier was walking toward her. He wore a frock coat lined in a yellow-buff color.

Cavalry. And an officer. She couldn't be her father's daughter and not know that.

He wore a handsome plumed hat, and his sword was encased in a sheath belted around his hips.

She closed her eyes, wondering what a Southern soldier had done to end up buried out here.

Please, please go away, she thought. Because she was afraid. The air here on top of the bluff was growing chilly in the dark, and she still felt as if she could hear—in her head, at least—the soft sound of sobbing.

The cavalryman was still walking toward her.

Screw the damned club. What an idiot she'd been.

"Don't worry, I'm going to help you."

At first she thought it was the ghostly Confederate who had spoken. But it wasn't. It was someone made of flesh and blood, someone real, and that realization startled her so badly that she let out a horrified scream.

"Hey, hey, hey," he protested, stepping closer and starting to work at the ropes that bound her. "It's all right. I'm Ethan Delaney. I'm here to help you."

She blinked. *Ethan Delaney.* She knew him, even if she didn't know him well. His father was a teacher and had recently taken a job at a music school in New Orleans. His mother taught piano. Ethan had graduated soon after she'd gotten to high school; he was three years her senior. She'd really only seen him from afar. When she'd been about eight or nine, he'd gotten stuck babysitting for her and some other kids because their parents were all friends.

What she knew about Ethan—what everyone knew about him—was that he was considered special, but not in a bad way. In a good way, in fact. He'd excelled at sports and qualified for scholarships at a bunch of schools. He'd ridden a motorcycle—when he hadn't been riding around on Devil, his dad's big buckskin quarter horse. People nodded when they heard his name and said things like *That boy's gonna make something of himself.*

He'd been gone from town for a while now. Gone off to college in New Orleans. Soon his parents would move to New Orleans, too, and there would be little reason for him to come back to town.

But—amazingly—he was here now and about to free her from her misery.

"Ethan. Delaney," she said, still not entirely sure that he wasn't an apparition. She hadn't seen him coming; she'd been distracted by the Confederate soldier just in front of him.

She stared as he kept working at the ropes. She could smell him, and he smelled good. He'd been riding earlier, she thought. He smelled of leather. He leaned back, focusing on one of the knots. She watched him as he concentrated. He had cool eyes. They were a golden green color. He was tanned. He had a lean face, and a thick strand of dark hair fell over one eye.

He was gorgeous.

She wasn't in his league.

But here he was, helping her.

"Thank you," she managed to say.

"How the hell did you get here?" he asked.

"Pledging," she told him.

"Stupid."

"I know. I told them I'd had it, I didn't want to be in their presence, much less their club," Charlie said, her voice tight. "They didn't listen."

"I see that."

She was suddenly freed, and immediately she tried to stand. Her legs wobbled, and he reached out to steady her. She looked up.

Suddenly she was in love.

She couldn't let him see it.

Charlie cleared her throat and fought to quickly maintain her balance on her own as she forced a smile to her lips.

"Thank you, Ethan. I owe you big-time."

"It was nothing…" He hesitated. "Nothing at all."

He doesn't even know my name.

Their parents were friends; he'd been to her house. But had he ever thought of her as anything other than a little kid? Did he even recognize her?

He was smiling at her. "Listen, I walked here. I don't have a car. But when we get back to my parents' old place—he's in NOLA, and Mom is there picking up stuff, 'cause she's in the middle of moving—I can use her car and drive you home."

"I hate to trouble you. I can walk home now that I'm not tied up, thanks to you."

His smile deepened. She noticed that he had a dimple in his chin. "I'm sorry, miss, but I was raised Southern, and my mama would probably still tan my hide if I didn't see you home safe."

He turned, holding her elbow—probably worried that she might trip on a gravestone, she thought.

"I have a name," she told him, sounding more strident than she'd meant to.

He stopped and looked down at her, that shock of hair still covering one of his eyes. "Of course. I'm so sorry. It's just that I don't know—"

"Charlie. Charlene, actually. Charlene Moreau."

Something flickered in his eyes. "Moreau. You used to hang at my house when you were little. Our parents are friends. Your dad is Jonathan Moreau, right?"

"Yes." She waited, afraid that somewhere along the line her father might have done something to bug him.

"Wow," he said with admiration. "He's brilliant. He knows more about local history and politics than anyone I've ever met."

"Yep, that's him."

"Come on, then. My mom can make you some tea or something, and then I'll take you home."

He started to walk, not holding on to her this time, and she followed. "How did you know I was here?" she asked him. "I mean, you don't seem the kind to be spending his Friday night hanging out at the graveyard."

He paused, his back to her.

"Was it the Confederate cavalryman?" she asked softly, not even worrying that if he hadn't seen the ghost he might think she was nuts. "Did he lead you here? If so, I wish I could thank him."

He turned then and stared at her. "You saw…a cavalry soldier?"

"I did," she said.

He studied her intently. Then he nodded slowly. She felt the intensity of his gold-green eyes. He'd heard exactly what she'd said, and he seemed to accept her words at face value.

"Best not to mention such things," he said simply, and started walking again.

And, once more, she followed. Except that the sobbing she'd heard earlier suddenly echoed in her mind again.

"Come on," he called back.

"Wait!" she said.

"What?"

"There was—there was someone there before. By the tree. Give me just a second."

She hurried over the tree roots, fallen branches and broken headstones that stood between her and the tree in question, hoping he noticed that she didn't need any help, even in rough terrain.

"There!" She saw something shiny in the grass and sank to her knees—her jeans were already filthy anyway—then parted the weeds and grass to reveal a bracelet. It was gold, with a single gold charm studded with what might have been a diamond or might have been glass.

Suddenly Ethan was there, too, down on his knees beside her, reaching curiously for the bracelet.

She picked it up and handed it to him. "A bracelet," she murmured, completely unnecessarily.

He looked up at her suddenly, those strange eyes of his intent on her. He flinched, staring at her.

"What? What is it?" she whispered.

He opened his hand. The bracelet lay on his palm, but she saw something else there, as well. Something gleaming and darker than the night.

"What is it?" she repeated.

"Blood," he said quietly.

Charlie didn't realize then that, for her, the night, along with the rest of her life, was just beginning.

1

West Feliciana Parish, Louisiana
Ten Years Later

They rose from the earth one by one, spectral shapes that slowly crept to the top of the high bluff where the church had long held dominion over the landscape. If a watcher blinked, they might have seemed like a part of the mist, they were so ethereal. And yet, seen with eyes open and focused, they were clearly real, soldiers rising from their graves, worn, war-weary, dirty, sweaty and exhausted, yet ready to stand and fight for what they believed to be right. Here in this narrow strip of Louisiana between Baton Rouge and Port Hudson, the Civil War had one day come to a halt, and thus the men who rose from the earth wore both tattered butternut and gray or Union blue. They had been good men all, fighting for what they believed to be just when death stopped their fighting, though not forever. They rose together now, for even at a time when the nation had been torn apart in tragic and horrific conflict, they had found moments of peace and friendship.

They were a ghost army, ragged and unearthly, chilling and terrifying shadows of vengeance in the moonlight.

Now they moved slowly in unearthly splendor, spectral shapes, faces hardened, joined together to protect the innocent and destroy evil.

Charlie Moreau kept running forward, through the mist and straight toward the ghostly apparitions. They were no threat to *her*; it was the men in pursuit behind her who threatened her with fatal danger, those men whom she had to escape. She brushed by the apparitions, feeling a cold mist against her flesh. And then she fell...

She heard screaming from the men pursuing her, who were now being stopped in their tracks by the ghostly Civil War soldiers who had risen in her defense. She rolled over, braced herself on an elbow and looked back, both fear and a glimmer of hope in her eyes.

"Cut!"

Brad Thornton, director of the movie, stood and smiled broadly, applauding. "Wonderful! Charlie, you're the perfect Dakota Ryan. The rest of you guys, you were everything you were supposed to be. All y'all, come on over here. You've got to see this footage. It's fantastic."

Charlie smiled and called back, "Great!" She was pleased to see how happy Brad was. He'd put everything into this, his heart, his soul and his best fund-raising efforts. Young, earnest—not to mention darkly good-looking—he was extremely professional and had done well in a tough business. Even so, he was still an independent filmmaker, so he needed every break he could get. She was happy to work with him as lead actress on his latest film.

Jimmy Smith, an extra who'd played one of the ghostly soldiers, reached a hand down to her. One of Charlie's best friends from both high school and the Tulane Department of Theater and Dance, he had a quick grin and shaggy hair, and his smile was warm. "Come on, Charlie. Sounds like this is one scene our mighty captain has decided he's gotten in one take."

"I'm kind of muddy—sorry," she apologized, happy to take his hand. He'd tried to help her on that horrible night long ago when the Cherubs had tied her up in the cemetery. He'd even cried as he'd apologized to her afterward. They'd stayed friends through everything, and she was glad to be working with him now.

Jimmy laughed. "And I'm a lovely mix of sweat and makeup and mud myself. We're both fine. Except they made me play a Yankee. That *was* the winning side, of course, but I doubt that mattered much to the men who died in battle, whether slowly and in pain or quickly, life snuffed out in an instant."

"I think most of them believed in what they were fighting for, other than the ones who fought because they'd been drafted and had no choice."

"All I know is I'm damned lucky I didn't opt to go into the military," Jimmy said, grimacing. "Whenever I see a reenactment, I shudder. Even when I'm part of one. I mean, those soldiers walked straight toward a line of people firing right at them. They had to know they could be hit by a bullet any minute, but they had to keep on walking."

"Never sure myself how people managed to do that," Charlie said. "We're playacting when we do a reenactment. I can't imagine what it must have been like for real. I can't imagine what it's like for the guys who go in the military today."

Suddenly she found herself thinking about Ethan Delaney. She knew that he'd gone into the service out of college.

Jimmy knocked at his ear. When she looked at him curiously, he said, "Just mud—I hope."

"No bugs," she assured him, studying the dirt caked on him from the ground where the "troops" had lain before rising. "Just mud."

"If only I didn't have to play a Yankee," he said, grinning.

"Remember the guy who played Robert E. Lee for the flashback scene?" Charlie asked. "His great-great-grandfather was a Union general. That's the biz. Around here, history is especially near and dear to us, that's all. Anyway, this movie is contemporary—these stupid shoes I'm running in are far *too* contemporary—but I love that the ghosts from both armies rise up to save the heroine from the bad guys."

"I like it that we get some of the soldiers' past, too. It's really sad, what with the captain killing himself," Jimmy said.

"The captain was fighting a terrible fever. He wasn't in his right mind. I forget the statistics—my dad could tell you—but more soldiers died of sickness and infection than gunshot, cannon fire or bayonet."

"I know—I've played a surgeon in a few reenactments."

"Oh, yeah. Nurse Moreau, here," Charlie said. "I think that's why people keep coming to reenactments, because of the human side of war. I mean, the generals who fought each other were often friends—some of them had studied together at West Point—or even family. No matter how you look at it, the Civil War was probably the most heartbreaking era in this country's history. I'm so happy we didn't live back then."

Jimmy grinned. "I agree, and I actually love the point Brad is making with this movie. You know, that people are people, flesh and blood, beating hearts, the same desire to find love and happiness. There may be a constant tug-of-war between environmentalists and oil companies, but I love how he doesn't make everything black or white."

"I love Brad's script, too, especially the way he shows how the Confederate and Union soldiers found common ground before they died, and then their ghosts work together to save me from being killed."

Jimmy's grin disappeared. "Speaking of which, did you hear about the murder?"

"What murder?" Charlie said. "When?" She'd been in bed early the night before, because her call that morning had been at the crack of dawn, so they could film the just-completed scene when she'd confronted an oil exec and a state senator after discovering the oil exec had bribed the senator to let him drill where his efforts would destroy the water source for their fictional town of Mary Elizabeth. That had led to tonight's scene, with her on the run from an oil exec and a crooked senator.

She hadn't seen any news before bed, and she hadn't had time to catch any that morning, either.

"They haven't said what happened yet. Only that a man was murdered. He was from Baton Rouge, and I feel like we might know him, because he was a reenactor, too. His name was Albion Corley. A nice guy, they said on the news."

The name sounded vaguely familiar to Charlie. She wasn't sure why. Maybe he'd been someone she'd met through her father, who was often brought on as a consultant for the local reenactments.

"Where did it happen?" Charlie asked. "Was it anywhere near here?"

"Between here and Port Hudson. His body was found just outside an old family cemetery, poorly buried under less than a foot of earth."

"How awful," Charlie said, genuinely dismayed. This was a small, close-knit area. The population of St. Francisville was under two thousand. They were just over thirty miles north of Baton Rouge. Of course, the population there was growing and spreading out. Still, murder wasn't common around here.

Ten years ago, yes, there had been a local serial killer, but he'd been crazy, plus they'd caught him. He'd killed nine people; he'd nearly killed Charlie. Ethan had saved her, and the killer had died five years ago of a stroke while still on death row.

"Is that all you know?" she asked.

"Yeah. It was major-league news this morning, but

that was all they seemed to know. They did show a quick clip of a press conference, but it was just double-talk by a Detective Laurent. He basically said they can't give out any information because the case is under investigation."

"I can't believe no one mentioned it all day today."

"The news just broke this morning, so most people on set probably don't know about it. I wasn't on call until later in the day, and that's why I heard about it. It'll probably turn out to be some family thing, a fight between friends, or even some idiot playing around with a firearm. It's sad, but something terrible happens somewhere every day." He paused and looked around. "And, as your dad once told me, we just never seem to learn our lessons about cruelty and violence."

"I'll bet my dad knew him," Charlie said. "The victim, I mean."

"I didn't realize it would upset you so much. I'm sorry I told you."

"Why? I had to know."

"But we're making a movie, and that needs to be our focus. Yours, especially. And Brad's calling," Jimmy said, brushing a smudge of caked mud off her face. "Let's go see that footage."

"Hey, guys, come on," Grant Ferguson—another friend who was working as one of the ghosts—said, joining them. "Let's hurry and see what Brad's so excited about, because after that we get to bathe."

Grant was playing a soldier who'd been gruesomely wounded before his death. On top of that, his face prosthetic was peeling off in the heat, which made him look all the more ghastly. At forty-two he was older than most of the others, which was a plus, because soldiers of all ages had fought in what, down here, was still called the War of Northern Aggression.

Charlie struggled to shake off the news she had just heard and tried to smile. "Grant, you look horrible," she said. "And I mean that as a compliment. Jennie outdid herself."

It was true. Jennie McPherson, the makeup artist, had worked wonders on a shoestring budget.

Despite the fact that they were all unpaid, every person involved in the film was glad to be there. In exchange for volunteering their efforts, they were all shareholders in the film. Of course, it needed to achieve a pretty broad distribution and earn a fair bit if they were to make any money, but they were all friends, along with a few friends of friends. Most of them had gone to school together and most of those had even graduated in the same class. Some had become friends through other acting jobs. Charlie had met Grant when they'd filmed a spot for a local car dealership. And he, like many of the other extras, had a day job. He was an accountant when he wasn't acting. That had proved to be a huge asset, because he was also an associate executive producer and kept the books for the film, making sure they spent the budget wisely, especially the state's money.

Louisiana had made a concerted effort to woo the film industry, and Brad had received a state grant to help him cover expenses for props and equipment.

Charlie and her friends weren't tabloid names—yet. But most of them were making a decent living at their craft, just like thousands of other actors who weren't yet

household names and might never be. This film was her
first chance at a lead role, and since she hailed from St.
Francisville herself, she was also in love with the historical incident on which Brad's script was based.

It had occurred one day in the middle of the Siege
of Port Hudson during the Civil War. Port Hudson had
been incredibly important to both sides, since it was at
the junction of the Red and Mississippi Rivers. Admi-
ral Farragut from the North wanted it taken, so the US
Navy was determined to take it.

In that effort, they shelled Grace Episcopal Church.

But one day, suddenly the shelling went silent. And
a small boat, bearing US Navy men and a white flag of
truce, made its way to the shoreline below the bluffs.

The commander of the *Albatross*, one of the ships involved in the shelling, had died by his own hand. Since
he'd exhibited no signs of depression in a loving letter
written to his wife just days before, it was later assumed
that he'd grown despairing during a fit of delirium, perhaps due to yellow fever. A good commander and a
Mason and a kind man full of concern for the wounded
of both sides, he had been well loved.

Two of his officers and best friends aboard ship hadn't
wanted to consign his body to the waters of the Mississippi, so they'd gone ashore to find out if there might
be brother Masons anywhere near, and if there was any
way that Commander John E. Hart could be afforded a
proper service and burial. One of the largest Masonic
lodges in Louisiana—Feliciana Lodge #31 F&AM—was
nearby. The White brothers, who lived in the area and

were touched by the plea of Hart's friends, set out to see what they could arrange.

The Grand Master of the lodge was serving in the Confederate Army. But the Senior Warden, William W. Leake, also with the Confederate Army, had his "headquarters in the saddle" and was in the area. The White brothers found him and explained the situation, and Leake said he couldn't imagine any military man—not to mention a brother Mason—not having a proper burial.

Word was sent back to the *Albatross*, and the ship's surgeon and a few fellow officers made their way, carrying the body in the June heat, swearing and determined, up the bluffs to the church. They were met by the White brothers, W. W. Leake, a number of other Masons, the Reverend Lewis and a company of Confederate States Marines.

For a few precious moments in time, on June 12, 1863, there was peace. Commander John E. Hart was buried with full military and Masonic honors in the Grace Church graveyard.

Of course, the war went on afterward. Vicksburg fell on July 4, Gettysburg turned the tide in the East on July 3, and Port Hudson was surrendered on the 9th, following the longest siege of the war. There were five thousand Union casualties and more than seven thousand Confederates. Once Vicksburg had fallen, General Gardner felt that to continue to hold out would simply cause more useless bloodshed and death. He was right, but he was overruled by his superiors. From then on it was more blood and the tragic loss of life for both sides until the day at

Appomattox Courthouse almost two years later when, for all intents and purposes, the country was reunited.

William Leake went on to become Grand Master of the Feliciana Lodge, and for forty-nine years, he tended to Hart's grave. When Leake died, he was buried next to Hart, and the two were now honored every year with a reenactment ceremony called *The Day the War Stopped*.

The whole story was covered in Brad's movie, which made it very special to Charlie. Her mother's great-great-grandfather had been one of the Confederate States Marines who had attended the funeral services for Commander Hart. She'd always loved the story, because it was about the goodness that could be found in people even amid the tragedy of war.

But Brad's movie wasn't historical; it was a suspense movie about a piece of land hallowed by the blood of the soldiers who'd died there and was now threatened by drilling, people trying to save it and other people sabotaging efforts at negotiation, while a few evildoers were ready to kill to have things their way. It was timely, and those on both sides were drawn as complex characters. At the end, the would-be killers were stopped by the very ghosts who made the land so special. Or, possibly, by what they saw in their own imaginations. The truth was, the ending of his movie was left to the eye—and the imagination—of the viewer.

As Charlie and the decaying soldiers, along with Harry Grayson and Blane Pica—who played the scuzzy oil baron and sleazy senator trying to kill Charlie—and assorted crew members got a look at the footage, she had to agree with Brad. It *was* great. Also really creepy. If the rest of the footage was as good, they would have a surefire hit.

"Thank you, and that's a wrap for the day," Brad said, smiling. "You're free—until your 7:00 a.m. call if you're in the fight scene. Check your schedules and have a good night."

Grant laughed and called out, "Brad, check *your* schedule. It's a 7:00 *p.m.* call tomorrow."

Brad winced. "Sorry. Go and enjoy your night."

Charlie smiled at Grant. She wasn't on call at all for the next several days. Due to her commitment to a web series she was also filming, she had returned to Francisville only five days earlier, and she'd been on call pretty much nonstop since. Now she had only a few scenes to go.

"Sounds good to me," Jennie McPherson said, as she glanced over at George Gonzales—another Tulane classmate—who was doing double duty in set design and as a prop master. The extras had been returning their hats, swords, guns, belts, buckles and the rest of their accessories—everything but the period uniforms they were still wearing—and George was frowning.

"Missing a belt buckle, a canteen and a knife," George said.

"Come on, let's go. Showers for one and all," Jimmy said, wrinkling his nose as he got a whiff of himself.

"I'm going to stay and help George and the set guys retrieve whatever fell in the fields," Charlie told him. "We can't afford to lose any of our props." She loved George. He was one of the hardest-working and funniest friends she had, claiming descent from both slaves and also from their Confederate masters. He loved to chime in on their historical discussions, especially since his mother—who, confusing things even more, was Israeli—had been born in New York City. He considered himself a Confederate/Yankee/African American, and liked to say that gave him a unique perspective.

"Yeah, don't want to leave George in the lurch," Jimmy said. "I guess I can stay, too."

"You have a call tomorrow night. I don't. Go have fun, then get some sleep," Charlie said.

"Oh, man, thanks, Charlene! There is so much we have to be so careful with! Money, you know," Jennie said. She was a petite blonde, and with her hair in a ponytail, as it was now, she looked to be about fifteen, but she'd actually turned thirty on her last birthday. Brad had met Jennie working on a project in New Orleans. She liked to lord it over George, who was her junior by a year. "We have to be so careful about costs."

"I'll stay and help, too," Grant offered.

"No, you do the books, you do the budgeting, you write the checks—and you're an extra every time Brad needs one. I've got this," Charlie said. "Go."

Jimmy and Grant left, looking more like ghostly apparitions than ever as they headed toward their cars. Brad didn't notice; he was studying shots with Mike, his brother and main cameraman.

"I'm off to look for your missing props," Charlie said. "Can Barry light up the field for me?" Barry Seymour was in charge of lighting. He was also an electrician, which made him perfect for the job, because he could fix any problems at minimal cost. He came from Baton

Rouge, and like Grant, he was in his early forties. He could not only take the time to work on the film but he could invest in it, as well, because he'd once worked as an electrician on one of the big oil rigs in the Gulf. He'd taken his pay and invested heavily in the oil company, and it had paid off.

"Barry! Light the field!" Jennie yelled.

Charlie cringed. She could have yelled herself.

"I can help, too," Luke Mayfield, their sound engineer and another friend, just a few classes ahead of Charlie and Brad at Tulane, walked over and said to Charlie.

"Great," she said.

She hurried toward the field where they'd been filming, followed quickly by Luke and George, and then Barry, Mike and Brad.

Even the director worked at keeping costs down.

As she walked, head down, eyes searching the ground, she was glad to be alone with her thoughts. Jimmy telling her about the murdered man had been unnerving. Especially here. She couldn't help but remember the past. And now something bad had happened again.

Yes, something bad happened somewhere every day, but that was no consolation.

She paused for a minute and looked up at the church.

The area held strange memories for her—some pleasantly nostalgic, some not so great. Now, though, the church and the surrounding landscape had an eerie beauty in the moonlight. The church wasn't immense or grand, like a cathedral, but it stood proud on its bluff overlooking the Mississippi, and there was even something unexpectedly poignant about it. The cemetery around the church was filled with graves of all kinds, in-ground, "box" graves—literally stone or marble in the shape of boxes—and family mausoleums. Cherubs and angels stood guard everywhere. Grace Episcopal Church still served the people of the parish, and the building and graveyard were well kept without looking manicured.

The mist created by their fog machines was dispersing, but slowly, so a low fog still hovered over the ground, making her search difficult and rendering the scene deceptively surreal.

For a moment Charlie found herself thinking that she could see a distant past when war had raged—and a temporary peace had been found. She could almost see those soldiers, some who had lived and some who had died, making their way through the mist and the moss-draped oaks.

She remembered being young and playing in the graveyard when she shouldn't have. She'd imagined seeing things then, too....

And then there had been that night in high school when she'd been pledging the Cherubs and ended up tied to a headstone, even though they all knew there was a killer at work not far away.

A serial killer who targeted young women.

Ethan had found and freed her. And she knew, though she hadn't said anything to Jimmy, that she was especially upset because...

Because she'd become entangled in that last murder when she'd found a dead girl's bracelet.

Charlie gave herself a serious shake. She'd been living

in New Orleans since she'd graduated from college; that's where the work was. She'd done some national commercials and even a few guest spots on network shows. But…

This was home. She loved it here. And she would be damned if she was going to be afraid out here now. She wasn't tied up; she wasn't a kid. She was an adult—ten years older, and making a good living in her chosen field.

Still, she couldn't help but remember the past.

She'd looked up information on the men who had died in and around the area, especially those who had been buried here. She was pretty certain she'd found the cavalryman whose ghost she'd seen all those years ago; his name was Anson McKee. Anson had been a married man with one son, and he'd been a graduate of West Point. The week before his death he'd written the most beautiful letter to his wife, a letter now preserved in a museum in New Orleans. He'd written of his love for her, his fear not of death, but of leaving her.

Know that I will whisper your sweet name with my last breath. Know that whenever Almighty God may choose to take me home, my time on this earth was the sweetest and most precious any man could ask for. I was blessed to know you, to live with you, to hold you and call you wife.

She sometimes wished that she could see him again and tell him that she'd been blessed because of him.

Anson was buried in hallowed ground. She had visited his grave and brought flowers to it.

And while the cemetery could feel very creepy at

night, there was no reason for her to be afraid—not now. Any ghosts there had been good people. Good people did not return to do mischief.

Her own mother had been interred in the family mausoleum at Grace Church. It was a handsome and historic old family tomb that she and her father kept in immaculate shape.

She bit her lower lip. The dull throb of that loss always lived with her, just below the surface. But she and her dad both remembered the good and the love, clinging to the beauty of their memories.

Still, she had too many recollections associated with the graveyard, and that one memory was very scary. If it hadn't been for Ethan, things might have been much, much worse.

Someone surely would have come back for her—eventually.

But would they have come in time?

The moon shifted. She was close enough to the edge of the bluff that she could see the *Journey*, the meticulously restored paddle wheeler on which her father worked and lived for large parts of every week, as she made her way up the Mississippi.

The *Journey* had been in port earlier and would be there early tomorrow morning, as well. She'd gotten to see her dad when he'd had a few minutes of free time after taking his tour group through the Myrtles Plantation and on to see Rosedown Plantation. She would have a few minutes with him again in the morning before the *Journey* headed to New Orleans.

She was glad of the chance. She was an only child,

and her mom was gone, but she had her father, and while these days he was almost always aboard the *Journey*, its home port was New Orleans, so she was able to see him often when she was home.

"Charlie."

She turned when she heard her name, trying to figure out who'd called her. The others were busy searching farther away, and no one seemed to even be aware of her.

She caught her breath. The mist from the foggers should have dissipated by now, but it seemed that a real one was rising.

"Charlie."

There it was. Someone had spoken her name again, and her coworkers were still involved in their own searches.

She could have sworn she saw shapes moving in the mist, just as she had seen ghosts, long ago as a terrified teenager tied to a tombstone before being rescued by a young man who also saw the ghosts in the moonlight but was not afraid.

The ghosts hadn't been out to hurt her. Ironically, Brad's movie had hit on the truth—or her truth, at least. She and Ethan had never spoken about it, but she knew that the ghost of the cavalry officer had led him to her that night. He'd seen her distress and found help. She'd wondered time and time again if there was a way to help that soldier. Did he want to pass on? Or did he stay to help others?

Or did he stay because he wasn't alone? There had

been others with him, just none she had seen as clearly as she had seen him.

A long time ago now.

She reminded herself that she was supposed to be working. She was the lead actress and a shareholder. And given their budget, she was also looking for costly props.

She straightened and gave herself another mental shake. She was letting the shadows and the moonlight and history infiltrate her mind and strip away all the logic and common sense she had acquired as an adult.

But she could never be here without first remembering her mother, and then that time, before she'd lost her mom, when she'd been tied to that tombstone.

When she'd heard the sobbing. When Ethan had come to save her...

When she'd found the bracelet that had belonged to a murdered girl...

"Hey!" she called, wanting to hear her own voice. "What are we looking for again? A buckle, a knife and a canteen?"

She didn't need to be afraid. Jennie, George, Mike and Brad were within easy shouting distance. She could see them moving across the ground where the "ghosts" had so recently walked.

"Yeah," George called back. His voice came from much farther away than the sound of her name had.

"Found the belt buckle," Mike announced.

"Got the canteen," George said a moment later.

Charlie walked closer to the outskirts of the church,

moving slowly and carefully over the ground, nearing the old outer, unhallowed, graveyard.

"I see something!" she cried, noticing a gleam in the moonlight.

She told herself to forget about the past—and the ghosts of the past.

She was safe now, surrounded by friends, and any ghosts here were helpful ones.

She dropped to her knees, reaching for the shiny metallic object.

"Think I've found something," she called over her shoulder.

At first she wasn't sure what she was seeing. It was just something shining in the dirt. It wasn't until she reached for it that she realized that it was a ring. A signet ring.

And it was attached to a finger....

A finger that was attached to a hand, a hand that was protruding from the earth...

Because it was attached to a barely buried body.

It took a few seconds to resonate in her mind, and then...

A dead man. She had found a dead man.

Only then did she begin to scream.

It was happening again.

2

Ethan Delaney tapped on the partly open door to Jackson Crow's office, then pushed it wide and walked in.

He'd been with the Krewe a little more than a month. He was still becoming accustomed to working in this office in Northern Virginia, which had its own low-key friendly ways. It wasn't that he hadn't been used to camaraderie among agents—he was. He'd been in the New York office for the last several years, and, due to the stress level that went with working in the Big Apple, the agents there often resorted to humor to lighten the tension.

Here, though, office doors were seldom closed, and they were never locked.

Crow was their Special Agent in Charge, directly beneath Special Assistant Director Adam Harrison, who made himself equally available. Adam had helped Crow interview Ethan before inviting him to join the elite unit. They had both treated it like an easy dinner out, but he'd known full well that his answers had been carefully weighed, and that they'd been keeping track of his body language, as well.

Relief.

He hadn't really thought about it before, but that was exactly what he felt in his new position. In his customary work in the criminal division, he'd often needed to watch his words carefully. He'd constantly had to come up with explanations for his decisions. He'd read about the Krewe of Hunters and in fact had a good friend who had transferred over before him. Aiden Mahoney had been professional when they'd talked, not lying to him and not trying to hedge, but not saying exactly what the Krewe's specific rules and responsibilities were, either.

But now that he was here, he'd discovered the rules weren't written down or formally agreed upon; rather they were *assumed* and tacitly understood by every member of the Krewe.

He was learning, day by day, to relax completely in this new realm. Here he could be totally honest about what he saw and sensed, things others might consider extrasensory. Truthfully, most solutions were based on logic and physical evidence, but others, the solutions to the crimes the Krewe investigated, included something more.

He had all the right training for his position: Loyola, where he'd studied criminal psychology and forensics; a stint in the military; a master's degree in forensic sciences from George Washington University; then the FBI Academy. He knew that training helped, but it by no means superseded something he'd been born with, something inherited from one or more of his ancestors, a mixture of Spaniards, Creoles, English, Irish, Italian and, as with so many Louisiana natives, Haitian and Choctaw. He had one living great-grandmother on his mother's mother's side who believed in the mysterious ways of true voodoo. He also had a great-grandfather from his mother's father's side who loved to teach him Choctaw legends. One great-grandmother on his dad's side had emigrated from Norway, while one great-grandfather had come over from Scotland and married a woman of Italian descent, all of which meant that the stories Ethan had heard growing up covered a vast array of myth and legend.

The tales were different and yet, oddly, much the same. In most of them, the supernatural played a key role, and since that agreed with his own experience of the world, it had caused him a few problems early on in school. He'd quickly learned to guard his thoughts in regard to the world around him and to keep his mouth shut about many things he might have had to say, and he'd pretty much stuck to that plan into adulthood.

Then he'd heard about the Krewe.

On their most recent case, his first, he'd discovered that his quick ability to communicate with the lost and disfranchised—the dead—was a bonus and not something to hide. One of the dead men, a powerful lobbyist, had spoken to him, and after that the clues had been easy to follow. The murders had not been politically motivated, but rather rooted in a family financial dispute.

Ethan was glad he and the Krewe had been able to solve the case and especially pleased that he had proved his worth.

"Jackson?" he said now.

His supervisor was busy reading through a file and frowning as he did so. He quickly looked up as Ethan spoke.

"Ethan, thanks for coming so quickly," Jackson said, indicating the chair in front of his desk. He passed the file across the table.

There were two pictures on the first page, men between the ages of thirty-five and forty-five, both in business suits, one a muscular Caucasian, the other handsome and looking to be of mixed African American and Caucasian descent.

"Farrell Hickory and Albion Corley," Jackson said, indicating the men in the pictures.

"And they're both...?" Ethan asked.

"Dead," Jackson clarified. "Local police are investigating. Everything they've got is all there in the files, and I've also emailed you."

"They're sure the murders are related?"

"Both men were found in replica Civil War uniforms in shallow graves—and not *in* graveyards but *near* them."

"Union uniforms?" Ethan asked. A twisted get-even spree by a deranged local? The Civil War had ended in 1865. Reconstruction had officially ended with the Compromise of 1876.

Long over—or so one would think. But down here, things were different.

As much as Ethan wanted to believe people, in both the North and the South, had escaped the prejudices of that era, the Klan, neo-Nazis and various supremacist groups were still around. While laws could protect people, they couldn't always deal with old hatreds that still had a pernicious hold on too many minds. Still, he believed he lived in a better world now than the one he'd been born into. And being of such mixed ancestry himself, it was painful to suspect that any murder might be motivated by prejudice.

"Here's the interesting thing," Jackson told him. "Farrell Hickory was in a Confederate cavalry officer's uniform. Albion Corley was wearing a Union naval uniform."

"That *is* interesting. You wouldn't kill your own side, so that seems to rule out someone still stuck in the Civil War," Ethan said.

Jackson nodded. "Anyway, both men were stabbed in the heart. The forensics experts believe that both men were stabbed with a bayonet or something similar that could be wielded with a certain precision."

"If a bayonet *was* the murder weapon, that seems to indicate the killer is a Civil War reenactor," Ethan said.

"That's what the police think. But what's the motive? And why these two men? Both of them were descended from men who fought in the Civil War but on opposite sides. Both of them had roots in or around the area, but their jobs weren't related, and there doesn't seem to be any obvious connection between them."

Ethan listened, surprised he hadn't seen anything about the murders on the news yet. He believed the country was trying to change the mind-set that had been so common at one time. He would have seen a clearer motive if descendants of known Klansmen had been murdered, for example, even more so if the victims were current members of the Klan or one of its spiritual cousins.

He didn't know the particulars of either man, since he had yet to read the files, but he was sure Crow would have mentioned anything that obvious.

And he had yet to hear why the Krewe were involved. Unless the local police had asked for help. Unless one of the men had been kidnapped or state lines had been crossed.

Under most circumstances, three murders with the same signature were seen as the calling card of a serial killer, which was when the Bureau got involved, and so far they only had two. Of course, since the War on Terror had begun, everything, even in the FBI, had changed. And especially with the Krewe of Hunters, there really wasn't such a thing as a norm.

"Jackson, I need to look through that," he said, indicating the folder.

Jackson nodded. "You can study it on the way."

"On the way? Where am I going?"

"Baton Rouge," Jackson said, watching him for his reaction.

"Okay," Ethan said slowly. "I'm just curious, and I'd like to play with a full deck. The Bureau has an office in New Orleans. Granted, it's not a Krewe office, but even here I'm not the only Louisiana agent on staff. Am I going with someone else? Were we invited in? Or will I be stepping on toes when I get there?"

"Adam is speaking with the proper authorities. You won't have any problems, though you'll be working with a local detective—Randall Laurent."

"Randy!" Ethan said.

"You know him?" Jackson asked.

Ethan nodded. "We're both from St. Francisville. He's a good guy," he added, pausing to grin. "He quit opening beer bottles with his teeth years ago and became a solid, tough and decent man. Seriously, he's a good guy. We were actually at Loyola together, too. But—"

"I'm sending you because Angela referred the call to me. She receives all our 'invitations' and inquiries, and she has a great way of reading between the lines and determining if the case is right for us."

Ethan knew Angela, a special agent with the Krewe who handled a lot of the administrative and back-end business. They were often inundated with cases, and she had an amazing ability to determine which ones might best benefit from the Krewe's assistance.

She and Jackson were also married and had been among the original six members of the Krewe.

"Yes, of course," Ethan said.

"I believe you're the perfect man for this situation. You know the area. If I'm not mistaken, you even used to live in the parish."

"I've been gone a long time," Ethan said. "I have family in the area, but they're mostly in New Orleans now."

"But you know people there. The lead detective is an old friend, you said. That's always a good thing."

Ethan was still curious. So far he'd always worked with at least one other Krewe agent, but it sounded as if he was being sent on his own.

He knew there were other Krewe agents who came from Louisiana, even if they didn't come from West Feliciana Parish. Jude McCoy, another recent addition to the Krewe, had been an agent in New Orleans before he joined the Krewe.

"If you find something, I'll head down with Jude McCoy by the end of the week," Jackson said, as if he'd read Ethan's mind.

"All right," Ethan said. He hesitated and then shrugged. He might as well just throw it out there. "I love this job. I'm ready to go wherever the assignment leads, do whatever needs to be done. You know that. But I'm surprised. There are other agents who've been with the Krewe a lot longer than I have. Even Jude. He's pretty new, but not as new as me. We've even become friends because we're both from Louisiana. The Krewe started out in New Orleans. So…not to take anything away from my own abilities, but…why me?"

"We were specifically asked if you were available," Jackson said, his light eyes, so striking against his dark hair and tanned flesh, hard on Ethan.

"By?" Ethan asked.

"A woman who found one of the bodies. She spoke with some friends of hers with connections here, and they made a persuasive case. She's a local actress, name of Charlene Moreau."

"Ah." Ethan hoped that the memories suddenly flooding through him weren't visible on his face.

"You do know her, then?" Jackson asked.

"I *did* know her," Ethan said. "When we were kids. And I know *of* her now. I've seen her on a new cop show they're filming down there, and in a couple of commercials. I haven't actually seen her, though, since I was nineteen. She must have been fifteen or sixteen."

"How close were you?" Jackson asked.

How close?

Jackson must have seen his confusion, because he went on. "When we're young, we're often more open to what's around us, to seeing the kinds of things we here in the Krewe see every day."

Ethan remembered being home from college, talking on the phone to his mother about something boring like his laundry. He was already taking criminology courses, and his mother brought up the killings that had occurred just north of Baton Rouge and how people were growing nervous in the entire area around the capital city.

And then he'd seen the soldier at the window. A Confederate cavalry officer. The man had seemed to be beckoning to him, and at first he'd naturally thought the man was a lost reenactor needing help.

But the soldier had led him across fields, pausing only to glare at Ethan when Ethan stopped, irritably demanding that the ghost explain what he wanted. Somehow Ethan felt compelled to follow him despite his silence and his strange behavior.

In the end he'd followed his spectral guide to Grace Episcopal Church.

That was when he'd seen Charlene Moreau. She'd been tied to a gravestone.

Her head was bent as she pulled against the knots that had held her there, and despite the situation she'd been ethereally beautiful in the moonlight, hair tumbling over her shoulders, a flesh-and-blood version of the worn stone angel that stood over a nearby grave with her head bowed deep in prayer.

Ethan pulled himself back to the present when Jackson spoke.

"Apparently Ms. Moreau is friends with Clara Avery and Alexi Cromwell, two young actresses I know from previous cases. They're here in our area at the moment, involved with Adam Harrison's theater project—he's restoring a historic theater and has hired them to deal with creative management—although they're both from the New Orleans area originally. Both of them are also gifted—or cursed—the same way we in the Krewe are." He paused, then went on. "And speaking of previous cases, there's another strange association here, too," Jackson said.

"That being?"

"We've recently worked two serial-killer cases involving the Celtic American cruise line. The cruise company wasn't at fault, of course, but both killers carried out their work aboard their ships."

Ethan frowned, wondering how the recent deaths of the two reenactors could be related to the cruise line.

Then he saw it. A slim connection, but a connection nonetheless.

"The *Journey*," he said. "Celtic American owns the *Journey*, and she does a run from New Orleans to Vicksburg, with a stop at St. Francisville. And of course, I know about the cases involving the *Destiny* and the *Fate*. Anyone in the world with media access knows about the cases." He hesitated. "We're sure there was no direct connection to the cruise line or the *Journey*?"

"We can't know for sure, not yet," Jackson said, his tone tight. "But not as far as the owners, operators or employees of Celtic American go. But Charlene Moreau's father is the cruise director and resident historian aboard the *Journey*."

"I know Charlene's father. I promise you, he had nothing to do with murder."

"I'm not suggesting anything like that. But here's where the connection to the cruise line comes in. Both of the dead men took part in a reenactment aboard the *Journey*. The ship does themed cruises. A week ago, the theme was the Civil War. Considering the route, a lot of their cruises are Civil War–themed, but this was their once-a-year extra-special Civil War cruise. Celtic American's claim to fame is that they specialize in historic cruises. Interestingly, the *Journey* offers ghost tours as well as your standard history-based ones."

"The *Journey* actually has a legitimate historical claim of its own. She was conscripted to move Southern troops up and down the Mississippi when the war began. She was seized by the Union forces when they took New Orleans in 1862, then used to move wounded Union troops. For a brief time she fell back into Confederate hands, when a small troop of Confederate soldiers slipped aboard and took her over. She went back to the Union, though—a trade was arranged that allowed for injured Rebels being held by the Union to be exchanged for the Union men aboard the ship. There had been an outbreak of fever on board, so the Confederates were only too happy to hand the ship and the men over to the Yankees, and the *Journey* continued on her way, mainly doing hospital runs for the rest of the war."

"See?" Jackson said softly. "You know your local history—something that can be invaluable in cases like this. So…back to the connection," he continued. "Both the murdered men were involved in that extra-special reenactment aboard the ship about a week ago. That's one of the reasons the police are so sure the killings must have been planned by someone in the reenactors' group."

"But you don't believe that," Ethan said.

"It's certainly possible, given what we know so far. But I don't like to grasp at the easy answer."

"Sometimes the obvious answer is the truth," Ethan said.

"And sometimes it's not."

"No," Ethan agreed, and stood. If he was heading to Baton Rouge and then up river to St. Francisville, he was eager to get started. "What are my travel arrangements?"

"A car's waiting to take you home to pack and then to the airport. The plane leaves as soon as you're aboard."

"As soon as I'm aboard?" Ethan asked.

Jackson smiled. "I guess you haven't gotten used to our form of 'troop movement' yet. We have a nice, new private jet. Adam financed it himself. No taxpayer dollars."

"Ah. Well, then, nice I won't have to change planes in New Orleans."

Jackson grinned. "Report in to me as soon as you have a feel for what's going on. Jude and I can join you

early if you think we can help. That plane goes back
and forth whenever we want it to."

Ethan took the folder and headed out of the office.

Within an hour he was on the private plane provided
by Adam Harrison.

As he flew, he read the dossiers on the dead men.

Then he looked out the window and gave himself up
to memories of Charlie Moreau.

"It's going to be all right, Charlie—really. This situation has nothing to do with you or Brad or the movie.
You stumbled on something very bad that someone else
did. You can't go letting it affect your life. In fact, you
should be glad you found the poor man, because now
the police can try to find some justice for him."

Jonathan Moreau set his arm around Charlie's shoulders and hugged her gently.

She was sitting with her father on a bluff high above
the Mississippi. It was a short distance from Grace
Church and the place where she'd found the body of a
man who'd been identified as Farrell Hickory dressed
in his Confederate cavalry uniform.

That area still had crime-scene tape around it.

From her perch atop the bluff she could see the people she assumed were forensic investigators searching
the area. The police had told her that they hoped to finish by that evening. Meanwhile, Brad had rearranged
the shooting schedule until they were free to use the
fields again.

Since then she'd spent a lot of time on the phone in
a three-way conversation with Clara Avery and Alexi

Cromwell, good friends she'd worked with a number of times in the past. They were now working with the FBI and knew a number of agents, including Ethan.

"You can't let it get to you, Charlie," her father said.

She knew he was right. The murder had nothing to do with her or the film crew. A vicious killer had murdered Farrell Hickory, and it was likely that the same person had murdered Albion Corley, as well. He'd been of mixed African and Caucasian descent, and had been wearing a replica Union uniform when he'd been killed.

Not long before Albion's death, he and Farrell Hickory had performed with a number of other reenactors on the same riverboat, the *Journey*, where her father worked, as part of an in-depth Civil War–themed cruise.

Charlie turned to her father and asked, "Why, Dad? Why them? This is nuts! I mean, one victim was half black and one was white, one was reenacting the Confederate side and the other the Union side. What was the killer thinking?"

"Maybe he's just someone who hates war," her father said.

"That doesn't make any sense. He hates war, so he commits cold-blooded murder instead?"

"Charlie," her father said, "if you ask me, murder never makes sense. Taking another man's—or woman's—life is brutal, cruel and ultimately senseless. But the police are investigating, so leave it to them. You're an actress, and a darned good one. You're not a cop. You…" He paused, looking off into the distance.

Charlie loved her father. Her mom had died suddenly the summer after her first year of college. It had been an aneurysm—one day a minor headache she laughed off, the next day…gone. She and her dad had been devastated. Her father was a handsome man, fifty-four years old. But he still hadn't even gone on a date. When she'd actually tried to get him to go out with one of the entertainers on the riverboat, he'd just smiled and told her, "Maybe one day I'll be ready for someone, but let's face it—in my heart and mind, no one can begin to live up to your mom."

She'd decided to let him be. When he was ready, she would be ready, too. She knew that—right or wrong—if he'd gotten involved with another woman right after her mother had died, she would have been bitter. Now, though, enough time had passed that she could deal with equanimity with the idea of him falling in love again. More than anything, she wanted to see him happy. Of course, she knew he loved her, and she made him happy—as did his work. He loved the old riverboat—the *Journey*—and he loved talking to people about history. He excelled at it. Still, she thought he would be happier if he had someone in his life. However, finding someone who loved the Mississippi, an old riverboat and being regaled with historical tales at every turn might be a bit of a challenge.

"You're not a cop," he repeated softly. "Even if you do play one on TV every now and then," he added lightly. "Sometimes you know things, but you're not trained law enforcement. You know how to shoot because I taught you when you were a kid, not so you'd shoot anyone or anything, but because we live out in the sticks, and I wanted you to be able to defend yourself. But snooping around…well, that could be dangerous. So don't even think about it, okay? No matter what you…know."

She understood he was talking about what her family called "insight." It wasn't really insight at all, of course. Most people called it the "gift" or the "sight." Her family seemed to think if you referred to seeing ghosts or speaking with the dead as *insight*, people wouldn't immediately think you were slightly daft or totally out of your mind.

Her father didn't see the dead. Her ability had come from her mother's family. However, Jonathan Moreau didn't doubt the existence of the insight for a minute. He'd delighted in her mother's abilities. How else could he possibly have learned some of the historical detail he cherished so much?

"Dad," Charlie murmured, and then hesitated. She looked at her father. He had deep blue eyes, the color of her own, but now they seemed even darker with concern. He knew what she was going to say, she thought.

Now, that was *actually* insight.

"He called my name, Dad. The dead man, Farrell Hickory, he called me by name. Or at least I think it was him." She hesitated; she had never told her father about the Confederate cavalry officer who had led Ethan to her that horrible night ten years ago. She'd told her mom, but her mom was gone now. Her father had been so upset about the entire situation that she'd never told him the whole story. Would it seem strange to him now that she thought a different dead man had called to her for help? "He called my name," she said again. "That's how I found him."

Her father shook his head. "Charlie, *I* barely knew

him. How would he have known your name. Did you know him at all?"

"I don't think so. I mean, if I'd met him, I didn't recognize him. I haven't been around that much in years, so I don't know how he'd know my name."

"Farrell Hickory's family's owned a sugarcane plantation downriver for over two hundred years," Jonathan reminded her drily.

"I think I've been there once," Charlie said. She loved history, too; she had to, to survive in her father's house. But few people had his passion for the past. "Now that I think about it, I'm pretty sure he was part of a reenactment I saw that revolved around the Confederate capture of the *Journey*. That was years ago, though." She paused, then asked, "Did you see him the day he and Albion Corley worked together?"

"I might have, Charlie. It was a crazy busy day, and I didn't really have much to do with the reenactors. I just put on my white cotton shirt and period breeches, added a straw hat and a pipe, and stepped ashore to give lectures in the old boathouse at the dock. And while we're a pretty small parish, I move in a pretty circumscribed orbit, and like a lot of locals, he might not have been around that much. Lots of people hail from here, but head down to New Orleans for the oil business."

"I doubt he was in the oil business, Dad. Like you were saying, his family has that plantation on the river. I was there with a school group when I was a sophomore in high school. The teachers love taking classes to the Hickory Plantation for a firsthand look at what working a plantation really meant. Mr. Hickory kept his private rooms on the second floor, and the ground floor was open to the public. I know the Hickory Plantation isn't grand like Oak Alley or San Francisco or some of the others, but I loved the fact that it was all about the way life was and the work people did and still do."

Her father looked at her, nodding. "Charlie, I know. And I'm sorry he's gone, even if I can't say he was a friend or even a close acquaintance. But I'd met the man, and I know a fair amount about the family planta-tion." He sighed. "According to the news, he left behind a twenty-four-year-old son. I hope he'll keep the planta-tion running, not just the tourist part but the sugarcane business, too. I probably saw his son around sometime over the years, but…"

"I don't know him," Charlie said. "He would have been two years behind me in school." She looked out over the water for a long moment, then said, "It just doesn't make sense, Dad. At first the press were theorizing that Albion Corley was killed because of some dispute with another reenactor. Something about him getting better parts than someone who'd been part of the group longer. But now, with another reenactor murdered, too… The two of them had nothing in common, other than that they were both reenactors and they were both in that program on the *Journey*."

"Don't forget, both men were born in Louisiana," her father reminded her. "And both of them were apparently killed with what looks to be a Civil War–era bayonet or a damn good replica."

"You know how they were killed?" She couldn't keep the amazement from her voice.

"I heard about Corley on the news yesterday, and I heard a cop theorizing about Hickory at the diner this morning."

She fell silent, thinking back to everything that had happened after she'd discovered the body. The police had arrived quickly, and she'd told a uniformed officer what had happened. Later a Detective Laurent had shown up, and she'd told him what had happened, too. But she had talked, and the police had listened. She hadn't thought to ask questions. She'd screamed once when she found the body, but after that she'd become almost numb, unnaturally calm, when she spoke to the police, her usual curiosity tamped down by her shock.

Every member of the crew had been questioned, as well. They'd all been asked if they'd seen any strange people hanging around the set.

In their ghostly makeup, half the actors had looked very strange indeed, but nobody had noticed anyone who might have been the murderer. Brad had told the police he had lots of film of the field, and they were welcome to see the footage. Naturally they'd accepted his offer.

Charlie had heard the medical examiner talking to Detective Laurent, telling him that Mr. Hickory had been dead at least twenty-four hours. But she hadn't heard anything about how he'd been killed, and it had never occurred to her to ask.

"I wish I had thought to ask the police more questions," she murmured.

"You should go back to New Orleans," her father told her gruffly.

"I can't! I can't walk out on Brad's movie."

"You're with me today."

"I'm not scheduled to work today."

Jonathan sighed deeply. "Well, I am. I've got to get back." He stood, reached down a hand and pulled her to her feet. "Stay and film your movie, Charlie. But go home—"

"Dad, I told you—I can't walk out on Brad."

"I mean our home, the one you grew up in. And stay there unless you're surrounded by friends. Stop fixating on this, sweetheart. You don't need to be asking any questions. Leave it alone and watch out for yourself. Promise?"

"I promise. I'll go home right now," she told him, then kissed him on the cheek. "Our home—the one I grew up in. And I won't fixate. Okay?" She smiled, feeling like a horrible liar even though she hadn't actually lied. She had simply neglected to tell him that she'd asked to have Ethan Delaney assigned to the case because she knew he had joined the FBI and was part of an elite team tasked with dealing with the unusual.

Was it unusual that two men involved in Civil War reenactments had been murdered?

Maybe not. Maybe it should be a matter for the local police. Except…

Except she was certain a corpse had called her name.

"You can always come and stay on the *Journey* with me. I've been with them so long that my original cabin has been upgraded to a pretty nice suite. It's not huge, but you could have the bedroom, and I'd take the sofa."

"Dad. I'm fine. I promise. I love the *Journey*, but I'm

doing a movie, remember?" she told him. "I promise I'll go right home from here, okay?"

This was a beautiful spot, she thought. They'd been coming here to sit and talk since she'd been a little girl. He had to get back to the port now, though. The *Journey* was heading on to Baton Rouge, Houmas House and then New Orleans, where her passengers would debark, new ones would board, and the cycle would begin again, NOLA to Oak Alley in Vacherie to Houmas House in Darrow to Baton Rouge to St. Francisville, Natchez, then Vicksburg. The itinerary stayed basically the same, but specific tours with different emphases were planned for aficionados of country music, history, art, theater and fine dining. As her father said goodbye and bent to kiss her on the cheek, Charlie really did intend to go home. But as he walked away toward his car, parked behind hers on the road just below the bluff, she noticed that someone was walking up the slope from that road. Her heart began to beat too quickly.

It wasn't because Ethan was back, she was certain. The years had stretched into an eternity between them. She hadn't asked for him to come for any reason other than that she knew he would take her seriously when she said she'd heard the dead talking to her again.

It was just that his timing was so damned bad.

Her father turned and saw Ethan. And then he turned and looked at her, and she felt as if she'd run over a puppy or slapped an infant. Why couldn't he let go of the past, of the way he'd felt about Ethan ten years ago…

"You called Ethan?" he asked.

"Dad, I called on a special group of FBI agents who

are used to dealing with…insight. My friend Clara—you know Clara, she used to work for Celtic American, too—is seeing a guy who works with Ethan, so I asked her to contact him for me," she said quickly. "Ethan's law enforcement now, federal law enforcement."

It was actually impressive that she was making something resembling a living by acting, she thought, hearing the pleading tone in her own voice when she'd hoped to project confidence instead.

"I see," her father said, staring at Ethan as he approached them.

He'd changed. The Ethan she'd known had been a tall boy, still slender with youth, not muscular like the man walking her way now. His hair had been on the shaggy side, and he hadn't yet shed the small-town football-hero swagger half the young men she'd known at school had affected. He'd been nineteen.

He'd filled out since the last time she'd seen him. Character seemed to have been etched into his face. He'd been a striking teenager, but this Ethan, with those green-gold eyes, dark hair and features that could have been painted by an Old Master, was something else altogether. His hair was cropped short now, his eyes had a sharper edge to them, and his chin had squared. He'd been a boy, she realized. Now he was a man.

As he walked up to them, he slipped on a pair of sunglasses against the brutal rays of the sun, and suddenly he became a total stranger.

"Ethan Delaney," her father said in an unreadable tone.

"Mr. Moreau," Ethan said, his voice now deep and rich. "Hope you're doing well, sir."

"We were doing well enough," Jonathan said gruffly. He turned and looked at Charlie again, then nodded toward the two of them and started to head down the slope.

He stopped after a moment and turned back. He stood very tall and straight, and said, "Don't let her get involved in this, Ethan. You watch out for her. Don't you let anything happen to Charlie."

"I didn't before, sir," Ethan said quietly. "And I won't now."

Charlie watched her father go, feeling a little ill. She loved him so much.

Then he was gone, and she was left alone with Ethan Delaney.

3

They stood some distance apart still, neither one rushing forward to initiate a warm old-friends' hug.

It had been a long time.

But, looking at her now, Ethan wished he could just walk over and take her in his arms.

Charlie had changed.

He would never forget the way she had looked when he'd found her that night—truthfully, he would never forget anything about that night. Charlie had always been beautiful.

She had become more so over the last ten years. The bone structure of her face was sharper. Her eyes, the deepest blue he'd ever seen, seemed even larger. She had delicately shaped brows, a nearly perfectly straight nose and a generous, well-defined mouth. She was tall—five-ten, at a guess—and carried her height well. She was thin, but had all the right curves. Everything about Charlie was…

Pretty damned perfect. Her hair was a rich chestnut. She wore it long, and it seemed to move with her at all times, even when she was standing still. In fact, when she'd had a crush on him, it had seemed like manna from above.

But, of course, he'd been nineteen. In college. She'd been sixteen, still just a sophomore in high school. Any thought of a relationship was simply doomed. And so, despite every objection posed by his heart—and his libido—he had turned her away. He wondered if, with age, she'd understood. He hadn't seen her since Frank Harnett's trial. She'd never tried to contact him.

Until now.

He wondered if she had any clue to the way she had haunted his dreams. The way he remembered her face when she'd looked up at him, her beauty, her hope— her faith.

"So how are you doing?" he asked her quietly. "Other than stumbling across a dead man."

She smiled. "Good. Thanks. In a nutshell, college, performing-arts major, some theater, some webisodes, a few nicely paying commercials. I've really been enjoying filming here. I love the project, love that we're all a part of the production as a whole—and glad to be home again. I don't get here often—not on purpose or anything. It's just I've been living in New Orleans, because that's where most of the work is. But it's great being here, because I get to see more of Dad, though the *Journey*'s home port is NOLA, so I get to see him when he's in town. I'm talking too much. Sorry. How about you?"

He shrugged and smiled. Talking too much? She'd managed to cover ten years in a pretty compact nutshell.

"College, service, master's degree, FBI Academy,

a few years with a regular unit, and now the Krewe of Hunters."

"I heard."

He nodded. "So I gather. You're friends with Alexi Cromwell and Clara Avery, right? You've all worked together in New Orleans?"

"Yes, in *Godspell*," Charlie agreed. "Alexi was the musical director, Clara and I were in the show. They're both from the NOLA area. And I saw the news about what happened on the *Destiny* and the *Fate*, and how they were involved... So I knew from them what you'd been up to and the work you're doing now."

He nodded. "I know about some of your work, too." He grinned. "I've seen you on that new cop series they film in NOLA."

"It's just a recurring role right now, but I keep hoping that I'll get upgraded to series regular," she said lightly.

"I especially liked that condom commercial you did."

"Hey. I made good money on that!"

At that, he took off his glasses, and they both laughed softly.

Then the laughter faded, and they were left staring awkwardly at each other.

Business, he reminded himself. He was here on business. To break the tension he said, "Okay, so our head honcho is getting me on the task force looking into the murders, but in the meantime, want to bring me up to speed on what happened the other night?"

She nodded somberly. "I didn't know anything about the first murder until one of my friends on the film told me about it after we finished shooting for the day. Apparently the information hit the news after I left for the set, and I'd been blocking and rehearsing and filming all day long." Her face lit up. "It's really a good movie, Ethan. I think you'd like it. Brad's captured the flavor of the Civil War era in the historical scenes, a real sense of what people were thinking and feeling. There's a great scene with one of the ghosts. He talks about the way a man's home state was everything to him back then. You get a real feel for people, and why they did what they did. And the soldiers… Did you know they would throw away their pipes and playing cards before they went into battle, anything it might have upset their families to find if they were killed. Of course, the movie's really about our present day—ecologists, big oil, and the need to preserve the land while also making sure that people have jobs and can afford to eat."

Ethan nodded, loving how passionate she was about the project. "I'm sure it's going to be a great movie. But what I need to know now is what happened to you last night."

"Right, last night." She was quiet for a moment. "I'm never in that area without remembering, you know? I'm not afraid, not usually, despite what happened out there. I mean, the whole unhallowed ground thing doesn't matter to me, because…because too many people were buried there just because they weren't from here or up to local standards at the time, or whatever. But then I heard my name being called. I don't really know if it was the murdered man calling me or if it was Anson McKee— Captain McKee, the cavalry commander who led you to me back when I was stupid enough to think I wanted to be a Cherub." She let out a breath. "But I found him. Farrell Hickory, I mean. Brad called the police, and the rest you know."

"I gather both men performed aboard the *Journey*," Ethan said.

Charlie nodded, looking around. "Most reenactors own their own uniforms, swords and other props. So when someone's looking for actors to fill specific historical roles, they can find the people they need easily enough, and the same people end up working together a lot. Friends of mine do it for fun—and for pay, when they can. They filmed a Civil War epic down near Houma not that long ago, and a lot of my friends worked as extras and made nice money at it."

"Right. So we need to find out who has a grudge against one or both men, who else was on the ship when the victims were, who might have been fighting with whom...." He sighed. "Hell, maybe some idiot just decided to refight the Civil War."

"It's not some idiot refighting the war. The victims represented both sides of the conflict. If you were a bitter Confederate, you'd kill Union men. And if you lost a relative fighting for the Union during the war, you'd want to bring down the Confederates."

"It's not race. One man was half black, and the other one was white," Ethan said. "But they were both in that reenactment on the *Journey*, so my gut tells me it has to go back to that somehow."

"Maybe someone on the *Journey* had a fight with both of them," Charlie said.

Ethan shrugged. He still had a lot of investigating ahead of him. It was much too early to settle on any one theory. He'd just gotten to town—and he'd headed straight out to see Charlie. He didn't ask himself why that had seemed like the most important thing to do.

Now he'd seen her.

And while so much was different after a decade had passed, everything he felt about her was just the same.

"I have to meet with the police and find out what they know," he said.

"Can I go with you?"

"No, not this time, anyway. Besides, when I was headed up here, I overheard you telling your father you were going straight home." When she looked as if she might object, he added, "Charlie, this doesn't really involve you, you know."

"Neither did the last murder," she said sharply.

Once again they looked at one another in silence, and he thought back to that night in the graveyard.

She'd found the bracelet; he'd called the police. He'd known it would be important for them to know exactly where the bracelet had been found, so he'd insisted on waiting there until the cops arrived.

Restless, Charlie had gotten up and perched on a headstone, while he'd walked off and leaned against a tree. Neither one of them had seen the killer when he'd come, searching for the bracelet, his trophy from his last victim. Then something, a rustle, a whisper, a movement—maybe even the Confederate officer who had led him to Charlie—had alerted him, and he'd turned just in time to see a man bearing down on Charlie with a raised butcher knife.

Luckily for him, the killer was nothing but a coward with a knife—a sick little bastard who didn't even put up a fight when Ethan tackled him. He screamed and cried like a baby when Ethan brought him down, knocking the knife from his hand.

By the time the police arrived, the killer had been caught.

He and Charlie had been credited with bringing him down.

Charlie had quit the Cherubs and sworn she would never have anything to do with such a ridiculous organization again.

And Jonathan Moreau had despised Ethan ever since. He said a real man would have gotten Charlie to safety, not made her stay anywhere near the site of a murder when the killer could return at any moment. Charlie had almost been killed, and as far as he was concerned, that was entirely Ethan's fault.

Charlie's mother, on the other hand, had applauded the fact that his quick thinking and determination had saved Charlie.

And Charlie herself...

She'd visited him once after he'd gone back to college. They'd talked a lot about seeing the dead. They'd wondered why some spirits stayed and others didn't, wondered why, when loved ones died, the living rarely got to speak with them. They agreed that they would never fathom it, not while they were here on earth. They'd come so close....

And then he'd made her leave.

He hadn't wanted to. Even at sixteen, she was already elegant as well as beautiful. Some might have said that a three-year age difference wasn't enough to make him give up the attraction—intellectual as well as physical— that sparked between them.

But in his mind, it wouldn't have been right; she was still a kid, still in high school. He was grown and out of the house, already in college.

Not to mention that he couldn't help thinking maybe her father had the right to hate him.

Looking at her now, he realized she'd grown even more beautiful, even more elegant.

"The killer was caught and tried, and it was all over and done with quickly, Charlie," he said.

"Really? Quickly? It still haunts me," she said. "I'd really like to go with you to talk to the police, now that it's all happening again."

"Do me a favor," he said after a moment. "For now, just do what you told your father you would and go home, okay? I'll let you know if I learn anything after I've had a chance to talk to Randy."

"Randy?"

"Randall Laurent, the detective heading up the case. He's an old friend, so I'm hoping things will go smoothly between us."

"I can't imagine they won't. I only vaguely remember him from school. Like you, he was three years older—a huge difference back then—and I know you were both on the football team. He seemed like a decent man when I talked to him last night. He wanted all the facts, but he was very understanding about asking. I guess he knew I was pretty much in a state of shock."

"That sounds like him," Ethan agreed. He wished her eyes weren't so blue. And that she wouldn't look at him the way she was, as if he'd become a stranger.

She walked past him, moving toward the path down to the road. They still hadn't touched, but he could smell her perfume, something as light as air and yet inexplicably provocative.

"Charlie?"

She waved to him without turning around. "I'm going home. Call me when you've got something."

Ethan watched her go. She might be going home now, but he had a very strong feeling that she wasn't going to stay there.

With a soft groan he decided to locate Laurent and find out everything he knew about the victims and whatever they'd pieced together about the killer.

Charlie just might be investigating on her own, relying on that special talent of hers.

And that could prove very dangerous.

Charlie paced the old house her dad owned just on the outskirts of St. Francisville. It was a wonderful old place, built sometime right before the start of the Civil War. It wasn't a plantation house and had never been a working farm. It had been built by a man who had worked the riverboats, which made it a perfect fit for her father, with his passion for history and his current position on a riverboat himself. It wasn't a large place, but there had always been enough room for their family, with three bedrooms upstairs plus a living room, dining room, office and library/family room—and modern kitchen—downstairs. Each bedroom had a fireplace, as did the living room. It was furnished with a mishmash of antiques that somehow worked, and her dad knew the origin of each piece of furniture. Only the big-screen television and entertainment center were new.

She loved her home....

Loved to remember her mom working in the kitchen or the seasonal flower beds she was so proud of. The sense of loss remained, of course, but Charlie thought both she and her dad had adjusted well, loving the memories and embracing them, but also finding satisfaction, even joy, in the lives they led now.

Right now, though, she didn't want to be home. She didn't want to care for her mother's flowers, look through scrapbooks or even learn lines for her upcoming scenes. She didn't want to read or catch a movie on Netflix, not when two people had been murdered and either a newly dead man or a long-ago ghost had called out to her by name. She felt connected to this case, compelled to do something to help solve it, but Ethan had sent her home instead, leading to her current restless frustration.

Ethan.

She really didn't want to think about Ethan, which was pretty much impossible, seeing as she was the one who had asked him to come back and look into this case. Because while she wasn't afraid of graveyards—or even the dead, when it came to that—she *was* afraid. Something very bad was on the horizon.

No, very bad things had *already* happened!

And she knew he would help with the situation, because she could tell him things, like the fact that she'd heard a dead man call her name, things she couldn't possibly tell the police.

She just wished he'd turned stodgy and perhaps developed a giant beer belly.

No, she didn't wish that, she just wished...

Wished she didn't still find him so incredibly compelling.

She told herself to forget about Ethan for now.

Which was next to impossible when the rest of the day seemed to stretch out boringly forever, even if it was actually more than half over and so far talking to him had been the best thing in it.

She couldn't help marveling at the speed with which he'd arrived; she'd talked to Clara last night, telling her what had happened, but she hadn't reached Krewe headquarters until this morning.

She would definitely go crazy if she kept thinking about Ethan—and the dead.

She had to get out.

She hadn't lied; she'd come home just as she'd promised. Ethan couldn't possibly object if she hung out with other people and made sure she was never alone, could he? She quickly texted Brad.

Going crazy. Need any help on set? she wrote.

A few minutes later, he texted her back.

Always. Left the field to the cops. Filming at Dad's office downtown—he donated the space. Come on in. Help with mikes and lighting.

She quickly responded On my way, then grabbed her bag and keys, and headed out. It didn't take her more than a few minutes to reach the downtown office building Brad's father owned. The security guard downstairs, whom she'd known since she was a child, greeted her by name. He immediately directed her to the second floor, where Brad was filming in the back conference room.

She waited outside in the quiet hallway before she heard Brad call "Cut!" Then she knocked and went in. There was no crowd of extras on hand for this scene, just Jennie with her makeup box, Mike Thornton with his camera, Luke Mayfield handling sound, Barry Seymour for lighting and George Gonzales keeping an eye on continuity. The only two actors in the room were those playing the oil-company exec and the senator, Harry Grayson and Blane Pica. And Jimmy Smith was standing on the sidelines, observing.

Despite the unexpected interruption in his planned shooting schedule, Brad was going with the flow. He beckoned her over as she entered. She waved to the others and walked toward him. Brad immediately invited her to watch the footage he'd just shot.

She looked into the camera as he replayed the latest scene. Afterward she looked over at Harry and Blane, and smiled. "Great stuff. Do you two sound scuzzy or what?"

"Thanks," Blane said, accepting the compliment with a pleased nod. He was from New York, and had been a couple of years ahead of Charlie and Brad at Tulane. He was heavyset, though a lot of his weight was muscle, and he was slightly balding, making him a perfect movie villain. Harry, on the other hand, was older, a seasoned actor Brad had met when working on a music video in New Orleans for a major producer. He was thin and wiry, with a sharp face that usually wore a pleasant smile unless the part called for something else. When he chose to, he could do grim and threatening very well.

The scene Brad had just shot came before the one he'd finished the other night, when the two men had been chasing her, ready to kill her because she'd discovered their plans.

"They only look good because of the great lighting," Barry said teasingly. The actors only rolled their eyes.

"Yeah, right. Everyone goes to see a movie for the great lighting," Jennie said drily.

"Actually, sometimes they do. They just don't know it," Barry said. "Lighting can be everything."

Brad cleared his throat. "Movies really belong to the director. All film buffs know that."

"Go ahead and delude yourself," Mike teased. "Real aficionados know the cameraman is everything."

"Think what you want. I know what really matters," Luke said, waving one hand dismissively. "Ever since the 'talkies,' sound has been the heart and soul of a film."

"I don't even pretend people come to see who the makeup artist was," Jennie said.

"Or the prop master," George put in. "But if you want my opinion, I say we stop this ridiculous conversation and head out for something to eat—and a beer."

"But I just got here to help," Charlie said.

"Too late. You can help us choose a restaurant,"

George said. "What's the cool place to see and be seen in St. Francisville these days? Or, even better, relax and have a great, hassle-free meal?"

Charlie thought of Mrs. Mama's, a local café tucked away on a side street, where they could order some of the best shrimp and grits she'd had anywhere. "I know just the place," she said.

Twenty minutes later they were seated, and a waitress was hurrying over to them. Charlie was looking at her menu when she realized the waitress was standing behind her, waiting for her drink order.

"What will you have, honey? Beer? Iced tea?"

Charlie turned and started to speak, and then she gasped softly and said, "Nancy? Nancy Deauville?"

It was the same woman who, ten years ago, had directed the action on the night Charlie was tied to a tombstone.

Like everyone involved with that horror show, Nancy had apologized. She and Charlie had even managed to act cordial for the rest of the year; then Nancy had graduated, and Charlie hadn't seen her since.

"Charlie, great to see you here," Nancy said. She seemed a little anxious and a little shy.

As if she meant what she was saying.

Charlie nodded. "Good to see you, too." She meant it herself. Time had gone by; they were no longer teenagers.

Nancy nodded. "I hear you're a movie star now."

"Hardly. Just a working actress. How about you? How is everything?"

Nancy smiled, but Charlie thought it looked a little

forced. "I married Todd Camp. The quarterback. We have two kids."

"Congratulations."

"Twins."

"Great."

"Sometimes," Nancy said, then shrugged. "Sometimes when Todd is working at the garage all day, I bring the kids here with me, and sometimes they even behave. But I love them. Anyway, I'm so happy for you. You always wanted to act."

"Well, thanks. I'm not exactly a fixture on the red carpet, though, you know?"

"You're doing what you want to do, and that's what counts."

"Thanks. Hey, how's Sherry doing? You two were so close. Is she still around, too?"

"Sherry got married and moved to New Jersey."

"That's nice."

"New Jersey? After here? I don't know. But she has a family, became an LPN."

"So. Twins," Charlie said into the awkward silence that followed Nancy's updates. "No kids for me yet, but one day, I hope."

"I'm sure it will happen for you. As for me, I just hope for a vacation one of these days. Anyway, what can I get you?"

"Iced tea and gumbo, please."

"You got it," Nancy said, and moved on.

She and Jimmy chatted for a minute, and then Jimmy looked down the table at Charlie and mouthed, "Didn't know she was working here."

Charlie shrugged. It had been ten years since that awful night, and it was a relief to discover she didn't really care what had happened to Nancy and the rest of them.

Once Nancy left, they chatted companionably as they waited for their food; they were almost evenly split between gumbo and shrimp and grits, breaking along pretty much the same lines for iced tea vs. frosty beers. For a few minutes the talk revolved around how to film the upcoming confrontation between Charlie and an oil baron. Brad wanted a live location, but Luke was worried about getting the clean sound that he believed the scene warranted. And then, because it couldn't be ignored forever, the subject of the dead man, Farrell Hickory, finally came up. They were all a little spooked because he was the second reenactor to be killed.

"And we all knew them both," Jimmy said.

Charlie turned to look at him. "We did?" she asked.

"Most of us did, at any rate," Barry said, nodding solemnly.

"Can't say I knew either man well," Mike Thornton said, pushing back a lock of dark hair. He was a lot like his brother, in both looks and mannerisms. He and Brad had been making movies together since they'd been kids.

"And," Jimmy said to Charlie, "you didn't know either one of them, unless it's from when you were a kid, because you weren't there for the special reenactment they did on the *Journey* a week ago—like so many of us were." He was wearing a brave face, but she could see he was deeply upset by the murders.

He had never really forgiven himself for being involved the night a serial killer had almost killed her.

"Right, I was doing that webisode series. *Banshees on the Bayou.*"

Brad smiled. "I hope this film is as successful as *Banshees on the Bayou.*"

"A bunch of us were involved because there was a corporate sponsor, so we were paid pretty decently," Jennie said, then went quiet for a long moment. "That's when we met the men who've been killed."

"Who—who else was working that day?" Charlie asked, more worried than she wanted to let on.

"Well, your dad, for one," Luke pointed out.

"Yeah, my dad. I know. Who else?" she asked.

"Let's see," Brad said, looking around. "Me and Mike, Barry and Luke… Jennie did makeup."

"Todd and I were there, too."

Charlie spun around to see that Nancy Camp—née Deauville—was standing right behind her. "We earn extra money any time we can. We didn't hang around, just did the bit they were paying us for, then left. You have to try to make more money than day-care costs or it's not worth it to work. Tons of locals were there, not just us."

"Jimmy Smith and Grant Ferguson," Brad added, then shook his head. "We were just extras. There was a scene between Hickory and Corley, though. I'm sure you already know this, but there was supposedly a meeting between a black Union orderly and a Confederate cavalry captain when the *Journey* was turned over to the Union. We were extras in that scene. We brought our own uniforms, so they cast us a lot."

"I have my Confederate infantry uniform *and* a Union artillery uniform," Barry said. "I can make money on either side of the Mason-Dixon Line."

Charlie grinned at that. But her smile quickly faded. "Did you notice anything wrong, anything that was even a little bit off, that day? Was anyone fighting?"

"I think there was a bit of a tiff between Corley and Hickory," Luke said. "They were both convinced they were historians, not just reenactors, and they disagreed about some detail of the scene. It got a little heated, but then your dad stepped in and calmed them down. But...well, they're both dead, so it's unlikely they killed each other."

"It's pretty damned stupid for anyone to kill some-one over a reenactment," Jennie said.

Brad shrugged. "People can be crazy sometimes."

There wasn't much of an argument to be made against that, so they all fell silent, lost in their own thoughts. Then Jennie made a comment about how good the food was, and the conversation turned to everyone's favorite restaurants in their favorite cities.

Charlie found herself smiling and laughing along with the others. But all the while she was making men-tal notes of things she needed to tell Ethan.

Farrell Hickory and Albion Corley had both taken part in the special reenactment aboard the *Journey*.

They had argued, and her father had intervened.

A number of her friends had also been involved in the reenactment: Brad and Mike Thornton, Jennie McPherson, Barry Seymour, Luke Mayfield, Grant Ferguson, George Gonzales and Jimmy Smith.

She didn't want to think that any one of them could be the killer.

Of course they were all innocent, she thought, giving herself a mental shake.

Because if one of them *was* the killer, surely he—or she—would have acted strangely while they were filming the rise of a ghostly army so close to the place where one of the victims lay dead.

"Wow. Ethan Delaney! As I live and breathe. Back and slumming it all in small-town America."

"Nice to see you, too, Randy," Ethan said, greeting his old friend outside the parish morgue on Oak Street.

The two of them were only about a month apart in age. They'd been friends throughout high school, making a lot of the same mistakes, going through the same wild stages, cleaning up their act when the world demanded they had to be adults. They'd lost contact when they went their separate ways after college. Since Ethan's parents had moved to New Orleans, he hadn't had much occasion to get back out to St. Francisville.

"Never thought of us as coming from the slums," Ethan said.

Randy grinned. "Yeah, we were all right, growing up, huh? I love this part of the world. I guess you can tell, seeing as I came back here. Look at you, though—a real live Fed."

"And look at you, a big-shot cop," Ethan said. "Not

bad for a kid who got hauled in on more Saturday nights than anyone else I knew."

"Detective, West Feliciana Parish Sheriff's Office, I'll have you know. The deaths actually occurred in two different towns in the parish, so we were called in on lead," Randy said, and grinned. "*Special* Agent Delaney. I have to say, I'm kind of surprised to see you down here for something like this. Wait, no, I'm not surprised you're here at all. This has to do with Charlie Moreau being back in the area, too, right? Bad business back then. Though I never did understand Jonathan being so pissed at you. You threw yourself on the guy."

"That was ten years ago," Ethan said.

"Bet you Jonathan is still pissed," Randy said.

"Thing is, I really have been sent down here on the case," Ethan said. "So what have you got?"

He studied his friend, noting the man the boy had grown into. Randy was lean, but deceptively so. He had excelled on the school's wrestling team, as well as being the football team's top field-goal kicker. He'd told Ethan once that he knew he was never going to have the bulk and broad shoulders of some other men, so he had to make up for it with lean muscle.

"Nothing new. You probably know everything I do, since I'm sure they brought you up to speed before they sent you down here. You have the case folders, crime-scene photos, all that, right?"

"Yeah."

Randy met his eyes and nodded. "Okay, so West Feliciana Parish has just under fifteen thousand people. Our annual crime rate is about two murders a year, and that

includes negligent homicide, so it's not like you're looking at a major city where the cops are accustomed to
investigating murders. We're not total newbies, though,
so don't think we're all a bunch of toothless rednecks
doing alligator wrestling for reality TV."

"Randy, I grew up here. All my friends had their teeth,
although the way you showed off opening beer bottles
with yours, I'm surprised you kept yours."

Randy shrugged. "Guess I'm glad they sent you and
not some big-city know-it-all. Okay, so here's where
things stand. At first, when Albion Corley was found,
we were a little worried that some kind of race thing
might erupt in town. We thought maybe some bigot was
pissed at him for having the nerve to wear the uniform
and take part in that big-deal reenactment, even as a
Union orderly. Everyone liked the guy, though. Smart,
a professor. Passionate about no-kill animal shelters
and saving the wetlands and all that kind of thing. Then
Farrell Hickory's body turned up, found by your old
girlfriend."

"Randy, we were never a couple," Ethan said patiently.

"Proof of fatal stupidity on your part," Randy said.

"Might be true. She was only sixteen, though."

"Shakespeare's Juliet was thirteen, or something
like that."

"Wouldn't have been right," Ethan said.

"Okay, okay, Mr. Morality, I'm moving on," Randy
said. "So now we have one dead black man in a Union
uniform, and one dead white man who played a Confederate cavalry officer. Our investigations found that the

two of them had some kind of dustup during what was billed as 'Journey Day.' You probably remember that every year there's a big reenactment of *The Day the War Stopped*. But this year, because it's a situation that also draws a lot of interest, some enterprising person with a tour group of teachers had a brilliant idea—reenact the day the Confederates traded the *Journey* and her Union wounded to the Yankees for a bunch of their own prisoners. There was so much sickness aboard ship, the Rebels didn't even want it, but the Union didn't know that. Anyway, the cruise line offers special tours each year that focus on the Civil War, and this year they decided to feature a special reenactment of the *Journey* handover. To be honest, I'm surprised it took this long for someone to realize that there could be big bucks in that kind of thing, but then again, Celtic American has only owned the ship for six or seven years. The reenactment was subsidized by Gideon Oil, so the participants even got paid. Half the people I know around here were involved. Okay, that's an exaggeration. But a lot of locals turned up as extras. As far as we know, that was the last time the two victims saw each other. We actually questioned Farrell about Albion's death once we heard they'd been seen arguing. He had an alibi for the night Albion was killed, though, and then, of course, Farrell turned up the same way. I guess you're here to see the bodies?"

"It's a place to start," Ethan said.

Inside the morgue, they found Dr. Earl Franklin on duty. He had to be nearing retirement age, Ethan knew, but he was also one of the brightest and most thorough men Ethan had met in the field, and not only in Louisiana but anywhere. He greeted Ethan warmly. When he'd been young and had already set his sights on a career in law enforcement, Ethan had plagued the man relentlessly, wanting to learn everything he could, and Franklin had been unendingly patient, as well as informative.

"Great to see you," Franklin said to Ethan now. "Sorry you're here under such unfortunate circumstances, though."

The ME was a stout man with wire-rimmed glasses and a head full of white hair. He would have looked at home on a big front porch, wearing a white suit and sipping a mint julep, Ethan thought wryly. Instead the man preferred libraries and skiing vacations in Colorado to sitting around anywhere.

"Good to see you. Though I'm sorry about the circumstances, too," Ethan said.

"Well, both of you put your masks on and come in. I've got Mr. Corley and Mr. Hickory ready for your visit."

Both men were laid out on steel gurneys. Their autopsies had already been performed. Sheets draped their lower extremities, revealing the Y incisions on their chests.

"No reason not to get right to it," Dr. Franklin said. "Mr. Hickory was my only client this morning—both a good thing and a bad thing. My last was Mrs. Delsie Peterson. Do you remember her? Sorry to cut her up, but she died in her own home, alone in her bed, so the law required an autopsy, despite the fact she was ninety-eight. The old girl went easily. Just fell asleep and her heart stopped."

"Glad to hear that. I do remember Mrs. Peterson. She fixed all our collars when we were kids and on our way into church," Ethan said.

"Aren't you proud of the man, Doctor? He remembers his roots." Randy grinned.

"A very good thing. Meanwhile, here are my notes. Both men were in good health, other than stabbed through the heart by something long and sharply pointed. Like a bayonet," Franklin said.

Ethan took a moment to look over the notes the ME handed him. Then he studied each man in turn.

There was something incredibly sad about a person's earthly remains, no matter how they had died. When the spark of life left the body, it seemed to take everything important with it. No matter what, the body had a gray, pasty color. It didn't matter if the person had been Caucasian, or of African, Asian, Native American or any other descent, or represented a combination of nationalities. The flesh sank in until there was nothing real left of the person who had once made the physical being vital. He'd loathed open coffins all his life. What was the point, when the person was simply gone?

Most of the time.

He made a point of touching each icy cold body. He lingered, looking over the still-visible wounds to their hearts. Both men had exercised or at least been active enough to keep their muscles tight. Neither one had been young—the wrinkles creasing their flesh testified to that—but both could have looked forward to several more decades of life if they hadn't, somewhere and for some reason, crossed the path of a murderer.

"No bruising or defensive wounds to indicate a struggle?" Ethan asked, reluctantly accepting the fact that the dead weren't going to speak with him.

"If you ask me," Franklin said, "and I'm not the detective, of course, Randy is—it appears that both men were taken completely by surprise. They were facing their killer when he struck, and he murdered each man the same way. Quickly. No defensive wounds. I believe they knew their killer."

"And both men were killed where their bodies were found?" Ethan asked, though he knew the answer; he'd read it in the files Jackson had given him. It never hurt to have these things confirmed, though, especially when he was talking to the medical examiner who had been at the scene.

"Definitely. The soil beneath the bodies was drenched with their blood. We're still waiting for chemical analyses in the hope that something might turn up other than the victims' blood, but…like I said, I feel strongly that both men knew their killer and were taken completely by surprise."

"And dressed up in their reenactment uniforms," Ethan murmured.

"And for that reason we're looking at everyone—men and women—who were involved with the victims' final reenactment," Randy said, sounding very much like a cop and very little like the old friend with whom Ethan had gone to school.

Ethan nodded. "Last meals, Doc?"

"Gumbo—both of them," Franklin said. "Probably from someplace here in town. They died twenty-four to forty hours apart. They weren't at dinner together or anything. If they had been, they would have been at different stages of digestion, which they weren't. And, actually, I'm waiting for the lab results before I can be definitive with regard to Mr. Hickory. I'm going by my own gut, if you'll excuse the pun, in his case."

Ethan nodded; Franklin had been at this long enough to recognize what he saw and smelled.

"They eat long before they died?" he asked.

"A couple of hours," Franklin said.

Ethan turned to Randy. "Is there a reason why they would have been in their uniforms?"

Randy shrugged. "There's been a photographer in town paying people to pose. He said he hadn't asked either of them, though. He *was* at the reenactment, though, and took some shots there. As I'm sure you know, Brad Thornton and his brother, Mike, are making that movie with Charlie Moreau. Maybe they wanted to be extras. Hickory told his housekeeper he would be going out for a meeting, and she didn't need to leave him dinner. His people closed up the public part of the plantation right at five. The housekeeper was the last person to see him, right about that time, and he wasn't in uniform then. As far as Corley goes, no one seems to know anything definitive. He was on a research sabbatical, so he wasn't expected in class. He called a friend and asked her to feed his cats for the next few days, and that's the last we know of his whereabouts. His home is just this side of Baton Rouge, where he taught."

"He didn't happen to tell the friend what he was up to, did he?" Ethan asked.

"Said he had some meetings in St. Francisville. That was it," Randy told him.

"Well," Dr. Franklin said, pulling the sheets fully over both bodies, "I'll let these gentlemen get back to rest. Any more questions, Ethan?"

Ethan shook his head. "Not now, Doc. But—"

"You can call me anytime. You know that. I'm here."

"Thank you."

Ethan and Randy didn't speak again until they were back out on the street.

"You coming in to the office?" Randy asked. "You want to see what else we've got?"

"What else *do* you have?" Ethan asked.

"Nothing except a pretty damned good crime board with times and pictures and everything laid out in one place. I'm going to start interviewing the rest of the people involved in that *Journey* reenactment, and, after that, everyone else who was on board. Is that what the Feds would do?"

"Yep. It is."

"So…you coming?"

"Give me an hour?" Ethan asked. "There are a few things I'd like to do. Haven't even opened up my folks' old house yet."

"You all still own the place?"

"Yep. My folks rent it out, but they're looking for new tenants now, so it's empty. Worked out nicely for me."

"An hour, then. I'll make some phone calls while I wait for you, get some of the St. Francisville police going door to door to see if anyone heard or saw anything. It's always quieter and easier to call when the night shift's on," Randy told him.

"See you soon," Ethan said.

Just then Randy's phone rang, and he motioned to Ethan to wait while he answered. After a one-sided conversation consisting mostly of "Uh-huh" and "You're sure?" he thanked the caller. His expression serious, he turned to Ethan and said, "Ethan, I just got some news, and it's something you need to know."

"What's that?"

"Doc Franklin was right about the gumbo. Both victims were seen eating it at the Mrs. Mama's Café in town. And there's one man who was seen around the same café when the victims were there. One man who might have had a beef with both of them. A guy who knew them, and might've been dining with them," Randy said. "One particular man I want to interview—at the station."

"And who is that?"

"Jonathan Moreau," Randy said, then added softly, "Charlie's father."

4

Charlie was half listening as Brad talked excitedly about some contacts he'd made who might help him get broad distribution for their movie when she saw Ethan enter the restaurant. She sat straighter, frowning as he greeted the owner, Emily Watson. Emily had been there as long as Charlie could remember and surely had to be in her eighties. The two of them were smiling and chatting, but Ethan was clearly looking around for someone as they talked.

Her?

Yes.

She saw him thank Emily as she pointed to Charlie and the film crew where they sat toward the back of the restaurant.

Brad nudged her to get her attention.

"Look, it's Ethan Delaney," he whispered. He didn't wait for her to respond before he stood and called out, "Ethan! Hey!"

Ethan smiled and headed toward their table, where introductions were quickly made.

He wasn't wearing a suit the way FBI agents always

seemed to in the movies. He was wearing a tailored denim shirt, blue jeans and a denim jacket. He wasn't dressed as casually as most of their crew, though. Most of them—including Jennie and Charlie—were in T-shirts and jeans or khakis.

"Guess you're here to help solve the murders, huh?" Brad said. "I would have thought they'd leave this to the local police. Then again, maybe this counts as a serial-killer case, and that's why the Feds are in on it?"

"Who really understands why the powers that be decide these things?" Ethan said, taking a spare chair at the end of the table. "But despite the reason, it's good to be home, see some old friends."

"Glad you still think of this as home," Mike said, leaning forward. "And I didn't mean that sarcastically, honest."

"This will always be home," Ethan assured him. "We still own the old house. My parents will never give it up, and honestly, neither will I. But enough about old times." He turned to Brad. "I hear you Thornton brothers are tearing up the film world."

"Hardly tearing it up, but…trying," Brad said.

"You should be in the film! I'm sure we can find you a uniform and make you an extra," Mike said.

"I'd love to be in your film, but I'm on company time right now. The taxpayers might frown on me taking time off for fun," Ethan said. "But who knows? I hear it will be a few days before you can film out by the old church again."

"Yeah, we've had to switch the filming schedule around," Brad told him. "So, if you've solved the murders by then and you're still around, I'm going to hold you to that."

"It's a deal," Ethan said.

"I hope you'll join us for something to eat," Brad said.

"Thanks for the offer, but actually, I'm here for Charlie," Ethan said.

"Oh!"

Everyone around the table spoke in unison, as if perfectly on time for some predetermined cue.

Then they all turned as one to stare at Charlie.

Of course, even those who had never met Ethan knew that, ten years ago, she had found a bracelet belonging to a murdered girl, and that when the killer had come back, Ethan had tackled him, saving her life.

"So Nick and Nora Charles are back at it," Brad said.

"Brad, no one knows who Nick and Nora are these days," Barry said.

"Okay, think *Remington Steele*," Brad suggested.

"Still too far back," Luke said with a laugh.

"Oh, come on!" Brad protested.

"Try *The X-Files*, Dana Scully and Fox Mulder," Blane offered. "They just made a comeback."

"Booth and Brennan—*Bones*," George said.

Ethan looked over at Charlie and smiled. "Charlie's an actress. She's not involved in the investigation in any way. I just want her to go out to the field by the grave-yard with me."

"Relive old memories?" Jennie asked, shaking her head. "Not a good idea, especially when an old, abandoned cemetery is involved."

Brad cleared his throat. "I don't think they're trying to relive the past, Jennie. He wants her to show him where she found the body. Actually, I can help," he offered, turning to Ethan. "Spare Charlie from having to go through it all again."

Ethan and Charlie were already out of their chairs.

"Brad, I'm fine. It's not a problem, and I *am* the one who found the body. Besides, I know you. You're already thinking about revising the shooting schedule yet again, then calling everyone to let them know the latest plans before you look over the dailies and moan about the fact that you have to be your own editor. Just call me when you have a final shooting schedule, okay?"

"She knows me," Brad said to Ethan, smiling, then added, "We went to college together. We're kind of like a sister-brother team, you know?"

"Sure," Ethan said. "And as soon as I can get away, I'd love to hang out on set."

"Cool. Anytime," Brad offered.

Charlie was already heading for the door, waving goodbye to everyone over her shoulder. She wanted to smack someone, she just wasn't sure whether that someone was Ethan for being so smooth or her friends for being so naive. Sure, he wanted to hang around on set, but not because he had any interest in being in the movie. He was suspicious of everyone involved with the film because, as far as he was concerned, any one of them could be a killer.

Ethan quickly joined her on the street.

"That was pretty rude, making them think you're interested in their movie when all you really want is to figure out if one of them—one of my friends—is a murderer," Charlie snapped at him.

He shrugged, looking at her as if he was trying to figure out what changes the years had made. "You're the reason I'm here, and I assume it's because you want the truth. Because we both know that it will haunt you forever if these murders aren't solved. And, yes, some of your friends are under suspicion, though they're hardly the only ones. But I'll also have you know I was in one of Brad's movies before."

"You were not!"

"Yes, I was. I was ten, Brad was seven. My mother made me. She and Brad's mom were pretty tight. He and Mike were already playing with cameras. He wanted to make a cowboys and Indians movie. He made me be a cowboy."

"You don't like cowboys?"

"In Brad's film, the Choctaws were victorious. Cowboys had to die. I did so pretty dramatically, if I remember correctly."

"So you'd really be in Brad's film?" she asked him.

"Why not?"

"You wouldn't get in trouble with the FBI?"

"With enough makeup, no one would even recognize me. And extras aren't credited, so who would even know?"

Charlie looked at him doubtfully. "Whatever. So, I've got my car. I can meet you on the bluff and—"

"No, we'll leave your car here. I'll drive." He met her eyes, his expression serious. "This is important, and we both know why." He started walking toward his car.

"Because a dead man spoke to me?" Charlie asked.

"That would be it, yes. But afterward, you've got to stay out of the investigation," he told her firmly.

She'd been walking briskly alongside him, but now she stopped abruptly.

"You said it yourself. You're only on this case because of me," she reminded him.

"Yes, and I'm not taking chances with your safety again."

"We didn't take chances. You called the cops. We waited for them to get there. It was the right thing to do. Period. No one could have known the killer was going to come back to find the bracelet," she said emphatically.

"And no one can deny the terror we felt when we saw the bastard with his knife out," Ethan said.

"You weren't terrified. You always planned on being a cop, and you knew just what to do," she said.

"I *was* terrified, because I saw him coming at you with a knife," Ethan said quietly. "And I was lucky he was nothing but a skinny coward who relied on the fact that his victims were weaponless and not as strong as he was. I was a fool kid. I just jumped at him, and he went down."

"Yes, and even though you didn't plan to, you stopped a serial killer," she said firmly. "I found Farrell Hickory. I didn't start out the day wanting to find a body. It happened. I'm part of this."

"Do you have a death wish or something?" Ethan demanded.

"No. Do you?"

He let out a sigh of aggravation and walked ahead of

her. Charlie followed. If he wanted to drive, he could drive.

He opened the passenger side door for her, and she slid in. They didn't speak as he headed toward the bluff.

They still didn't speak when he stopped the car. She hopped out quickly and headed toward the place where she had found the body. Trampled crime-scene tape remained, but the crime-scene techs had finished their work and the site was deserted.

"Here, obviously. Right here," she said quietly.

She stood still. There was a gentle breeze blowing that high up, and it was the time right before true darkness fell. The nearby trees seemed to sway and move like great dark beings with a life of their own. Traces of sunset remained, thin, quickly fading streaks of color in the sky. She stood there and relished the sensual movement of the breeze across her skin.

Ethan walked over and stood beside her, but she knew he wasn't feeling the breeze. He looked toward the area with the unhallowed graves, and then beyond, toward the church.

"So he was killed right here," he murmured.

"Could the killer have brought the body here?" Charlie suggested.

Ethan shook his head. "Died right here." Then he added quietly, "The ME could tell by the amount of blood in the ground." He hesitated. "There was a lot—he was stabbed in the heart. Thing is, what the hell was he doing up here? In uniform?"

"He wasn't part of the movie," Charlie said. "And

we'd been out here for several hours before I...before I found him."

"He told people the night before that he had a meeting, but he didn't say where. We do know he was killed with something long and sharply pointed, like a bayonet."

"Are you suggesting that his meeting was with someone involved with the film? Someone with access to props?" she asked, trying to keep a defensive note out of her voice.

"I'm not suggesting anything. I'm saying that both of these men put on their reenactment uniforms, went out to meet with someone and wound up dead. I'm trying to think of reasons for why they were in their uniforms. If you can come up with any, please feel free to share."

"People are always doing things in uniform around here. There are historical reenactments around every corner, living-history plantations... There's the *Journey*, the riverboat my dad works on, and when it's in port—"

Charlie broke off. Something in Ethan's face had changed. She stared at him for a moment, realizing that the police *were* suspicious of reenactors, which meant they were suspicious of her friends on the film.

Worse, she could tell that they were also suspicious of everyone involved with the *Journey*—including her father. And the way Ethan was looking at her...

"No! Oh, no, no, no. You can't possibly think my father had anything to do with this in any way," Charlie said.

"I don't," Ethan said.

"Of course not," she said. But something in his eyes,

an evasiveness she had never seen from him before, told her that he wasn't telling her the whole truth.

"But there are those who do."

She froze, staring at him in shock.

He took a deep breath and said, "There's no one person who's a prime suspect at the moment. What we know is that Farrell Hickory and Albion Corley had some kind of a disagreement when they were working that reenactment and your father stepped in. From what I understand, it was heated, and he wasn't pleased with either of them, but in the end he got them calmed down. He was also seen at the restaurant, having a meal with them."

"You don't kill someone because you've had an argument!" Charlie insisted vehemently. "And certainly not if you ate with them after!"

"No, and as I said, I don't believe your father had anything to do with this."

"But you—you don't even like my father," Charlie said.

"Charlie, I don't *dis*like him. *He's* the one who doesn't like *me*. But whatever our feelings, they have nothing to do with the situation. Right now, I'm floundering in the dark. I'm looking for motive, a reason why the killer targeted these two men. I'd hoped if we came out here together, we might find some clue, that if a dead man did call your name…"

"You know I didn't make it up."

"I know. I'd hoped he might come back again," he said quietly.

Who was he hoping might come back? she wondered. A Confederate cavalryman? Or had it been Farrell Hickory himself who'd called to her?

Charlie stood there silently for a minute, then shrugged. "I'm sorry," she said. "No one came back."

"We have two groups of people to consider," Ethan told her. "Reenactors, including the people on your film, and everyone who was aboard the *Journey* the day of the fight."

She stared at him, but night was falling in earnest, making it hard for her to read his expression.

"Let me get you back to your car," he told her.

"Yes, thank you," she said tightly.

He turned away, and she followed right behind him, then paused to look back.

Right where she had been standing, something seemed to be taking form in the air, a deeper shadow forming against the darkness.

And then she saw him. The Confederate cavalry officer she had seen before, Anson McKee.

He looked at her gravely, then pointed toward the river.

Seconds later he was gone, leaving Charlie to wonder if she had really seen him at all, or if he had been only a shift in the light or a haunting figment of her imagination.

"Charlie?" Ethan turned back to her.

"Sorry," she said tersely. "Coming."

She had seen a ghost. She knew she had seen him. And she knew she should have told Ethan—after all, he was here because she believed in his ability to find the truth.

But the ghost had pointed to the river.

And she knew exactly where he had been directing her to look....

To the *Journey*.

Ethan's family home was outside the historic downtown section of St. Francisville. It was, however, equally as old. Someone back in his family's history had raised horses. They'd largely been sold or conscripted by the Civil War, and in the 1880s the stables, paddocks and the bulk of the property had been sold off. Now, to the one side of his house, there was a housing community called Golden Acres, and to the other was a sprawling manor built in the 1890s. The Delaney family residence was two full stories, with a half-story attic above. His mother had been in love with the idea that the family had once kept horses on the property, and there were paintings of the animals all over the house.

It was furnished as a hunting lodge might have been, with heavy wood pieces, and leather sofas and chairs. There was a large-screen television set up to work with a gaming system. His parents didn't keep cable hooked up, but they had Netflix and could stream TV and movies anywhere in the house.

He wasn't sure he was going to spend enough time here to worry about entertainment, but he was glad he could connect his laptop wirelessly and see his photos on the giant screen.

He'd taken a shot of Randy's board, which was as impressive as promised. There were pictures of Farrell Hickory and Albion Corley as they had been in life.

There were also the crime-scene and the autopsy shots, along with a fact sheet on each man estimating time of death, last meal and everything the police had put together regarding his last movements.

The only place where the men's timelines had crossed, at least as far as they knew, was for the special reenactment on the *Journey*. There was a note that a local photographer, a man named Chance Morgan, had spoken with both men about taking some shots the Celtic American Line could use for PR, but he claimed he hadn't been able to arrange a time with either man.

Ethan had called Morgan himself as he'd left the station earlier. Along with everyone else he was looking at, he had to consider the photographer, who was known for his photos replicating those taken during the Civil War. He'd told Randy Laurent that he'd been in Baton Rouge on the days when the murders had been committed, and he had hotel bills to prove it. But in Ethan's mind, Baton Rouge just wasn't far enough away to clear him. Randy had, however, verified Morgan's claim to have been shooting stills for a local catering company.

When Ethan had reached him, Morgan was shooting a wedding at the Myrtles, but he'd told Ethan he could see him the following day any time he wanted. They'd made an appointment for nine o'clock the next morning.

He examined Randy's board on the big screen. Examined it over and over again. Randy had dispassionately told him that Jonathan Moreau made a damned good suspect. He'd argued with both the dead men. Either of the men might easily have planned to meet him to discuss a new project. Jonathan Moreau knew about

Civil War weapons, including bayonets. He knew the area like few other men.

But when Ethan looked at things closely, even considering the fact Moreau was Charlie's father and he had an emotional connection with Charlie from the past, he came to the conclusion that Randy's reasoning was really only a lot of speculation.

They didn't have anything concrete. No witnesses. No physical evidence. Just two men who had died wearing reproduction uniforms, killed by a weapon that could have been a Civil War bayonet.

Ethan turned away from the screen.

It was tempting to believe the murders had something to do with an old grudge that led back to the Civil War, or at least someone's interpretation of it. Even when he'd been a kid in school, there had been teachers who referred to "the War of Northern Aggression."

So many terrible things had happened back then. The war itself. Reconstruction. The rise of the KKK. Murder and mayhem and resentment for years and years to follow. At least in the world they lived in now equality was the law of the land, although that wasn't always true in reality.

You could never tell what was really going on in a man's heart or mind, no matter what the law dictated.

And the fact that, based simply on the identities of the victims, the murders appeared to have a connection to history and those who reenacted it bothered Ethan, in part because the connection was so obvious.

When it came to solving crime, the obvious explanation was often the true one.

But sometimes it wasn't.

Ethan turned and looked at all the information again. He needed to be objective.

Objective, yes.

Whoever had killed those men...

He was damn well sure it hadn't been Charlie's father.

"It's wonderful, Charlie. You have to see it," Clara Avery said excitedly over the phone. "It's in Northern Virginia and was actually built as a theater in the early 1800s. It was a venue for political speeches, as well. It became a movie theater in the 1930s, and then it was a bowling alley for about forty-five years. Then someone started to develop it as a theater again, ran out of money and interest, and headed west, abandoning it. But it's beautiful. The architecture is stunning, and the sound is fantastic."

"It does sound wonderful," Charlie said.

She suddenly heard something slam against the door, and she took the phone with her as she went to look out the peephole. There was no one there, and no one on the street.

She shrugged. She must have imagined the sound.

"I'm so happy for you and Alexi. Your own theater! But...wow, that's a lot of work, choosing shows, casting, hiring a permanent crew to do lighting and set design and...wow," she said again.

"You have to come perform here," Clara said.

"Yes, of course," Charlie said distractedly, still wondering about that noise at the door.

"Charlie, you don't sound like yourself. Ethan is there, right? He'll figure out what's going on. And—"

"Clara, you know those murders I told you about? My father is a suspect."

"What? You can't be serious."

"I'm sure there are other suspects, too, but he's among them."

"Oh, no." Clara was quiet for a minute. "Thor Erikson—the agent in Alaska who worked with Jackson there and is now…now with me!—told me that Jackson might be going down himself, and probably Jude McCoy, too. I can come and stay with you if—"

"You've got a theater to manage."

"We're still in the early stages of renovation. We have a fabulous contractor who's handling everything. Alexi and I can both come." She was quiet for another long moment. "We both know how you're feeling," she added.

"Well, the two of you *could* be in the movie," Charlie said. "But you know I didn't call you to cry on your shoulder and try to get you to come down here and take care of me."

"I know that, but we're happy to do it, and this really is a good time."

"Well, then…" Charlie hesitated. "If you think you can both come, there's something else I want to try to work out."

"Oh?"

Charlie was about to start explaining her idea when she heard another thump. No, not really a thump, more of a…a scrape. Against the side window of the parlor.

She hurried over there, forgetting that Clara was still waiting for her to say something.

"Charlie?"

"Oh, um, sorry. I think the murders are connected to the Celtic American Line. So, my idea has to do with the Celtic American Line! You and Alexi used to work for the line," she said. "My dad works for Celtic American. Between the three of you, we must have an in. We need to find out more about what happened on that ship."

Her old softball bat was in the hall closet, or it had been. Charlie went to get it. She knew there was a gun somewhere. Her dad had taught her to shoot because their neighbors weren't that close and you never knew what could happen. She hadn't taken it to New Orleans, but she had no idea where it was now. Her father would have made sure that it was kept somewhere safe, but where the hell that was, she didn't know.

The bat would have to do.

"Clara, I'll call you back tomorrow. But do me a favor. Do talk to Alexi. And I'll talk to you again in the morning."

"You sure you're okay?"

Charlie gripped her bat. "I'm fine," she said.

She hung up, then turned on the television, thinking that outside noises wouldn't bother her if she couldn't hear them, or at least had something to distract her.

But just as she clicked the remote, she thought she heard scurrying outside.

A possum or a squirrel, maybe even a rat, she told herself.

And still, though she didn't know why, she felt her

heart thumping far too quickly. Some innate sense warned her of danger.

She almost jumped sky-high when she heard the next noise.

Someone was out there. Someone was walking around her house, looking in the windows.

Watching her.

It was growing late. Ethan suddenly found himself reaching for his phone. He had to know that Charlie was all right.

He hesitated, then told himself not to be ridiculous. He had every right to call her. She was the reason he was there.

He found himself thinking about the last time they had seen each other.

After that night in the graveyard, they'd been drawn to each other. She'd been in awe of him, and he'd been as ridiculously attracted to her as only a teenage boy could be. She was too young, and he'd known it, but she was still...Charlie. Lithe and graceful, with her deep blue eyes and long chestnut hair. She had the most captivating laugh, and she'd had a way of looking at him that...

Friends...it had been great to be friends.

But he'd known that in everyone's eyes—even, if he was honest, his own—she was simply too young. And when she'd come to New Orleans on a school trip and broken away to visit him, when she'd been alone with him in his dorm room, he'd already known how she felt about him.

He should have been prepared.

He hadn't been.

He'd come back to his room after dropping off a book to a friend, and there she'd been. Exquisite and tempting as any Eve, her perfect body bared for him alone as she'd stretched out on his bed, her hair falling over her breasts, her smile as sensual as that of the most seasoned lover.

He'd nearly headed straight to her. Older, better men might have done exactly that.

But he'd been raised to do the right thing.

He didn't think he'd ever wanted any woman more— or ever would—but giving in to the attraction, no matter what she thought she wanted, would have been just plain wrong.

As torn as he was, though, his voice had come out too harshly.

"Get dressed, Charlie. Get dressed now," he'd told her.

Then he'd left the room.

When he'd gone back to talk, she was already dressed and on her way out. When he'd touched her arm to stop her, desperate to explain, she'd shouted, "Don't touch me, Ethan Delaney. Don't you dare touch me!"

"Charlie, let me explain," he'd all but begged.

But she was already gone. He'd left her messages. A score of them. She'd finally left him one in return. "Stop worrying. We'll always be friends."

He'd tried to call again, but she hadn't answered.

That was when he'd realized she was embarrassed, and the only way she could be his friend was not to see him at all.

She *had* seen him, though. He'd gone to her mother's funeral. She'd been polite but distant. And, given her deep emotional pain at the sudden loss, he'd provided her the distance she'd needed.

And for the life of him, he'd never understood how every time he'd had any relationship since then—easy and casual, or deeper, with the potential to go somewhere—things just never worked out. Because no one would ever compare to the girl he'd walked away from.

And now, well...

Now she'd only called him because she needed his expertise.

Because he was the only law-enforcement professional who knew she not only talked to the dead, she could also see them.

He looked at the phone in his hand. And he dialed her number.

To his surprise, she answered.

"Ethan?"

"Yes. I was just checking that you were okay."

"I'm fine," she said, sounding a little breathless.

"Really?" he asked.

She laughed softly—the laugh that had always seemed to wrap right around his heart.

"Honestly, I'm fine. The authorities have cleared us to film on the field by the cemetery tomorrow, so I have an early call."

"Okay, great. I, uh, just wanted to make sure."

"Thank you."

"You're alone there, right? I mean, sorry if I sound like I'm intruding, but it's my job. Your dad is staying on the *Journey*, right?"

"Yes, he's on the *Journey*. I'm locked in. I'm fine."

"Okay, then. Well, I'll talk to you later."

"Sure."

"Night."

He was about to hit the "end call" button when she spoke again.

"Ethan?"

"Yes?"

"I'm *not* fine. I'm scared. I don't know what's going on, but I keep thinking someone is outside. I keep hearing things."

"I'll be there in five."

"I'm not propositioning you, I swear. I mean, you're not going to get here and find me... Well, it's not like that. Nothing sexual. Really."

"Got it. Nothing sexual." *Too bad.*

He hung up and headed out on the run, barely remembering to log off his computer and lock up his own house.

Nothing sexual.

Hell.

It was always going to be sexual between them, whether they ever acted on it or not.

5

Charlie heard the sound of a car driving up and hurried to the door to look through the peephole.

She let out a sigh of relief when she saw it was Ethan. He was driving a small black SUV that fit her image of the Bureau.

She threw the door open as he came up the walk. He was in a light pullover and jeans. No glasses. He looked...

Like Ethan. The Ethan she had known, but with closely cropped hair. His expression was tense, his eyes filled with concern, and as soon as he was close enough he took her by the shoulders, searching her face.

"Are you all right?"

"I am. I shouldn't have asked you to come over. It's just... I don't know. These murders...they're unnerving me."

"It's all right. I'm going back outside to look around. Lock the door. I'll just take a walk around the house and make sure no one's around and nothing looks out of place."

"Okay, thank you," she murmured. He went out, and

she immediately locked the door. A few minutes later, he was back.

"No one around now, anyway," he told her as he entered.

"Thank you, and I'm sorry for making you come out here for nothing. You have to be tired as hell, what with traveling and everything you've been doing today. Here it is, nearly midnight, and you're still on the clock, as they say."

"I was awake."

"Well, I'm glad. Did you eat?"

"I did."

"Want a drink? Some tea—hot or iced—or I think—"

"Tea would be great. Hot. No milk or sugar."

"Sure. Make yourself comfortable."

She left him in the living room and fled to the kitchen. Everything seemed to be all right. Whatever had gone bump in the night—if she hadn't just been imagining everything—was gone, and Ethan was here. Of course, he was only here because he was an FBI agent, and she had requested his presence for protection. And protection was all she wanted. Right?

She set water on to boil and looked through the cupboards. Her dad kept staples in the house, but not much else, and she hadn't had time to do any shopping. In the freezer she found some frozen blueberry pastries and was happy to see that they were microwavable. She popped them in while she waited for the water to boil. A few seconds later she had a tray fixed with two cups of tea and the pastries.

Ethan was still standing when she returned to the

parlor. He had one of her dad's history books in his hands. It was a very specialized book, dealing with a group of Union generals who had risen and fallen—and sometimes risen again.

"You don't think his choice of reading material makes my father a murderer, do you?" she asked, aware her tone was sharper than she'd intended it to be.

"I don't think your father is a murderer at all—I've told you that."

"But he is in the suspect pool."

"Charlie, at this moment half the town and beyond is in the suspect pool."

"Of course," she murmured, lowering her head, not wanting him to see her flush. She quickly set the tray on the coffee table and sat in one of the old upholstered chairs nearby.

"So," she said, once he, too, had taken a seat, "what's going on? How's life?"

He shrugged. "It's good. I like being with the FBI. I wanted to join the Krewe. And now I'm a member of the Krewe."

She reached for a pastry. "That's great. I'm glad you like your work, but you always knew what you wanted to be."

"So did you."

"Alexi and Clara have both told me they're alive because of the Krewe."

"We do good work," Ethan agreed. "How about you? I see your face on the television now and then."

"Mostly commercials, I'm sure," she said. "Not that I'm complaining. They pay well. Theater—not so much.

But I still love it. And I'm doing the movie now. We've all invested our own money in it in exchange for a cut of the profits, so we're hoping.… I think it's going to be a good movie. It combines a lot of genres. The history in it is really solid. And it contains some social commentary, too. Plus, there's the added benefit that I got to come home and spend some time with Dad."

"You live in New Orleans these days, I gather."

"That's where the work is." She took a sip of tea, but it was still too hot, so she quickly set her cup back down. "So how about you? What's up? You're living in DC now?"

"I'm living in Virginia. An old town house in Alexandria. I've been all over, though. Worked in New York for a few years, which was great, but I love the office I'm in now. I haven't been there long, but long enough to know I enjoy it. It's cool getting to work with Jude, of course, and Jackson Crow is an amazing guy. I'm really learning a lot from him. And our real boss, Adam Harrison, is like some kind of wizard or something. So, yeah, life is good."

She nodded, then finally asked the question that had been nagging at her ever since she'd seen him again. "Any little Delaneys running around yet?"

"Nope. How about you? You gotten married since I last saw you?"

She shook her head. "What can I say? Obsessed with my career, I guess."

"You've got to have a life, though, you know."

"I *do* have a life! A great life," she told him. "I'm sure you do, too."

He smiled and shrugged. "No, not so much."

She found herself trying to slug down hot tea. "I guess that's your choice."

"Yes, I guess it has been."

Suddenly uncomfortable sitting so close and talking almost personally, Charlie stood, taking her cup with her. "I guess I should go to bed. Early call tomorrow."

He smiled. "No problem. Get some sleep," he told her as he rose and started heading for the door.

"You're leaving? I—I thought you were going to stay. There's the sofa—or one of the other rooms. There are two more bedrooms upstairs, my dad's and the guest room."

"I'm not leaving. I'm just going to take a last look around outside."

"I'm not going to bed until you're safely back inside."

"What did you hear exactly? What spooked you? Was it someone…?"

"It was someone living," she said flatly. "Not that I'm all that experienced with the dead, but I'm pretty sure if someone wanted to haunt me it wouldn't matter if I locked the door or not."

"Not that any of us is an expert, but I agree with you."

"I'm going with you," she said, coming to a sudden decision, ready to insist if he denied her.

"Okay."

Surprised, she followed him to the door and stuck close behind him as they walked out.

"There was a thump against the front door," she said, slamming a hand against the wood. "Sounded like that. But I looked out and didn't see anyone. Then, a little while later, I thought I heard someone at the parlor window."

"Okay."

She followed him past the row of bushes growing in front of the house. He got to the window she'd mentioned, then left and walked to the next, where he ran his fingers along the outer sill, producing a noticeable scratching sound.

"Is that what you heard?"

She nodded, biting her lower lip.

He didn't say anything as he continued walking around the entire house, checking the foliage as he went. He checked the back door, but it was firmly locked. They kept going until they came around to the front again. He opened the door for her to go on in.

"You think I'm hearing things," she said, pausing. She prayed it wasn't worse, that he didn't think she'd made up a story to get him over to her house.

He shook his head. "I know you don't make things up," he said softly, then urged her inside. "Early call," he reminded her. "You should go up to bed."

"I should. I will. Right now," she said.

"Good night, then."

"You're not leaving?"

"I'll be here," he promised her.

"Okay. Thank you. I'll see you in the morning."

"You got it."

Charlie hurried up the stairs. She didn't turn on the light, just closed the door to her room and walked over to the window. There was nothing to be seen. Even so, she couldn't shake the feeling that someone had been outside the house, watching, waiting for her to step out alone.

But Ethan had come when she asked, and she wasn't alone anymore.

She dressed for bed and lay down, listening. Whatever he was doing downstairs, she couldn't hear anything.

She knew she was only fantasizing when she hoped he would come up the stairs. If he did, of course she would tell him to go away.

No, she wouldn't.

She tried to fall asleep, thinking of that early call.

It didn't help. No matter how hard she tried to fall asleep, the effort went badly.

Charlie didn't imagine things.

Once she was upstairs, Ethan stepped back outside. He'd never been much of a hunter. He just didn't take pleasure in killing things. Odd, maybe, that he'd wound up in the FBI, where there were bound to be times when he had to kill a person. He wasn't sure what a shrink would think about that.

He'd been hunting enough, though, to learn a fair amount about tracking.

And he didn't need to be the finest tracker in the world to be able to verify what he thought he'd seen when he'd been out with Charlie.

Flattened grass, broken twigs and a scratch on the windowsill, as if someone had tried to pry at it.

He hunkered down and studied the ground by the window. He was pretty sure whoever had been there had covered their shoes, explaining the vague shape and flatness of the indentations in the earth. That made him equally sure they'd been wearing gloves.

That would have stood out if they were downtown, where people were everywhere. But out here where Charlie lived, most houses were set on several acres. It would be easy to dress like Godzilla and go unnoticed. Gloves and bootees were nothing.

He stood, went back in and studied the house's security measures. Good windows that closed tightly, latches snug, and locked, bolts on the doors. Even so, no place was impregnable, and there was no alarm. That wasn't good.

He had a gut feeling that tonight had only been a trial run. Someone had been checking to see just how hard it would be to break into this house. He was pretty certain no one was coming back tonight, at least.

Even so, he elected to sleep on the sofa, closest to the doors. He'd learned to sleep lightly, a useful skill for nights like tonight.

As he lay down, he thought about Charlie, sound asleep in her room upstairs.

He couldn't help but remember her face as they'd waited for the police that night ten years ago, her leaning against the grave marker, himself leaning against a tree.

And then the killer, bursting suddenly out of the woods like a berserk, heading straight for Charlie, as if he knew she had something to do with the end of his spree.

She had stared at him, as he raced toward her, and started to rise in defense. She would have fought like the devil, he knew. He'd seen the emotions fly across her face:

terror, anger, determination, and the look that meant she wouldn't go down without fighting.

He didn't remember actually thinking about anything himself. He just flew at the man, glad he played football and was a good tackle.

Someone had asked him once if he feared the dead.

He didn't.

He feared the living.

And he hadn't been haunted by the dead for the last ten years.

He'd been haunted by memories of Charlie.

When her alarm woke her early the next morning, Charlie could hear Ethan downstairs. Of course he was up. Not that she really knew his habits, but for some reason she'd doubted he was a late sleeper.

That meant she had to hurry. She quickly called Clara, hoping her friend would answer.

"Charlie! Hey, you good?" Clara asked anxiously.

"I'm good. Just reporting in," Charlie said, relieved that her friend had picked up.

"Did anything else happen?"

Charlie told her about the strange noises she'd heard the night before—and about calling Ethan. "Probably got spooked by a squirrel," she said.

"I'm just glad Ethan is there," Clara said. "And you don't need to worry. After I talked to you last night I told Alexi what's going on, and we made some calls."

"To?" Charlie asked.

"There's a new guy who took over recently as head of all entertainment at Celtic American. I worked for him when I first started with the company, and he was entertainment manager for the ship I was on. Anyway, to make a long story short—"

"Too late," Alexi said, having seized the phone. "Charlie, we can get on the *Journey* as Southern belles— and you should join us. We've already talked to Jackson Crow, and he's going to run it past Adam Harrison. I'm not sure how soon we can start, but we'll get back to you as soon as we know something."

"You two are incredible," Charlie said.

Clara laughed softly. "Well, we like to think so, anyway."

Charlie glanced at her watch. "Call you later today, okay?"

Then she dressed quickly and went downstairs.

Ethan was in the kitchen. He'd had no problem figuring out the coffeepot, and the smell of fresh coffee was nearly as appealing as the man.

"Good morning," she said, helping herself to coffee.

"Morning. You slept okay?"

She smiled. "Helped a lot that you were here. Thank you."

"Not a problem. And, as it happens, I'm going your way this morning."

"You can't be. I'm due on site in…" She paused and glanced at her watch, a gift from her mom. "I'm due in makeup in forty minutes."

"I know. Me, too."

"I'm filming a scene with the oil-company boss and the senator."

"I know."

"There are no extras in it."

"I know that, too. I talked with Brad this morning. I know more about the schedule now than you do. As soon as you film that scene, he's going to use a day-for-night filter and shoot some extra shots for the scene where the ghosts start to rise from their graves to protect you."

"You didn't say anything yesterday about being on the set today."

"I didn't say anything because I didn't know I would be. I had—and still have—an appointment with a guy named Chance Morgan—a photographer. He's going to find me some time during the day and ask Brad if he can get a few shots out by the bluff. So now this is my plan. I'm flexible, just like your filming schedule."

"Oh. Okay. Well, maybe I'll have a long enough break between scenes for us to catch a bite together in the catering tent. But how can you do that and work a murder?"

He just looked at her, and she sighed.

"Yeah, right. I forgot," she said. "The cast and crew are all suspects."

"Not all of them. Still, it never hurts to get to know the people you're looking at."

"Well, I have to head out now, and you—"

"Showered this morning. After Mike suggested being an extra, I realized that would give me a good reason for hanging around the set. I'm prepared for whatever may happen."

"I see. Wow, you're good."

"I do this for a living, Charlie."

She laughed. "Not movies." Then she sobered. "The

FBI, being an agent, it's more than a living for you, Ethan. And that's great. Listen, I won't be a sniveling coward forever. I won't take up all your time, or you'll never be able to do what you came here for."

"I'm not worried. I know you don't plan to monopolize my time, and anyway, I actually know how to manage my own time. I've cleared the decks, so I can spend the day on set. So…" He paused as he went to wash out his cup. "Whenever you're ready, Ms. Moreau," he said, setting the cup in the dish drainer.

"I'll just grab my things."

As they headed out, he turned and looked back at the house. "You should get an alarm," he said.

"We've never needed an alarm. We've had the same neighbors for ages."

"You need one now."

She fell silent as he opened the door to his SUV for her, and she stayed silent as he got behind the wheel and started to drive.

She couldn't help thinking about the way she'd felt the night before—afraid. Certain someone was outside.

Someone who was watching her.

And just might want to get in.

"Kind of ridiculous of me," she said aloud as they stopped at a light. "Two men were killed. Not women. And men in uniform, too. I've done my dad's reenactments, but I've never played a soldier. Some women did disguise themselves as men and join the army, and some of my friends have played those women, but I've always been a nurse, except once when I was a general's wife.

So it really was kind of silly of me to get so spooked last night."

He glanced her way. "Nothing is silly when people have been killed," he said.

"Well, I don't usually... I don't know why I was so frightened last night. If someone *was* hanging around outside, it was probably just some homeless guy feeling desperate and just looking for a place to sleep out of the elements. Anyway, I'm sorry, and thank you."

"Like I said before, not a problem."

When they reached the filming location, Charlie was surprised to see how pleased everyone seemed to be that she had brought Ethan. They were all staring at him like some kind of savior.

"Did you see the way they were all looking at you?" she whispered to him when they were finally alone before he headed out to the makeshift dressing rooms.

He laughed. "There's at least one forensics show on cable almost every hour of every day. People think every case can be solved in an hour. Too bad it's not true."

"Is there such a thing as a perfect murder? Do people get away with it?"

"In my opinion, no, there's no such thing as a perfect murder. But do people get away with killing? Yeah, sadly. Sometimes. But not this time, Charlie. We're not going to let it happen this time."

He gave her an enigmatic look and moved on.

Charlie headed to a bigger tent where she would have her hair and makeup done, as well as get into costume. They put her in spike heels and a pencil-skirted business suit, miserable clothes for running around in a field. She was playing an executive assistant who had just discovered fraud and shady dealing at the highest level in the film's fictional oil company.

Her scene took place just prior to the one they had been filming the day she'd stumbled upon the dead man.

She tried not to think about that.

To distract herself, she ran over the backstory for her character, Dakota Ryan, in her head. Dakota had been concerned for a while about things going on at the company. Now, having driven out to the bluff to deliver an important message to one of her bosses, she was about to come upon him in a clandestine meeting with a state senator. The senator planned to rig things so that the oil company could drill and lay pipe in an environmentally sensitive area, where it would damage the riverfront, but the increase in production would provide a huge profit to the stockholders. Once they discovered her presence, the two men took off after her, clearly intent on murder.

She went over her lines in her head as she changed.

When she stepped out, she froze for a minute.

The Confederate cavalry officer from that long-ago night was standing right there.

No, she realized, he was there in the flesh.

This wasn't a ghost, it was Ethan Delaney.

He was wearing a Confederate cavalry officer's uniform, complete with gloves and rakish plumed hat, not to mention a blond wig. She couldn't help being taken aback by his startling resemblance to a dead man.

A ghost…

A ghost who had come to her aid.

"A wig?" she asked him.

He grimaced. "Yeah. Jennie thought it would be perfect."

"It is, but you do know..."

"I do know what?"

"You look like him."

"Him?"

"You mean you don't know? You look like Anson McKee—Captain Anson McKee. You know who I mean. You *must* know."

"Are you talking about the ghost who brought me to you?" He shook his head. "I didn't realize. It must be the wig. The uniform's pretty typical for Confederate cavalry captains of the day."

"Maybe," she murmured. "You seriously look like you could be his great—well, I don't know how many greats, but his many-greats-grandchild."

"Seems unlikely. I'm an all-American mutt," he told her. "But I did look him up back then," he said softly. "He left behind one son and a wife he apparently loved with his whole heart. No evidence that he was messing around and might have produced an unknown bastard to procreate into the twenty-first century. As I recall, he was killed in the fighting in this area, right before Vicksburg fell."

Just then Brad summoned Charlie and her coactors for the scene. She excused herself and hurried over.

They were going to film uncomfortably close to where she had found the dead man, though Brad had been careful to avoid the exact location.

She was to come up a path, hear her boss and the senator speaking, and duck behind one of the crooked stones half-hidden in the tangle of overgrowth filling the abandoned unhallowed graveyard.

A sad place, she thought. Whoever lay there had been buried outside the bounds of the church's protection.

She pushed her thoughts aside, and smiled and waved to Brad, then started up the path, concentrating on her work.

She'd thought it would be so easy to work here, in her home. And it should have been. St. Francisville was normally a peaceful city, not the kind of place where people tripped over bodies every day. Except for her, apparently.

She neared the place she was to stop and listened while the two men said their lines, then slipped into hiding behind the gravestone. At the proper point in the script she moved—Brad would insert the sound of a twig snapping when he got to postproduction—and the men all turned to discover her. She leaped to her feet, told them the world was going to know about what they were doing and then turned to run.

"Cut!" Brad called. "Great—we need the opposite POV now, please. Once more—" he said, pausing to chuckle softly "—with feeling!"

And so they repeated the action for another camera angle. And then another.

Finally Brad was pleased with the results, and Charlie was free to watch as he called on his Confederate ghosts so he could film individual shots of them rising from the ground.

After watching for a while, she grew restless and found herself walking through to the church, out of range of the cameras. She wandered into the graveyard and searched until she found the grave of Confederate Cavalry Captain Anson McKee. She pulled weeds from the ground around his headstone and spoke aloud. "I don't know why you're still here. I don't know why Ethan looks so much like you. I don't know why people kill other people. I wish I could help you, because you certainly helped me."

She felt his presence the minute he came to stand beside her. She rose, stumbling a little in the ridiculously high heels. There was a solemn expression on his face as he reached out to her and said urgently, "Go. Go!"

She shook her head. "Go where? Please, tell me what's happening. Please...."

"Go!"

"The murders have something to do with the *Journey*, right? With what happened on the *Journey*?"

"Go!" he said again, and reached out as if he would shove her if he could, force her to move.

She nodded and turned to head back toward where Brad was filming.

As she turned, she felt a rush of air as something flew by her cheek.

She caught a glimpse of it in her peripheral vision. It was shiny.

She started to run, her mind struggling to process what she'd seen.

Only one object made sense, as much as she tried to deny it.

A knife.

6

"Look like a hero."

"Pardon?" Ethan said, jolted by a voice from behind. He was standing out on the bluff, along with Brad, Mike, Grant and Jimmy. Barry Seymour was also there, holding a light reflector, and Luke Mayfield was positioning the microphones.

"Dammit, Chance!" Brad exploded, turning to the man who had just arrived, balancing a camera and a gear bag. "When you told me Ethan had asked you out here, I said you could take still shots as long as we could use them. I didn't say you could plow into the middle of a scene."

"Sorry, sorry," the newcomer said earnestly. Then he turned to Ethan. "Man, you really look the part. You have to be Agent Delaney, right? Nice to meet you. You certainly look different from anything I've seen on TV, and not only because of the uniform."

Chance Morgan industriously pumped Ethan's hand. The photographer was a thin, wiry man of about forty, with sparse wheat-colored hair that grew long and scraggly. His smile and eagerness reminded Ethan of a puppy who expected nothing but fun and kindness from the world.

"Thanks for coming out here," Ethan said to the man.

"You two have to talk, I get it," Brad said. "Just take it off to the side somewhere, so I can shoot Grant and Jimmy."

"Thanks," Ethan said.

Brad shrugged off his irritation, then grinned. "You do look the part of a hero."

"That's the FBI for you," Barry said.

Ethan just nodded as he carefully unclipped the tiny mic he'd been wearing and handed it to Luke. "These are great," he commented.

"Easy on, easy off," Luke agreed.

Ethan set a hand on Chance's shoulder and led him across the field as he spoke. "So you knew both the dead men?"

"Knew them because of the show they did aboard the *Journey.* I got tons of great shots that day. Asked them if they wanted private sessions to get some shots they could use for PR, maybe to get more jobs. They both said yes but that they'd have to get back to me to schedule something. Needless to say, they never did."

"You didn't ask them to get into uniform and meet you anywhere, did you?"

"As God is my witness, I did not," Morgan said solemnly. "That sounds nice and Southern, right? I'm actually from nowheresville up in northern Wisconsin, but I love all this Southern atmosphere so much. The history, the reenactments…great stuff, especially for a photographer."

Ethan nodded. "So after the event on the *Journey*, you went…?"

"I was in Baton Rouge until yesterday, then I was out at the Myrtles, shooting a wedding. Man, would I have loved to own a plantation. Anyway, if you're worried, I can prove where I was. There were witnesses everywhere, and the metadata on my camera will back them up. I liked those guys, so why would I kill them?"

"All right, so tell me about the day you shot the reenactment on the *Journey*."

"A*mazing*," Morgan said. "It started out with the Confederates on deck. The narrator was super—what a voice. The story just soared."

"Jonathan Moreau?"

"Yeah. I think that was his name."

"What about the argument? Between Corley and Hickory?" Ethan asked.

"Oh, that was before the performance. They had the deck cleared while they got set up, no passengers allowed. I got the feeling when they weren't fighting, the dudes were friends. They called each other by their first names, were talking fine before they started arguing. I think Hickory started it. I heard him yell something about wanting to be authentic. Said no Southerner at the time would have handed the ship over to a man of color. That's the way he said it, too. Not black man, not African American, but 'man of color.' Then Corley shouted back that he had records proving such a man had accompanied the Union troops aboard the ship, and he told his friend to quit being a bigot. Hickory was all offended at that. Said he was the least prejudiced man he knew, if he did say so himself, and that Corley knew it. That's when that historian guy—"

"Jonathan Moreau?"

"Yeah, him. That's when he broke in. Calmed them both down. Said the records were a little vague, but that it was more than possible. Said there were records of a unit of freed African Americans in the area, mostly digging trenches, bringing in the wounded, but because there were so many wounded, some of them ended up working with the surgeons. Anyway, it was settled."

"What about the other people around? Anybody voice an opinion?"

"Everyone," Morgan said drily. "Oh, my God, if it weren't for Moreau, it might have turned into another war right there, and they might never have gotten the program started. It was really cool, too. You saw everyone being enemies at first, but by the end everyone was suddenly acting human. When the commanders transferred control of the ship, then shook hands and wished each other long life, they meant it. I'm telling you, I almost cried."

"Before things calmed down, do you remember anyone who might have been angry with both Corley and Hickory?" Ethan asked.

"No, it was just like the reenactment. At first, the actors were all arguing, but by the end they were all laughing and man-hugging each other. I was shocked when I heard Corley was murdered. I figured it had to

be some kind of hate crime. Then Hickory wound up
dead, too, and now I don't know what to think."

"You have photographs from that day, obviously,"
Ethan said.

"Is Wisconsin known for beer and cheese? You bet
I have photos."

"I'm going to need them. For the investigation. I
won't be posting them on social media or anything that
would mess with your copyright."

"Okay, sure. Want me to bring them to you? I can
get you prints by tomorrow, or I can send the files tonight or tomorrow morning."

"Send me the files. If I need prints, I can make them
at the police station."

"Whatever you need. Um, I'd still like you to pose for
me, if you wouldn't mind. You know, you look like one
of the guys whose picture is in the museum in town. I
was just there… Let me think. McKee! Anson McKee.
Yeah, that's it. There's a picture of him in New Orleans, too. There's a great traveling exhibit there now—
'Letters to Loved Ones.' Anyway, if I could take a few
shots… I mean, if you wouldn't mind?"

"I have to get back to work, but if Brad gives the
okay, as far as I'm concerned, you can take whatever
pictures you want."

Ethan headed back over to where Brad and Mike
were waiting, and let Luke reattach his mic before he
left, saying something about joining the others for a bite.

He was getting a bit tired of being compared to a
man who was long dead.

Even if he did consider the man's ghost to be a friend.

* * *

Charlie hurried over toward the catering tent—at least as much as she could hurry in those ridiculous heels—craving the company of a crowd.

She'd seen Ethan out in the field with Brad and Mike as she headed past.

For a moment, as she'd watched them all talking, she'd felt as if she were alone in the world.

She knew she should go over and tell Ethan what had just happened, but she wasn't ready for the others to know she saw ghosts or even that she was afraid a flesh-and-blood killer was after her. She was safe—for now—and there would be time enough later to fill Ethan in.

Bizarrely, when she got there she found the catering tent empty. She sat down at a table, and a moment later Jennie came in, flopped down in one of the folding chairs with an exhausted sigh and said, "Whoa, hope this film does well, 'cause these are long days we're putting in."

She was followed by Grant and Jimmy, headed for the cooler first to grab a couple of bottled waters, then they joined them at the table.

"Know what we need out here?" Jimmy asked.

"What?" Grant asked.

"A bathtub!" Barry said, walking in to join them.

"I was thinking a shower," Jimmy said.

"Same deal," Luke announced, coming over. "I'm grungy from tramping around this damn field."

"Yeah, and you don't even have to do the whole makeup thing," Jimmy told him.

"Nope. That's one reason why I'm in sound and not an actor," Luke said, grinning.

Charlie suddenly felt thirsty and went over to the ice chest herself, though at that moment, a large bottle of whiskey might have been preferable to water. She didn't know what to do. They were all so normal, so nice, people she'd known and worked with forever. None of them could have been waiting down by the church to throw a knife at her.

Could they?

Had she made up the whole thing? Had the wind picked up and blown a twig past her, but she was so spooked by the murders that she'd imagined it was a knife?

"Hey, girl, where're your shoes?" Jennie asked, reaching past her for a water of her own.

"By my chair. I took them off when I came in. It's not easy walking around here in stilettos."

They were all acting so normal, so natural. No one was winded.

And yet…they hadn't been there when she'd come in. The only people she knew for certain had *not* been anywhere near the church were Brad, Mike and Ethan.

"Thank heavens we're nearing the end of the day," Jennie said. "Lord, it's been a long one. I'm starving."

"Hey, all." Chance Morgan walked into the tent and introduced himself, though most of them knew him already, at least casually. "Got some great shots out there today." He paused in front of Charlie. "I took some of you earlier when you were up on the bluff, standing by an old grave marker. There's one that's spectacular."

Charlie smiled at him, but the truth was, she wasn't

sure she liked the idea of being photographed without her knowledge. Chance Morgan was a good photographer, though, and she knew that Brad wanted him on set so he could use his still shots for publicity when the time came.

"Nice," she said.

"I'll show you," he said, and hunkered down by her chair. "Gotta love the digital age," he said, turning the camera so she could see the LCD screen. "Here, look."

He *had* gotten a great shot of her. She was standing very straight, her hair flowing behind her. Decaying gravestones surrounded her, with the church and the river in the background.

"I love it," she said.

"If you'd like it for your portfolio, it's yours," he said. "I got some great ones with your friend, too. You know, the FBI agent."

"Oh?" Charlie said.

"Took 'em at the same time," he said.

She arched a brow. Ethan hadn't been on the bluff with her. But maybe Chase had gotten a shot of whoever had been out there and thrown that knife.

Assuming she wasn't imagining the whole thing, of course.

He frowned as he started clicking through his shots. "That's odd—they're gone. I thought they were right here, but all I have is shots of you. Well, I'll download everything later and get it all figured out."

She was too shocked to tell him that she hadn't been with Ethan.

He had seen the ghost.

She set a hand on his arm, and he looked up at her. "I'd love to see all those shots, Chance. Would you email me the whole batch?"

"Sure. I just wish I could find the others...."

He started searching through his camera again, and she watched over his shoulder.

She didn't see Ethan, of course, because he hadn't been there. And, not surprisingly, ghosts didn't show up in pictures.

Most worryingly, she didn't see anyone else. Except...

There *was* someone, she thought, over in the trees near the church. And maybe, just maybe, once he downloaded the images and she could see them on screen...

Charlie rose. "Thank you so much. I'd love to have the pictures for my portfolio. It's so generous of you to offer them."

She realized she was being too effusive. But she was nervous, keyed up, and couldn't seem to stop babbling.

In fact, she was tempted to tell Chance Morgan that he'd seen a ghost.

Charlie was behaving strangely, to say the least.

She was walking around shoeless, although that was understandable. It was ridiculous for her to run around the area in spiked heels. And Ethan had to admit that she was incredibly attractive in the skinny suit and mile-high heels.

But she looked as if she was about to scream, except she didn't. She almost visibly pulled herself together, then smiled and waved at him as if everything was fine.

He'd been watching her from a distance all day. He

hadn't seen anyone suspicious anywhere near her. In fact, other than a tour group heading into the church, he hadn't seen anyone at all who wasn't part of the film.

On the other hand, trees and brush and the jagged landscape had periodically obscured his vision. He made a mental note to tell Charlie not to go wandering off in the future.

He'd tried to keep an eye on the others, too, but at this point most of them had retreated to the dressing rooms or the catering tent, a makeshift creation of a few poles draped in canvas, and a bunch of folding chairs surrounding a few folding tables. The weather was changing. The dead heat of summer was no longer upon them, and in the shade, the day was almost pleasant.

For the most part, it had been easy watching Charlie, and it was a bonus to be on the set, because it gave him the chance to speak with the rest of the cast and the crew during breaks. He hated having to consider them suspects, but it was a necessary part of the job, and it was great to be able to form his crucial first impressions without letting them know that was what he was doing.

Jennie McPherson was effusive and charming, casually confident. She was excited to be a shareholder in the movie but not particularly worried about whether her investment earned out or not. She was a good makeup artist and could always find work in New Orleans, because the film industry was booming there.

Grant Ferguson was older and an established accountant. Jimmy Smith had freely admitted that he was praying for the movie to do well. Acting was his life, but he wasn't exactly earning the big bucks. Barry Seymour was also heavily invested in the project, but he was quick to say that he would never have invested if his financial security depended on it. He had a fiscally conservative father who'd lectured him about investing since childhood. He was going to be all right.

"The best money a lot of these guys made in ages was for that special reenactment on the *Journey*," Barry had told Ethan. "Most of them are so in love with history that they'll spend stupid amounts of money to be involved in something like this movie. Not me. I'm happy to invest, but not to risk anything I can't afford to lose." He'd looked across the field to where Charlie was standing. "Some are smarter than others. You take Charlie's dad. History is his life, but he's no fool. Jonathan Moreau knows his own value, and he makes sure he's well paid for doing what he loves."

Jonathan Moreau's name again. But he could no more see Jonathan Moreau stabbing a man in the heart with a bayonet than he could see *himself* doing it.

"So most of you were involved with the programming on the *Journey*," Ethan had said. "Did any of you get in on that argument between Farrell Hickory and Albion Corley?"

"Oh, God, no! I made a point not to get involved," Barry had said.

"Did you see who started it? And was anyone passionately opposed to one man or the other?"

"I think Hickory started it," Barry had answered. "And I think he was being an ass. I mean really, who the hell cared? It was all about whether a black man had really been there, but Jonathan said there's no real proof either way. And in New Orleans these days, we're such a mixed bag, no one notices anyone's skin color any more than they notice hair color. I know we're talking history, but…" He'd shrugged. "It just wasn't worth fighting about, you know?"

"Cut!" Brad called, jerking Ethan abruptly back to the present.

He had been kneeling, head bowed, as he contemplated the earth he'd risen from and to which, he assumed—he hadn't read the whole script—he would return when his protective presence was no longer needed.

"Damn, but you look the part," Mike said.

"Thanks," Ethan said.

"Too bad you're a Fed," Brad told him. "You look great on film. You could make a career of this, if you wanted."

"Thanks. I have to admit it's fun," Ethan said, keeping his eye on Charlie. He could see the catering tent from his vantage point. She'd looked a little lost when she went in and found herself alone, but she was now speaking with Jennie and Jimmy. Something about her body language seemed off, though, as if she were trying too hard to act casual.

"Excuse me," he said. "I'd just like to make sure Charlie is doing okay, seeing as you're filming so close to where she found the body and all."

"Yeah, this is kind of awkward for all of us," Mike said. "I feel like we should do more to respect the dead, but at the same time, we paid for permits. And we've all got our lives and finances wrapped up in this thing, so we've pretty much got to keep going."

"You moved the filming as far away from the burial site as you could. Nothing else you can do," Ethan said.

He'd known both Thornton brothers forever, though he was older, so they hadn't been close friends.

"You know," Brad said, suddenly passionate, "we'd never let anything happen to Charlie."

"We'd die for her," Mike added softly.

Brad nodded.

"Yeah. I believe you," Ethan said, nodding, then walked away, anxious to get to Charlie. It was already late afternoon. Where the hell had the day gone?

She spotted him as he entered the catering tent, and smiled broadly—too broadly.

"I'm done for the day," she said. "I'm going to go change clothes. What about you?"

"I'm done, too, though I think I need a bath," he said.

"I think we all need baths. Even those of us who didn't roll around in the dirt," Jennie said. She raised her voice and asked the larger group, "Anyone want to meet for dinner?"

A round of "okay" and "sure" answered her.

Ethan looked at Charlie and found her looking at him.

"Yeah," she said. "I'd like to walk over to the grave-yard first, though."

"Charlie, you're obsessed with that place," Luke said. "If you ask me, you should stay away."

"Hey, my mom is buried there," she reminded them.

"Leave her alone," Jennie said. "How does two hours sound? That gives everyone time to clean up, and hopefully, the café will still be open."

"They serve until ten," Luke offered. "We should be fine."

The group began to split up, actors heading over to the "dressing rooms" to change or down the road to their cars, crew gathering equipment. Ethan and Charlie both left to change. He asked her not to head out to the graveyard without him.

"Nope. Don't intend to," she assured him.

She looked almost wild, he thought, her chestnut hair tousled, her eyes so dark they were almost indigo.

He was ready before her, his Glock tucked into the back of his jeans.

She appeared a few minutes later, and they headed for the graveyard. In place of her stilettos, Charlie now wore sneakers as they moved through the tangle of high grass, brush and weeds.

She still didn't seem like herself, so when she didn't say anything he demanded, "What happened?"

He'd expected her to dodge the question, but instead she answered honestly right away.

"Someone threw a knife at me," she said.

He paused, staring at her. "What? Who?"

"I don't know—if I knew, I would tell you."

"You're sure? Where did it happen? When?"

She inhaled deeply, then let her breath out in a rush. "No, I'm not sure, but… I went to Anson McKee's grave. And then he appeared and kept telling me to go. I tried to ask him what he was talking about, but he just kept telling me to go, so I went. I ran. And then I could swear I saw a knife go flying past my head."

"What kind of a knife?"

"I don't know! I was running. I barely saw it," Charlie said.

"Okay, so where were you exactly when it happened?"

"That's where I'm trying to take you now," she said, exasperated.

"All right, all right, let's retrace your footsteps."

"I think I know almost exactly where it happened," Charlie murmured, walking ahead of him.

He followed closely, unwilling to let her get too far away.

She paused. "I was right about there," she said. "I'd left the grave, which is over there." She pointed. "Whoever threw the knife had to have been standing in the trees, those oaks right there."

"So the knife would have landed in the unhallowed section of the graveyard, right?"

She nodded. "I think so."

They headed that way and started examining the ground, looking for the weapon. Ethan could tell from Charlie's tense expression that she was uncomfortably reminded of the night she'd found a body while searching for a missing prop.

"Hey!" called a friendly masculine voice from behind them.

Ethan turned and saw Jimmy Smith heading toward them, a broad grin on his face. Ethan was used to sizing up suspects, and the first thing he noticed was that Jimmy wasn't particularly tall or well built, not that those were requirements for knife throwing, nor was he particularly handsome. On the other hand, his thatch of brown hair, hazel eyes, freckles and lopsided grin added up to the kind of cheerful manner that probably helped him deal with the vicissitudes of an actor's life.

"Hey, there. What are you doing over here?" Charlie asked him.

"It looked like you two were searching for something, and I thought maybe I could help. We always seem to be missing stuff. Charlie, you didn't lose one of your 'fuck me' shoes, did you?"

"No, I didn't lose a shoe," she said.

"I hope to hell you don't find another body." Jimmy turned to Ethan. "You haven't gotten any further on figuring out who the killer is, have you? I sure hope you catch him soon. It's spooking everyone out, knowing a murderer was so close."

"I think we're all handling it just fine," Charlie said.

"Yeah? Well, *I'm* sure as hell spooked out," Jimmy said. "I look at everyone—some of them friends I've known practically forever—and can't help wondering if one of them has blood on their hands."

"We're following every lead," Ethan said.

Jimmy looked worried, but he nodded. "I hope one of them leads somewhere soon. Anyway, sorry—I thought I could help, but to tell you the truth, I don't really like being out here when it's getting dark. Catch y'all at dinner."

He waved and left them.

"*Are* you following every lead?" Charlie asked Ethan.

"At the moment we don't really have any leads," he admitted.

"Except that the cops think my father might be involved," Charlie said.

"Let's see if we can find that knife, okay?" Ethan said.

"What if Jimmy's right and we *are* all spooked, and I just imagined the knife?" Charlie whispered.

"I don't think you imagined anything. And I'm not sure you should be around here right now. Aren't you done filming your scenes?" he asked.

She made a point of looking down at the grass.

"Charlie?"

"Mostly," she said.

Ethan turned suddenly, a shiver running up his spine, and saw that they weren't alone. Two people were standing near them on the bluff.

Barry Seymour and Luke Mayfield.

"Are we missing another prop?" Charlie asked as soon as she noticed them, too.

"Yeah, but, don't worry, we'll find it," Barry called back.

Ethan grabbed Charlie by the hand and led her over to the others. "We'll help," he said.

"It's all right," Luke said. He glanced uneasily at Barry.

"What is it?" Ethan demanded.

Luke let out a sigh.

Barry spoke. "An Enfield rifle. With a bayonet. And we didn't lose it today," he added in a rush. "Luke and I were just helping some of the others—Brad and Mike, Jennie—go through the props. But...when we counted the Enfield rifles—reproductions, not collector's items—we realized we were missing one."

"How long has it been missing?" Ethan asked sharply.

Barry and Luke looked at each other again.

"We're not sure," Barry said.

"The last time we had a record of anyone using it was a couple of weeks back—first day of filming some retro shots." Luke hesitated again. "It was before...before the whole special programming thing we did on the *Journey*. And it was just one of a bunch of props we signed out, so there's no record of who, specifically, was using it."

"Brad's calling that cop, Detective Laurent, right now," Barry said. "But Luke and I thought we should search the field one more time. We were thinking that maybe it got lost on the field."

"We were just hoping against hope that we could find it before we had to tell *you* about it, too," Luke said.

"We'll help you look," Ethan said.

He created a grid, scratching lines into the ground with a tree branch, and then all four of them went to work.

It was a lot of ground to cover, so it was a relief when Brad and Mike arrived, looking embarrassed and upset, and joined the search.

To no avail.

An hour later, there was no sign of the rifle and bayonet.

And no sign of a knife, either.

"It's too dark to keep going," Brad said. "We can try again in the morning." He cleared his throat. "I told Laurent, so—"

"So we can get the police out here to help once it gets light," Ethan finished for him.

Now, though, it was time to head back. Clean up. Have dinner.

And put in a call to Jackson Crow.

They were a glum group as they headed for their cars.

Still, Brad tried to be cheerful. "See you at the café," he said, forcing a smile.

They waved to one another, and then, at last, he was alone with Charlie in his rented SUV. He met her eyes. "You should know there's a leak somewhere. The media have the information that the medical examiner thinks both men were killed with a bayonet."

"And you think that the missing bayonet is *the* bayonet. The murder weapon," she added softly.

"Well, on the plus side, the fact that it's missing will make the local authorities think that the movie crew are as suspicious as your father," he said.

"Great," Charlie murmured. "I'm supposed to suspect my father or my friends."

"You've really got to stay away from that whole area now," Ethan told her. "Someone threw that knife for a reason, and until we know what that reason is, what someone—probably the killer—thinks you know, I don't want you out in the open that way."

She didn't reply. She was looking out the window.

"Charlie?"

"I hear you," she said, turning to look at him, serious at first, and then she smiled.

When they reached her place, she looked at him and

flushed slightly. "You're not just going to drop me here, are you?"

"Nope. I'm like a Boy Scout. Always prepared. I brought some things with me last night."

"Good planning. Thank you."

"Charlie, I don't like the idea that someone was snooping around here."

"I really might have imagined the knife, though. We didn't find it."

"No, we didn't." Whoever had thrown it might have gone back for it before they went back to search, but he didn't want to tell her that. She was worried enough as it was.

He stopped her just as she was about to slip the key into the lock, stepped forward and examined the door. Satisfied that no one had tried to pry it open, he nodded at her.

"We're going to be late to the café," she said, leading the way inside.

"Not that late. I'll see you back down here in twenty minutes—if *you* can be ready that fast, that is," he teased, trying to lighten the mood.

"Hey, you may be FBI, but I majored in theater. I can be ready to go in about fifteen minutes," she said, then turned and raced up the stairs.

He followed more slowly.

As he showered, he thought about the fact that they were both naked. Wet. Slathered in soap bubbles. And mere feet away from each other.

And he wondered…

If it didn't seem imperative that they actually make

it to the café that night, so he could have a chance to study the whole group in one place, he might have been tempted to make his way to her shower.

What was the worst that could happen? She could demand that he get away from her. She could be indignant and incredulous. Admittedly, she'd had a schoolgirl crush on him a decade ago. But that was all over now.

Or was it?

Maybe she would feel even better about him, like him more, once she'd had her chance to turn the tables but, he hoped, decided not to take it.

No, he couldn't take that chance, because something could happen that would be much worse than her simply telling him she was no longer interested. She could ask him to leave, and then someone out there, someone watching, might think that she knew more than she did.

He twisted the knob and made the water cold. Very cold.

7

Cold showers were good. They didn't tempt a man to stay beneath the steaming hot water and think equally steaming hot thoughts.

Ethan quickly got out and dressed and was ready to go. He grabbed his phone and dialed Jackson Crow before he headed downstairs.

As soon as Jackson answered, Ethan gave him a quick rundown of the case. The fact that a replica bayonet was missing from the film set was the best new information they had.

"That does seem to point toward someone working on the film being our killer. Still, I wish we had some idea of motive," Jackson said.

"There *is* a motive, there always is, and I'll figure it out," Ethan promised.

"Don't get ahead of yourself. You've only just begun your investigation. We've spent months—years—working some cases," Jackson reminded him.

And some cases, as Ethan knew, were *never* solved.

"We're working out some things here," Jackson said, "but more of us will join you by the day after tomorrow.

Meanwhile, I've got Angela digging up more detailed
information on the key players from the *Journey* and everyone involved with the film. Yes, there was some kind
of an argument about history. We can't figure a motive
for the murders based on that. The men didn't kill one
another. Someone killed them. And though they might
have worked together—and argued—on the ship, that's
not the only place where their lives collided. They both
belonged to the local Masonic lodge, and they were both
Shriners, as well. They contributed to and worked for
a number of the same charities. But we're still considering the riverboat, of course, and Charlene Moreau's
conviction that something connected to the riverboat
can lead us to the truth. We're also still considering the
plan to have her and the others work aboard the ship."

"I'm sorry, what?"

"I guess she hasn't spoken to you about it, then. At
the moment, it's only on the drawing board here. When
Charlene contacted us to ask for you to be assigned to
the case, she went through her friends Clara Avery and
Alexi Cromwell. The three of them were talking again
recently, and Charlene seemed to feel strongly that the
answer can be found aboard the *Journey*. The three of
them have proposed a plan to work aboard the boat as
part of the entertainment staff. Clara and Alexi have an
in, having worked other cruises for Celtic American."

"I see," Ethan said. "No, Charlie hasn't mentioned
this to me. Just what exactly is the plan?"

"They can accept a week's contract and go aboard as
a trio of singing Southern belles performing Civil War–
era songs. They proposed it as a test run to see whether

the line would like to hire them for future cruises, not
that the details really matter. Adam could have gotten
them on board if necessary. Anyway, they'll probably
join the staff for the *Journey*'s next cruise. And with
the situation as it is, I'll come down and probably take
over in St. Francisville while you tackle the riverboat."

"The murders happened on land," Ethan reminded him.

"Yes, I know. But from what Charlene told Clara and
Alexi when she asked them to intercede, there's a local
ghost who's appeared to her several times."

"Captain Anson McKee," Ethan said.

"Charlene feels he's indicated that the riverboat holds
the answers."

Ethan had felt his temper simmering before; now it
was boiling over. But Jackson was still speaking, so he
kept his mouth shut, though it was a struggle.

"The *Journey* leaves in three days out of New Orleans. And you'll have plenty of coverage. Jude will be
coming down with Alexi Cromwell, and Thor Erikson
will be down, too, though he's not a Southerner like
you and Jude. Alexi and Clara aren't agents, but they're
smart, and they've been through a hell of a lot themselves. Also, they have the same talents we all share,
and their perceptions might prove to be handy."

"Jackson, you've been with the Bureau a lot longer
than I have," Ethan said, "but the missing bayonet does
point to the film crew."

"You just said it's missing, and that means anyone
could have gotten hold of it."

"True enough. And there *is* a connection between a
number of the actors and the *Journey*. It turns out that

some of them took part in the same special reenactment as the victims," Ethan said. "So I suppose the likeliest explanation is that the killer is involved with both the ship and the movie."

"That's certainly what it sounds like."

"Or the killer could be setting things up to look that way," Ethan said. "It's possible the murders were motivated by something that has nothing to do with the film or the riverboat. According to the film crew, the bayonet was last seen before the program on the *Journey*. I can't figure out a motive, no matter what angle I look at it from—well, not yet, anyway. Farrell Hickory owned a historic plantation, Albion Corley was a professor in Baton Rouge, their paths crossed in multiple ways… There's got to be something else we're not seeing yet."

"Well, with no physical evidence and no real leads or witnesses, questioning and watching anyone who was even tangentially involved with both men seems to be the way to go," Jackson said.

"Agreed."

"And that involves the *Journey*."

Yes, Ethan thought, it involved the *Journey*.

And Charlie.

She had been busy, setting all this up and not saying a word to him.

"I'll go over everything we've talked about with Detective Randy Laurent tomorrow and see if the police have come up with anything else themselves. I'll let him know we're going to take a closer look at the riverboat."

"It's always best to work as closely as possible with local law enforcement. They always know more than we do about the area. Of course, in this instance, you're familiar with the area, too."

"But I've been gone a long time," Ethan said, "so Randy is much more aware of what's going on around here than I am. Things change—people change. The good thing is, people still gossip. And gossip can be the best lead there is."

"True. We'll connect again in the morning," Jackson said. "And if anything new comes up before then, call me."

"You got it."

They said good-night, and Ethan hung up.

He was still for a moment—both angry and amused. On the one hand, Charlie had gone behind his back. But on the other, he was only here because of her. So she had faith in him, apparently, but maybe not enough?

He looked at his watch. He'd used what was left of his twenty minutes on the phone. As he left the room he saw that Charlie was just coming out of her own.

He started down first, but near the bottom of the stairs, she tried to push past him. "Told you I'd be ready first!" she cried.

"Hey, no cheating," he told her, catching her by both arms as they reached the lower landing. He spun her around to face him. For a moment they were looking straight at one another, laughter in their eyes.

And for a moment he felt as if they were caught in time, as if his body were both frozen and searing hot all at once.

"Better get going," he said huskily, and released her quickly.

As if she had burned him.

Which, in a way, she had.

He smiled, curious as to when she would tell him about the plans she'd made with her friends.

She nodded. "Yes, let's get going."

They drove toward the café without speaking, as if neither one of them was quite sure what to say. It was late enough that it was easy to find parking on the street. As he exited the car, he looked up at the old wooden sign that identified the eatery as Mrs. Mama's. It was the same sign that had been there since he'd been a kid.

The café itself hadn't really changed, either. The place was still paneled in wood, with tile flooring. The building had originally been a hotel way back in the day, and at a later point it had been a school for young ladies. The Watson family had owned it for over seventy years.

The booths and tables were all solid wood. There was a bar that offered a view into the kitchen, and the lights were relatively bright. The kitchen itself was modern and busy. The café drew both locals and tourists.

It was especially busy whenever the Saints played. Emily Watson had seen to it that there were flat-screen televisions set high on the walls—along with pictures of famous Louisianans, Grace Episcopal Church, the Myrtles and other nearby plantations. There was also a striking picture of the *Journey* proudly moving down the Mississippi.

There was no Saints game that night, though, and the news was on, the sound muted.

When they entered, Mrs. Mama's was busy, though the crowd consisted mainly of the film's cast and crew. Everyone who had been working that day had shown up, from Brad and Mike Thornton to the photographer, Chance Morgan, who quickly came over and promised Ethan that he would get the files to him as soon as possible, but he was hungry and hadn't been able to resist the lure of a good meal first.

Ethan nodded. There were only two seats left, and they weren't together. Charlie wound up across the table from him, between Jimmy and George.

He took the remaining chair between Brad and Jennie.

Brad leaned toward him and said, "I heard from your friend Detective Laurent today." He laughed. "Randy! Whose high school claim to fame was popping beer bottles open with his teeth. But he makes a good detective, strange as that seems. Never acts like he's lording it over anyone, but he gets the job done."

"We were all kids once, and then we grew up," Ethan said. "So, what did Randy tell you?"

"He finally went through all the footage I gave him. Nothing. He said he didn't expect to see anything, that based on the autopsy, Farrell Hickory was dead and in the ground long before we started filming that day. I guess they're figuring he was killed the night before. And if Charlie hadn't found him, he might still be there, buried in a shallow grave." He was quiet for a moment. "Guess it might have gotten a lot worse if he hadn't been found. It would have looked like the North against the South all over again. Of course, now it looks like someone involved with my movie might be the killer."

"Yeah, I know how you feel," Ethan said. He liked Brad. He had also eliminated Brad and Mike Thornton from his personal list of suspects.

He believed someone had thrown a knife at Charlie.

And Brad and Mike had been with him at the time.

That still left a wide array of possibilities, along with the question of why someone was after her. Did it have something to do with her father? But what?

He glanced across the table at her. She was laughing at something Jimmy was saying. They had always been good friends, he remembered.

"Ethan, what are you having?"

He turned. Emily Watson—proprietor of Mrs. Mama's since he'd been a kid—was standing behind him. Despite being at least eighty, she was still slim and straight, and her face was beautiful, even with the passage of time. She was holding a coffeepot, and when she offered him some, he grabbed the cup in front of him and accepted with an enthusiastic "Thank you." He could see her age in her hands, but there was strength in them, as well.

He smiled at her. "I'll have your gumbo, of course, ma'am."

She nodded, pleased. Then her smile faded slightly.

"What's wrong?" Ethan asked her.

"I'm proud of my gumbo. It's my own recipe. But I can't help remembering that both Albion and Farrell were in here often, and they both liked my gumbo—and now they're gone."

"Did they ever get together here, Mrs. Watson?"

"Oh, my, yes. Those fellows were the best of friends," she said. Her eyes started welling up. "You find out who killed those two fine men, Ethan, you hear me?"

"I intend to do everything in my power," Ethan promised her. "Miss Emily, were they in here together before they were killed, by any chance?"

"I don't remember exactly, Ethan. I know they were both in here not long before they died, but not together, though."

Ethan nodded. "Thanks, Miss Emily. And I promise you again, I'll do everything I can to bring their killer to justice quickly."

Emily frowned. "Maybe Jonathan can help you."

"Jonathan?" Ethan said.

"You know. Jonathan Moreau. Charlie's daddy. He's in here all the time, too. Bless that man. He tells people on the boat that they have to come here for lunch. I saw him with both men together not that long ago. Maybe they told him something you can use. It was nice to see you come in here with Charlie, too." She winked at him. "You two make one handsome couple."

"Uh, thank you." He didn't try to tell her that he and Charlie weren't a couple. "So you're saying Jonathan was in here with Albion and Farrell recently?"

"Yes, a week or so ago, maybe. He's such a nice man."

A nice man whose name kept coming up in connection with two dead men. Even so, he couldn't believe Charlie's father had anything to do with the murders.

"You were always a bright and determined boy, Ethan. I know you'll handle this."

"Yes, ma'am."

Emily gave herself a little shake. "I'm going to get moving over yonder to see what Charlie would like to have—took care of the rest of these riffraff already," she said, smiling.

"Miss Emily knows everyone in town—and just about everything that goes on, too," Brad said. "And, of course, Nancy is working here now, too. What Miss Emily doesn't know, Nancy does."

"Nancy?" Ethan said.

"Nancy Deauville. Well, Nancy Deauville Camp now. She married Todd Camp. He works over at Perry's Garage."

"I remember her now. She was a year behind me in school."

"She was the pledge master who had Charlie tied to that gravestone the night you and she...encountered that serial killer."

"And she's working here now? I thought she wanted to work for one of the airlines, see the world," Ethan said.

"I guess she wanted to get married more. Todd was getting ready to go off and accept a partial scholarship to some big northeastern school. Nancy...needed him. She was going to have the twins. They got married, and Todd didn't go to college. Like I said, now he's a grease monkey at Perry's Garage."

"Our plans in life can change," Ethan said.

"They were there that day on the *Journey*. Todd had the afternoon off, and Miss Emily is always flexible when it comes to Nancy's hours 'cause of the kids. She doesn't take much time off, though. She needs to make money any way she can," Brad said.

"I guess if you have two kids, you don't have much choice," Ethan said. He remembered Todd better than he did Nancy. Todd had been on the football team and, like Randy Laurent, he'd been great at opening beer bottles with his teeth.

Ethan made a mental note to find out where Todd had been around the time of the murders. It was always good to know where everyone who could've been even remotely involved might have been.

"I half expected Miss Emily to be the 'detective' who solved this thing," Jennie said, turning to look at Ethan. "She knows more than any local reporter. I'm from NOLA, but I get out here pretty often, and I can tell you, Emily Watson probably knows more about me than I know about myself."

Ethan smiled, about to answer her when he found himself distracted by the television high above their heads near the counter.

He rose and walked toward the big screen.

The news was from Baton Rouge. He couldn't hear the details, but he heard enough to know the attractive reporter was giving out information on a murder. The picture of a taped-off crime scene was projected behind her.

"Mrs. Watson, would you turn that up for me, please?" he asked.

"Sure, honey," she said, then got the remote out from behind the bar and handed it to him.

The anchor was continuing with her story. "Mrs. Rodriguez was found this afternoon just outside the campus in a wooded section of town. Friends, neighbors and co-workers considered her a warm, friendly woman, and police are seeking help from anyone who can tell them more about her whereabouts or give any information whatsoever that could lead to the apprehension of her killer. In other news..."

Ethan quickly flicked to another station.

And then another.

Mrs. Selma Rodriguez, sixty-two, of Baton Rouge, a custodian at the college, had been found murdered just outside campus. She'd been reported missing when she'd failed to show up for work. Her purse, money and credit cards had been found with the body, ruling out robbery as a motive. As it was an ongoing investigation, police were not reporting the cause of death, and were seeking any and all help from the community.

He sensed someone standing next to him, watching the television, and turned to see it was Chance Morgan.

The photographer was shaking his head sadly. "This world's a real mess. Killing a hardworking woman—for what? Too many crazy bastards out there."

"Yeah. Crazy bastards," Ethan agreed. He turned to see Charlie staring at him. He smiled grimly back at her and returned to the table just as a young waiter was delivering his gumbo.

He felt her eyes still on him as he bent to eat his meal. Charlie was a good person and would undoubtedly be upset that a woman had been murdered.

But she would also be wondering why he found the case of such interest.

He was actually wondering that same thing himself.

And then he remembered that the *Journey* had been in port at Baton Rouge that day.

With Jonathan Moreau among those on board.

Had he spoken too soon when he told Charlie he didn't consider her father a suspect?

The silence in the car as they drove back to Charlie's house hung heavy, as if they were both harboring dark thoughts they didn't dare voice.

"Did you enjoy being on set today?" Charlie said finally. "I mean, minus me thinking someone threw a knife at me and the fact that the bayonet the killer used was likely stolen from the prop collection."

"I didn't mind filming," he said, but he didn't elaborate. His features looked cast in concrete as they were caught in the moving shadows created by the streetlights as they drove.

He wasn't showing any outward signs of anger, but she could feel him seething. And she had no clue why.

He would certainly be angry later, when she finally told him she was certain the answers to the murders lay aboard the *Journey*.

And that she would be aboard next time it set sail.

"It's sad about Selma Rodriguez, that woman in Baton Rouge," she said, since he didn't seem inclined to keep the conversation going.

"Yes."

Clearly talking wasn't going to help, so she decided to go back to dark silence.

They reached the house, and Ethan immediately got out of the car. While she headed for the door, he opened the trunk and took out a briefcase, then headed up the walk to join her. He inspected the door and nodded, and she slid the key in the lock.

Inside, he made sure the door was locked, then went straight to the sofa, sat down and pulled his laptop out of his briefcase. Without a word, he booted up the computer and started working.

Charlie hadn't moved away from the door; she just stood there and watched him.

At last he looked up at her, his head tilted at an inquisitive angle. "Yes? Is everything all right?"

"Fine, thank you. Thank you for staying."

He nodded, then looked at her expectantly, waiting.

"Well," Charlie murmured, "I guess I'll go to bed."

He stood suddenly and walked over to her. She was disturbed to realize she actually had to force herself to hold her ground. Her knees felt weak, and she felt hot as her blood rushed through her. She never had gotten over the way she felt about him. Ten years…a decade. A lifetime between them. She still loved the way he looked, the way he moved…even the way he breathed.

And yet, as she stood there expectantly, she remembered the absolute humiliation of throwing herself at a man who hadn't wanted her. She'd been so certain they'd been made for one another. But he had only stared at her in horror and walked away.

It was a moment never to be forgotten.

He stood for a moment, not touching her, just looking at her.

"Is there anything you'd like to talk to me about?" he asked her.

She wasn't sure if she lied at that moment because she still didn't know how to explain her near desperate determination to be on the *Journey* or because she was distracted because he was standing so close.

"No," she managed sweetly. "Just thank you, that's all."

He still didn't move, but she couldn't stand there any longer. He was, however, blocking the stairway. She put a hand on his chest as she moved past him, and she felt his body heat and the sudden sharp constriction of his muscles.

She fled. Up the stairs, into her room. She closed the door and put on a nightshirt. Got in bed.

And remembered…

She remembered the unhallowed ground where she'd sat as they'd waited for the police to arrive, then the man—the killer—suddenly emerging from the trees and racing straight at her, intent on murder.

She'd been so young, so terrified, but Ethan had been there, like a bolt of lightning, the wind of a hurricane, slamming into her would-be killer and taking him down.

She forced herself to consider the possibility that she had fallen victim to some kind of survivor's hero worship for the man who had saved her life. Maybe Ethan and her feelings for him weren't what she'd thought they were for so long. Certainly she could live without him, as witnessed by the last ten years.

No. He'd always been there, lurking in the far reaches of her mind, her heart.

And she knew.

This wasn't hero worship. Something inside her was captivated by the man. And she felt as strongly now as she had when she'd been raw and young and scared. From the moment he had come to her rescue that night, freeing her from "pledging" at the gravestone, she'd been connected to him. And she was forced to admit that it had been more than her knowledge that he could see the dead that had led her to ask to have him assigned to the case.

It had been the best excuse in the world, though, since it was real.

She realized she should head downstairs while he was still awake and at least tell him about her conversations with Alexi and Clara. It would be the right thing to do.

She started to rise. Just as she sat up, there was a knock at her door. She froze, afraid.

She suddenly wished she hadn't changed into one of the ragged football jerseys she used as nightgowns.

"Yes?" she asked.

The door opened. Ethan was there, silhouetted in the light from the hall.

There was something between them. They both felt it and always had, even though he'd fought so hard against it ten years ago. And now, at last, he had come to her. She'd felt his instant, sharp response when she'd touched him. He knew, knew that no one in her life had ever lived up to just the dream of him.

"Okay, so when the hell were you going to tell me?"

"Pardon?" she said, genuinely confused.

"About the *Journey*, Charlie. About the plans you and your friends made—and neglected to tell me about."

"Oh."

She plumped up her pillow and clutched it on her lap. "I'm sorry. I didn't exactly make any plans. I *can't* make plans. Neither can they. All we could do was imagine what might be possible, and then they were going to follow up with—"

"Oh, cut the bull, Charlie!" He walked over to the bed. He was like a tower of searing anger, completely restrained, of course, and possibly more shocking—or awesome—because of it.

"I know what you're doing, and I understand why you want to do it, but what I *can't* understand is why you made the effort to get me down here specifically, but then you didn't trust me enough to keep me in the loop. If you want me here, don't lie to me."

"I didn't lie!"

"Not telling me was lying. Don't do it again."

He turned and left her room.

So much for thinking they both knew they were meant for each other.

She lay back down, shaking and completely clueless as to what the morning would bring.

"A lot of times, when I'm working on a tough case, I think about Jack the Ripper," Jude told Ethan.

"Didn't know the Krewe worked that one," Ethan said with a smile.

"We've all studied the case, and drawn our own conclusions. And, actually, years ago, the Krewe did work a copycat case back in New York City. The thing is, there were all these conspiracy theories. The royal family was even implicated at one point. But I think, if the authorities had the forensic abilities we have now, they would have discovered that the killer wasn't a lofty prince but a poor butcher or some whacked-out laborer who hated prostitutes."

"And this is relevant how?" Ethan asked skeptically.

"I think sometimes we look for a complicated solution when there's a more obvious answer that turns out to be the right one."

"I'm not sure that applies to this case," Ethan said. "The killer is organized, and both murders were carried out in the same way. He—or she—made sure the bodies would be discovered soon, but not immediately. Both men were lured to their deaths, I'm certain of it. What we're still looking for is the reason for them to have been wearing their uniforms. I think we're on the right trail, but I agree to a point. I don't think the murders are part of a big conspiracy to start a race riot, or anything like that. I know there's a reason behind all this. We're just not seeing what it is yet."

They were seated at the table in the Moreau dining room, and it was seven in the morning. Jude and Alexi had flown into Baton Rouge late the night before. Alexi was on her way to New Orleans to make the final arrangements for the "Belle Sisters" to perform on the next voyage of the *Journey.* Clara, the third member of the trio, would arrive in New Orleans the following day, along with Thor Erikson, another recent addition to the Krewe. Thor hailed from Alaska, so the Southern heat was going to be a real shock to his system.

The more agents around, the better, Ethan thought, though he still wasn't so sure about the plan for the women to work aboard the *Journey.* Having to spend time worrying about their safety didn't seem like a plus in any way.

A number of the agents in the Krewe were partners, in every sense of the word, from Jackson Crow and Angela Hawkins on down. But Angela and many of the others had gone through the academy and joined the Bureau; they had training in both investigation and firearms. But in this case, all three women were *performers*, for heaven's sake.

It was good to have Jude there. They'd become friends quickly when they'd met up after joining the Krewe. They were both from Louisiana, which created an immediate bond, though unlike Ethan, Jude had been in the New Orleans field office before becoming Krewe.

Jude also knew Charlie's friends Alexi and Clara. Both women had been contract performers on the Celtic American Line's *Destiny* when a serial killer had been aboard. Jackson Crow himself had been involved in both Celtic American cases, and Ethan was certain Crow was poring over everything to do with this case, as well. Not only was another Celtic American ship potentially involved, incidents that had occurred on that same ship over a hundred and fifty years ago might also play a role in the current murders.

Ethan finished the last of his coffee and rose. He had an eight o'clock meeting with Randy, and, with Jude here, he could leave without worrying about Charlie's safety. It bothered him that—just like Albion Corley and Farrell Hickory—she was in the killer's sights and he had no idea why.

And despite the lack of any real connection, his gut told him that the cleaning woman who had been killed in Baton Rouge had run afoul of that same killer, too.

"I've got to get to my meeting with Randy. I doubt

he has anything new, unfortunately. He's a good cop, but there hasn't been a damned thing to go on with this case."

"I'll be here. The *Journey* arrives in New Orleans on Tuesday night and leaves again Wednesday, so we've got time before we need to board."

"Good." Ethan hesitated. "I'd like to stop in Baton Rouge on our way to New Orleans."

"Something going on there I should know about?"

"I know the police are on it, but a cleaning woman was killed right outside the college where she worked."

"The connection?" Jude asked.

"Same college where Albion Corley taught," Ethan said.

"I see. It's a thread—a slim thread."

"I know, but the way I see it, we've got no choice but to grasp at threads."

"You'd better wake Ms. Moreau first and let her know I'm here. I understand she's a crack shot, and I'd really hate for her to think I was an intruder and plant a bullet in me."

Ethan agreed. He headed upstairs and knocked on Charlie's door. She threw the door open a second later, easing any fear he'd had that he would have to wake her. She had showered and dressed for the day in jeans and a tank top—both blue, enhancing the sky blue of her eyes.

"I'm heading into town," he said, "and I didn't want you to freak out when you went down and found Jude at your dining room table. Your plan is certainly coming together."

"Hey!" she protested. "I wasn't sitting around cackling and plotting. I just wanted to help catch a killer."

He didn't reply, only turned to head down the stairs. She followed.

Jude stood to greet her, and she smiled and reached out a hand to him.

"Ms. Moreau, Charlie, I've heard all about you and seen your face often enough in Alexi's pictures and on screen. It's a pleasure," Jude told her.

"And I'm delighted to meet you, since Alexi is alive and well—not to mention happy—because of you," Charlie said.

Ethan watched the exchange between them. They were going to be just fine. "I imagine I'll be an hour or so."

"We'll be here," Jude said. "And if Charlie needs to go anywhere, I'll be happy to accompany her."

"Let me know if you head out," Ethan said, and caught Jude's eye. The reassurance he saw there confirmed what he'd already learned in the Krewe. They were a tight-knit group and always had each other's backs. "You'll want to get packed," he told Charlie.

"Oh?"

"We're leaving this afternoon."

She had the grace to look away, uncomfortable.

"For New Orleans?" she asked.

"For New Orleans," he said. "The *Journey* was in Baton Rouge yesterday, she'll be down by Houmas today, and tomorrow she'll return to New Orleans. She'll head out again the next morning. As you wished, you'll be on it. And so will we."

8

Charlie had a guard—or a babysitter. Whichever way she chose to look at it, Jude McCoy was here and not with Ethan or anywhere else because he was watching over her.

And she was grateful for that.

He was friendly and charming as he told her about the theater Alexi and Clara were renovating. It was an entirely new experience for both of them, though Clara had at least been a stage manager and worked as an assistant casting director several times, but neither of them had actually managed a theater. The building itself was historic, and they had plans to bring in both professional shows and to offer the space for community outreach, bringing in free children's theater to benefit the area.

"I'm sure they're going to do well," Charlie said. "They're both so talented, and I would know, because I've worked with both of them."

"I know. I've seen the pictures," Jude reminded her.

Charlie grinned. "It was great when we were all based in NOLA. It's a great place for performers of any kind. You can hear better music on the streets of the French Quarter than you can for big bucks in any city in this country."

"So how's the movie going?" he asked her. "It's good to know the film industry is busy here at home."

She smiled. Jude didn't much look as though he was "home." Of course, he was from New Orleans, but they were both from Louisiana. He was very formal in his dark suit. She'd always envisioned FBI agents wearing dark suits, and he was exactly what she'd imagined. Tall, dark, striking, assured—which made her very happy for her friend Alexi, since Jude and Alexi were definitely a couple.

"What are you grinning at?" he asked her.

"Are all FBI agents tall and fit and forced to wear suits?"

"Of course not," he protested.

"So you don't always wear suits?"

"No, we're not all tall," he told her. "So tell me about your movie."

"It's really good. It's not a horror flick, even though there *are* ghosts. It's social commentary wrapped up in a great suspense story. It should do a lot of good for the area. Of course, it was already doing a lot of good, providing jobs, getting some nice PR—until I found a dead man on our set," she added softly.

"What about your role? With you leaving for a week, will you mess up the filming schedule?"

She shook her head. "A lot of my scenes are already in the can, filmed before all the 'ghost' stuff happened. You know movies are seldom shot in order, right? We filmed some of the ghost scenes the first day I arrived. They shot some of the other characters' scenes before I even got here. I was finishing up a webisode."

"I've seen your webisodes. Alexi watches them religiously."

"She's a good friend."

"She says the same of you," he told her. Then his cell rang, and he excused himself and walked away to take the call.

When he returned, he told her, "Ethan's spoken with Brad Thornton and cleared you for the week. He had you penciled in for tomorrow, but he rescheduled you for this afternoon. Can you pack up and be ready to go in about thirty minutes? Brad needs you for about two hours, and then he'll do pickup shots when you're back."

"Um, sure," Charlie said. She leaped up, feeling guilty. She'd made a point of telling her dad she couldn't leave Brad and his movie, but when the ghost had pointed to the Mississippi, she'd known she had to get aboard the *Journey* somehow. Clara and Alexi had made it easy for her.

"Good. We'll probably get in fairly late. Ethan wants to stop in Baton Rouge on the way, so we'll probably hit NOLA around eleven or so."

"Okay," Charlie said. "I'll be ready to go ASAP." She hurried up the stairs.

As she prepared, she thought about Ethan's strange behavior the night before—not when he'd knocked angrily at her door, but before that, at the café, when he'd been riveted to the story of the cleaning woman who'd been killed in Baton Rouge.

That had to be the explanation for why he wanted to stop there on the way to New Orleans, but why did it matter so much to him when they had two murders to solve right here in St. Francisville?

Baton Rouge was a major city, the capital of Louisiana. It had more crime, and certainly more murders, than tiny St. Francisville.

But Ethan wanted to know more about this particular murder, and she didn't need Jude to tell her so.

But why?

And then she realized that the *Journey* had been in Baton Rouge yesterday. With her father aboard.

And no matter what Ethan said, she knew that her father was a suspect.

Ridiculous.

Ethan had said he didn't believe her father was the killer, and she was certain he wasn't lying. She didn't need to feel fear for her father—no matter what Detective Laurent might think.

But even though Ethan didn't suspect her father, for some reason he did think the murders of Albion Corley, Farrell Hickory and the woman in Baton Rouge were connected.

But how?

And more important, who was the killer and how could he be stopped?

Randy Laurent still had nothing. They'd spent time doing background checks. They'd sent officers to Baton Rouge to question anyone involved with Albion Corley. No one knew anything useful.

"I'm planning on a trip to Baton Rouge myself," Ethan told him.

"Don't trust us locals anymore, huh?" Randy asked him.

Ethan shook his head. "You know it's not that. I just need to get the feel of the place again, ask around myself."

Randy nodded. "Just remember those are my friends over there, okay?"

"I will. So on another note, what's going on with the Hickory Plantation?"

"Farrell's son is there now, and he's not a suspect. We have a dozen sworn witnesses who say he was in school when his dad was killed. And by school I mean Harvard, so, no, he didn't slip back here from Boston to kill his dad, then take off again."

"Was anyone besides his dad living at the place when he left for the semester?"

"No, there's a staff there during the day, but that's it. Hickory Plantation isn't that big, remember. They do tours, but they don't take overnight guests. The family keeps the upstairs for themselves. People come to do Rosedown Plantation and the Myrtles, then find Hickory once they're here. It hasn't been featured on every ghost show on TV, for one thing. Not that I don't think it's as historically interesting. It just doesn't have the same hype. In any case, they've always closed up at five o'clock sharp. The day Hickory was murdered, the cleaning staff and the last guide went home shortly after they saw him leave, wearing his uniform. No one there knows anything about where he went."

"I'd like to take a drive out anyway," Ethan said, then heard his phone beep and glanced down at it. Chance had texted earlier to say he was finally in the process of emailing the photos after a computer crash had caused an unexpected delay. "Chance Morgan is sending me some photos, but the files are pretty large. Can I bring them up on one of the computers here?"

"Of course."

"So we'll take half an hour or so, drive out to the Hickory Plantation, then come back and look at photos."

Randy shrugged. "Sure. Whatever you want. You know, we're not totally incompetent. I did talk to the plantation staff, and I didn't just take Farrell's son at his word. I went through the kid's phone and his iPad."

"I'm sure you did. But—"

"But we're all grasping at whatever we can," Randy said. "I know. I'm doing it, too. But what do you think you're going to find?"

"I have no idea," Ethan told him. "But I'm willing to try anything. I'm also working the cruise angle, looking at the reenactment on the *Journey*. I need to talk to the locals who were working as extras that day."

Randy grinned at him. "I had my men talk to each and every one of them."

Ethan hesitated. "What about Todd and Nancy Camp?" he asked.

Randy sighed. "Them, too. But they were out of town when Corley's murder took place, at a funeral in Gainesville, Florida. And, yes, I checked that out. Todd's grandmother died. And since the one thing we do know is that we're looking at a single killer, that rules them out. I can see how, given the past, you might want to look at the two of them. We've all been jerks at times. But being a jerk doesn't make you a murderer."

"No, being a jerk doesn't make you a murderer. But it doesn't make you innocent, either."

"But an ironclad alibi does," Randy said.

Ethan had to agree. "Okay, let's check out the Hickory Plantation. Because something has to lead us somewhere."

Before they headed to the set, Jude changed into something more casual. But when they went out to the car, Charlie had to wonder if—like dark suits—dark SUVs really were the FBI's vehicles of choice. Jude's rental was pretty much the twin of Ethan's.

On set, Jude stayed close by the entire time she worked with Brad, Jimmy and Grant, taking some extra shots for the scene after the ghosts took care of the men who had been trying to silence her.

During a break, she walked with him to the church, and they wandered among the unhallowed graves.

"You won't read about this in the guidebooks," Charlie said. "These graves are unhallowed. You wound up here if you killed yourself or were especially bad. My dad knows all about this stuff."

"I understand your dad's quite the historian. What about you?"

"I love it, but I don't know it like he does," Charlie said, then fell silent as, between where they were standing and the church, she saw her Confederate cavalry commander slowly appear.

"He's here," she said quietly.

"Who?"

"The ghost of Anson McKee."

Jude looked in the direction she indicated. Once again, the ghost was pointing to the river.

"I see," Jude said softly.

Charlie looked at him and realized he not only saw Anson McKee, he saw what the ghost was trying to tell them, as well.

He wanted them to go to the river.

Charlie nodded. "We need to get to the *Journey*," she said quietly.

McKee seemed pleased and slowly disappeared.

"Charlie! We're ready for you!" Brad called, his voice reedy, as the breeze carried it away. "Let's get going so we can get you out of here on time."

"Coming!" she called back.

"Amazing," Jude said.

"That you saw a ghost?" she asked. "I thought you were used to that."

He looked at her and smiled. "No, not seeing a ghost," he told her. "The resemblance. Throw a long-haired wig on Ethan, and that could be him."

Farrell Hickory had done a good job with the plantation.

The private quarters upstairs were comfortable and well cared for, and the public sections had been perfectly preserved for those who wanted to visit a smaller plantation. Those who wanted grandeur usually started with Oak Alley, San Francisco or Rosedown, or, in this immediate area, the Myrtles. They were all interesting and historically accurate, and as different from each other as the planters who had owned them.

While visitors could rent rooms at the others, the Hickory Plantation had never operated as a B and B. Guests could come for the day and see the downstairs, which was the heart of the plantation—the master's office, music room, grand parlor, dining room and ballroom. Outside, they could tour the smokehouse, the two remaining buildings from what had been slave quarters, and the stables. But there was also a private outside staircase, which led up to the balcony and an entrance to the second floor. There, Hickory had raised his son. His wife had passed when Jefferson, aka Jeff, Hickory was only a child, so Farrell had lived there with his son, and, according to Jefferson, it had been a happy life.

Ethan and Randy met with Jeff, who had come home from Harvard to arrange his father's funeral, in the upstairs parlor, which in actuality was simply a wide hallway that ran through the middle of the upstairs. The living quarters consisted of four bedrooms, one of them turned into an entertainment center, an office, a living room and a small kitchen that opened on to a dining area.

"Dad was a good guy," Jeff told them. He was earnest and direct and, at twenty-three, as clean-cut as a marine. "He was so proud of our family history. Naturally one of my great-greats was a Confederate officer in the Civil War. But Dad was proudest of the fact that his father marched for Civil Rights in the sixties. He was dedicated to keeping the house open to the public. Thought it was important for people to remember history so we wouldn't repeat it. I think we probably came out about even, what with the costs of operating and what we brought in." He let out a deep sigh. "I wish I could help you find out who killed him." Suddenly his control slipped, and tears filled his eyes. "I loved my dad."

"We're so sorry for your loss," Ethan said.

Jeff nodded. "Thanks. I know you're doing everything you can, but why Dad and Uncle Albion? Why in God's name would anyone want to hurt either one of them? They never did anything but good for anyone."

"*Uncle* Albion?" Ethan asked. "You called him uncle?"

"Sure. They were best friends. Oh, my God, did those two like to argue. Albion didn't have a family. I want to bury him near Dad, in the Grace Episcopal graveyard. When I can," he added softly, glancing over at Randy.

Ethan knew that the bodies hadn't been released yet. For this kid's sake, he hoped they could take care of that soon.

"He was proud of me for getting into Harvard," Jeff said.

"I'm sure he was," Ethan said. "When was the last time you talked to him?"

"He called me every Sunday. We'd talk for about an hour," Jeff said.

"What did you talk about?" Ethan asked. "The last time."

"I told him about a girl I've been seeing and promised

that it wasn't interfering with my studying," Jeff said, smiling. "Told him about one of my classes he would have loved—an elective, on the history of Boston and the Cambridge area. He told me they'd had a great time doing some special reenactment on the *Journey*, said he and Uncle Albion had gotten into a major-league shouting match over some historical point until their boss—a friend of theirs named Jonathan Moreau—stepped in and told them to cut it out." Jeff shook his head. "Dad said they provided the best excitement of the day and gave people something to talk about. But he was glad that Jonathan stepped in." He started to smile, and then his expression grew sad again. "God, I still don't believe..."

"Jeff, could we see your father's office?" Ethan asked him.

"Sure. Come on back."

Jeff led them to a room with a handsome antique desk but no computer.

Ethan glanced questioningly at Randy.

"We've got his laptop down at the station," Randy said. "I told you, we checked everything."

Ethan sat down at the desk. He wished Farrell would materialize in front of him.

No such luck.

Ethan looked carefully through the drawers. He found one drawer filled with key chains and magnets. "What are these?" he asked Jeff.

"Souvenirs from Dad's charities. They usually give some goodie or other to the sponsors. Dad gave to save abandoned animals, save the wetlands, all that kind of thing."

"Okay if I take these?" Ethan asked. "I promise I'll bring them back."

"Sure. You can take anything you think will help. I guess I shouldn't believe in the death penalty, and I'm not sure I did before, but...some bastard stabbed my dad in the heart. I don't know what will happen to that person, but I sure as hell don't want him walking this earth free."

They stayed a while longer, but Jeff had absolutely no idea who his father had gone to meet the night he'd been killed or why he'd worn his uniform.

"I'll tell you what, though. I graduate at the end of the semester, and then I'm coming right back here. Dad's death isn't going to stop me from keeping his dream— and this plantation—alive. Dad left me this place and a hell of an insurance settlement, so I've changed things up a bit. I've hired security. And they'll damned well know where I'm going whenever I go out."

As they left, Ethan and Randy passed a tour group and overheard the guide mention the recent murder of the former owner.

Randy shook his head and then turned to Ethan. "What the hell do you think you're going to learn from that collection of junk?"

"I don't know yet. But if nothing else, it might give us a better idea of who he might have been seeing or what he might have been doing."

Brad was true to his word; he quickly finished filming the scenes he wanted and told her he would let her know if he needed anything else.

"You know I'll be on the *Journey* with Clara and Alexi for a week, right?" Charlie asked him.

"I do, and it's no problem. I'll find you if I need you. And anyway, you're free for the day when the *Journey* is docked here," he reminded her.

"Very true," she agreed.

She said goodbye and left with Jude. Once they were in the car, he asked her, "How much do you know about Anson McKee?"

"I know that his life was cut short by the war. According to the records I've found, he was from this area, joined the cavalry, was voted a captain by his men. He was married and had one son. He wrote his wife a beautiful letter before he died, telling her how much he loved her. Why?"

"The resemblance to Ethan really is uncanny," Jude said.

"You should have seen him in his wig," Charlie said.

"His wig?" Jude was evidently amused.

"Brad had him do some extra work as one of the ghosts, and those boys did not have FBI haircuts," Charlie said.

"Interesting."

"I looked him up—the captain, I mean," Charlie said. "The man helped save my life ten years ago. He led Ethan out to the unhallowed graveyard where my idiot high school friends had me tied to a headstone as a test because I was pledging their stupid club. Ethan freed me, then took down a killer when he came back looking for something he'd left behind earlier that night. If I'd still been tied to that headstone…" She shuddered.

"That's a hell of a story. And I still can't get over that resemblance."

"Ethan's got just about every nationality you can think of in his family tree, but he can't be descended from Anson McKee. The son moved west after the war and had a family, but his descendants all live in Nevada. A few years back, one of them came to St. Francisville when they were reenacting *The Day the War Stopped.* Nice man. And you should read the letter McKee wrote to his wife. He really loved her, so…"

"So he wasn't messing around elsewhere," Jude said, then shrugged. "Still…"

"Maybe that's why the captain comes back. Maybe he sees something of himself in Ethan. Luckily he seems to like me, too. And he's still trying to help." She glanced at him. "You saw the way he pointed to the river. The murders have something to do with the *Journey.* I'm sure of it."

"Hopefully, we'll find the answers—and soon." He smiled at her. "I gather you and Alexi and Clara have a plan, but seriously, do you really know that many Civil War songs?"

Charlie groaned softly. "Oh, yeah. Trust me, I know recipes, songs…you name it. I am my father's daughter."

She knew then it wasn't just her discovery of a dead man that had made her so determined to find the killer.

She was her father's daughter. And she was going to see that he was proved innocent.

And yet…

He had lied to her. He'd told her he barely knew Farrell Hickory, but according to what she was hearing, he *had* known Hickory.

He had known him very well.

Ethan and Randy Laurent were sitting in a conference room, staring at a flat-screen TV hooked to a computer while a police tech ran through the shots Chance had taken the day of the *Journey* reenactment. They watched as picture after picture went by, shots of the boat or the river. Finally they came to the shots of the run-through, when the two victims had their argument, and the crowd had gathered to see.

As Ethan examined the faces in the crowd, he thought about the historical events that had been commemorated that day. From what he knew, the moment when the *Journey* had been handed from one side to the other had actually been a beautiful one. For those few minutes, in that one place, the war had stopped, the killing had stopped. An injured Union soldier had risen from his bed and hobbled over to embrace the Rebel orderly who had cared for him. There had been plenty of ceremony, but there had also been a human factor. After all, both the caregivers and the injured had probably found it impossible not to swap stories, memories, shared experiences of a better time.

Based on what Ethan could see in the photos, the reenactment had been especially well-done, with the injured Yankees in their hospital beds laid out on the deck. The riverboat had pulled up as close as possible right below Grace Church, and small Confederate boats had clustered nearby, ready to bring the Rebels home once the ship had been handed over.

As for the reenactors themselves, the only one missing, Ethan thought drily, was Charlie.

The rest of her friends all seemed to be there. He saw Brad and Mike Thornton—Brad an infantry sergeant, Mike a private—Grant Ferguson, Jimmy Smith, George Gonzales, Barry Seymour and Luke Mayfield, all of them in costume. Even Jennie McPherson was there, dressed in a white nurse's apron, appropriately frayed from continual washing. Albion Corley and Farrell Hickory were front and center—especially once their argument had begun. There were dozens of consecutive shots of the two men fighting, and then showing Jonathan Moreau stepping in to intervene.

"See anything?" Randy asked, leaning closer toward the screen.

"Not yet. One more time," Ethan told the tech.

As the pictures rolled by again, Ethan watched closely, then he asked the tech to pause on a shot of Jennie whispering something to Albion.

After a long moment he asked the tech to move on, but by the next shot she was back with Barry and Grant.

"What are you thinking?" Randy asked him.

Ethan let out a sigh. "I'm thinking I'd like to know what Jennie was saying to Corley."

Charlie was grateful that Jude managed to come up with easy conversation as they made the drive to Baton Rouge. It wasn't a long trip, but Ethan was quiet, seemingly lost in his own thoughts. She herself felt unnerved, certain that he was still angry with her and worried that an explosion was coming somewhere along the line.

She assumed they were heading for a police station, and she would need to wait somewhere while Ethan and Jude did their FBI thing.

Baton Rouge was a beautiful city. Built along the river, it had fantastic museums, a blossoming business district filled with high-rises, but it also offered the old, charmingly mixed in with the new. The old Governor's Mansion, for example, which was now a museum, was an impressive building. She didn't know what area of the city they would be in, but she figured she could probably just walk around a bit.

They didn't head for a police station, but rather a quiet, lower middle income neighborhood. Kids were actually playing kick ball in the street. They stopped at a small house with a white picket fence, and Ethan, who had been driving, looked back at Jude, who nodded and said, "This is it."

Ethan got out, then came around and opened the door for Charlie. "Are you coming?"

She didn't ask him where they were or why he wanted her there; she just got out of the car.

They walked up the front steps, and Ethan knocked on the door, which was thrown open by a tall man with a thin, haggard face and a grim look. "Special Agents Delaney and McCoy?" he asked.

"Yes," Jude said. "Julio Rodriguez."

The man nodded and looked curiously at Charlie.

"This is Charlene Moreau," Ethan said.

"Charlie," she murmured, offering her hand.

"Mr. Rodriguez, we're truly sorry to intrude, but we need a few minutes of your time," Ethan said.

"I am happy to speak with you," Rodriguez said. "Please, come in."

Charlie lowered her head, wincing. She realized that they had come to the home of the murdered woman, Selma Rodriguez. A younger man, who seemed to be in his twenties, came forward as they entered, ready to rush to the defense of the older man—maybe his father, Charlie thought—if their presence was upsetting him.

"We've answered all the police questions," the younger man said angrily. "We're in mourning and need to be left alone."

"It's all right, Sean," Julio said. "They've come to help."

Sean nodded. "*Tio*, the family will be here soon." He glared at Ethan. "They questioned us, *us*! As if we would do this to Tia Selma."

"We only need a few minutes," Ethan said soothingly.

"Come, sit in the parlor. May I get you something? Selma would be very upset if I did not offer refreshment to guests," Julio said.

"We're fine, but thank you," Ethan said. "I promise we'll be quick."

"You'd better be," Sean said, giving Ethan a lethal glare.

Ethan ignored him and addressed Julio Rodriguez. "I know your wife worked at the college, Mr. Rodriguez. Did she ever mention a Professor Corley, Albion Corley?"

Before Julio could answer, Sean suddenly spoke up, pointing at Charlie.

"I know you!" he exclaimed. "You're Leticia from *Banshees on the Bayou*. Tia Selma loved that show. I had to show her how to watch it on YouTube."

Charlie flushed and nodded. "Yes, I play Leticia."

"This is so sad," he said. "She should be here to meet you."

"I wish I could have met her," Charlie said. "At least now we have the chance to help find her killer."

Sean suddenly turned back to Ethan. "Professor Corley? My aunt spoke of him often. He was a generous man and never forgot her at Christmas."

"He never forgot her birthday, either," Julio said. He frowned. "Professor Corley was also murdered. Do you think his death and Selma's could be related?"

"To be honest, we don't know," Ethan said. "That's why we're here, to find out everything we can that might help. Do you know if your wife had any enemies? Can you think of any reason why someone might have targeted her?"

"Tia Selma had no enemies," Sean said. "She was sweet, and she loved everyone." He drew a deep breath. "She would say what she thought, but she didn't argue with people. There is no reason for anyone to have murdered her."

"The police probably already asked you this, but did she keep an appointment book of any kind?" Jude asked.

Julio shook his head. "No book. Selma went to work and came home. We never had our own children, but we're

very close to our nephews and nieces. Every Sunday, whoever was free would come here."

"As I told the detectives, I talked to Tia Selma the day
she died," Sean said. "She was talking about Professor
Corley, in fact. The school had asked her to clean out
his office. She was very sad. He had said something to
her about meeting an old friend, and that he was worried that his old friend was changing."

"Changing how?" Charlie found herself asking.

He shook his head. "I don't know. I don't think she
did, either."

Ethan rose, offering a hand to the young man. Sean
took it and nodded. "I'll try to think of anything else
my aunt said that might help you."

"Thank you," Ethan said, handing him his card. "Cell
phone—you can reach me anytime."

Charlie and Jude got up and joined Ethan, ready to
leave, but Sean stopped her.

"Thank you," he said. "You made my aunt very happy."

Julio thanked them, as well, and walked them to the
door. He said he, too, would try to think of anything that
might help, though he didn't think that was likely. He
did, however, take Ethan's card.

They made one more stop, and that was at the college,
where they had arranged to meet up with Vince Raleigh,
the local detective in charge of the case.

Raleigh couldn't see any reason to associate the murder of a cleaning woman with that of a professor—even
though they worked in the same place—when the circumstances of the two killings were so different. He
accompanied them to speak with Albert Lacroix, the

dean of the college, who unfortunately had nothing useful to offer. They hadn't known that the professor was missing because he had arranged for time off and was supposed to be gone.

"I can't believe we've lost two members of our staff in such a short time, and to think they were both murdered..."

"We believe," Detective Raleigh said, "that Mrs. Rodriguez was walking in the wrong place at the wrong time, while Professor Corley seems to have been targeted. We're putting all our resources into solving Mrs. Rodriguez's murder, I promise you."

Charlie could tell that Raleigh was trying to hide his annoyance at the FBI's presence and their intrusion into his case, but his feelings simmered close enough to the surface for her to pick up on them.

"Dean Lacroix," Ethan said, "do you have any idea who Professor Corley might have been meeting with in St. Francisville?"

"Old friends—that's all he ever told me," Lacroix said.

Ethan and Jude thanked the detective and the dean for their time, and Raleigh led them out of the dean's office. The three men stopped in the hall to trade thoughts, and Charlie wandered away. She realized she was standing outside Albion Corley's office. The letters of his name had recently been pried from the outer door, but the "ghosts" of their forms still remained.

She looked back and saw that the men were still talking and found herself compelled to step inside, closing the door behind her.

She saw a tiny woman, dark-haired, older, with a pleasant face, standing by the window. She was wearing a faded blue uniform with a white apron.

And, of course, she was dead. Charlie realized that immediately.

The woman turned, caught sight of Charlie and walked over to meet her; then, smiling, she reached up as if to touch Charlie's face.

"Leticia…" the woman said.

"Charlie, Charlene Moreau," Charlie said softly. "But, yes, I play Leticia on the show. You're Mrs. Rodriguez, aren't you? We're trying to find whoever killed you."

The smile on the woman's face faded, and she looked as if she was about to cry.

Charlie wanted to kick herself for reminding the woman of what had happened to her. "I'm so sorry. Please, forgive me. But we really do want to help you."

The woman nodded and walked back to the window.

It was as if she wanted to feel the sunshine just one more time.

"Who did this?" Charlie asked softly. "Can you describe them? Can you tell me anything at all?"

Selma Rodriguez turned back to her and shook her head slowly. "I was walking to the bus stop. It was late, because my shift starts when everyone else goes home. I like working late, though. It's quiet, you know?"

Charlie realized Selma was speaking in the present tense, as if she still hadn't fully accepted her own death yet, and glanced back to the door, wondering what would happen if Detective Raleigh were to step in and catch her talking to the empty room. "I understand," she said. "Please...help us to help you."

Selma shook her head and said something softly in Spanish, then switched back to English and said, "I don't know anything." She suddenly appeared angry. "I am a nice person, a good person, but if I knew who the bastard was..." She clenched her ghostly fists at her sides. "I'd—I'd haunt him! I'd learn, and I'd trip him and shove him when he was shaving and..." She broke off with a little sob, her hand at her throat.

Charlie hadn't known how Selma had died. The police were holding on to that information, though she was sure Ethan and Jude knew.

And now she knew, too.

Selma's throat had been slit.

"He came from behind," Selma whispered. "I was so stunned, I barely felt the knife, just something warm, wet...the blood...and then the night faded, and I was looking down at myself, my blood drenching the ground."

"Selma, I'm so sorry." Charlie glanced at the door again. "Can you tell me... Did Professor Corley tell you why he was going to St. Francisville?"

"He said he was going to talk to an old friend and fix a...a situation. He said he knew what was going on, and so did others, and that they agreed it was wrong, and he said he would fix it."

"Did he mention a name?" Charlie asked.

Selma grew thoughtful, looking out the window once again. "Don...? No. Oh, I know! Jon. Jonathan. That was his name." She looked at Charlie with pride at having pulled the name from her memory.

Charlie had to force herself not to scream, not to reach out and try to shake a ghost, not to tell a poor murdered woman that she was a liar.

"Thank you," she managed, just as the door began to open.

Selma let out a little breath of air and vanished into the dust motes that played before the window.

9

Charlie hadn't thought to ask about what arrangements Ethan and Jude had made for themselves when they reached New Orleans. Thinking about it as they drove, she assumed they were planning to stay in the same hotel as Alexi, Clara and the third agent, Thor.

For herself, she had what she thought was an amazing deal: a very small duplex that was part of what had once been a single family dwelling on Dauphine Street in the French Quarter. Alexi and Clara could have stayed with her, but she couldn't fit everybody.

She loved her apartment; it was over two hundred years old and had survived the fires that had ravaged the city in its early days. The plumbing was debatable, the electric sketchy, and the cable went out whenever it rained, but she considered herself lucky to be able to afford the rent. She shared a courtyard with an older couple, Laurence and Loretta Harvey, who had the unit on her right. They had retired from the countryside around Houma to live in the French Quarter. They loved being able to walk to anything they needed. Their children had moved to Nevada but sometimes brought the grandkids for extended stays. That was fine with Charlie; she got along great with eight-year-old Matilda and six-year-old Jeremy. And Laurence and Loretta collected her mail when she was gone. She couldn't have asked for better neighbors.

As they passed the Superdome, she cleared her throat and asked, "So, where are you guys staying?"

"We're all crashing at your place," Ethan told her.

He grinned at her look of surprise, then laughed.

Jude leaned forward. "Actually, we're not going to your place at all."

"No?" she asked.

"My parents are in London at a symposium," Ethan told her. "We're taking over their place in the Garden District. It's just north of Magazine and near the port."

"Oh," Charlie murmured.

"We can stop by your place if you need anything, though," Jude said.

"I'm good," she said, then looked out the window, suddenly feeling a little guilty. She'd known Ethan's parents were in the city and only a cable car ride away, but she'd never made any attempt to see them.

In a little while they reached the sprawling late-Victorian house Ethan's parents owned. It was on a street filled with equally gracious mid-eighteenth-century homes with columns and porches and balconies. The Delaney home was painted white and surrounded by a cast-iron fence. The yard was shaded by magnolias and oaks. The place was the epitome of old Southern charm.

Charlie had no chance to feel awkward about the arrangements, because Clara and Alexi came racing down the steps of the board porch to meet them. They took turns wrapping Charlie up in a hug.

"It's late, but I'm glad you made it here tonight," Alexi said. "We've got to practice our harmonies tomorrow. It's going to be fun. I just hope you remember the words to all the songs."

Charlie nodded, but her attention was on a tall blond man standing at the top of the steps, waiting patiently. He wasn't wearing a suit, but he still looked like FBI.

Jude headed up the steps, while Ethan stood in the yard, waiting. Charlie realized he wasn't going to leave her unprotected until they were inside.

"Let's go in," he said finally. "I'll get the bags later."

They went inside, where she met Thor Erikson. She noticed how comfortable and easy they all were with one another and realized she was the outsider here. She might have known Alexi and Clara for years, working and even socializing together, but she was new to the group as a whole.

Clara had sandwiches ready, and since everyone was hungry, they immediately gathered around the table. Alexi produced a clipboard and went through the musical numbers she'd chosen for them to perform. "You've never worked on a riverboat, have you?" she asked. "Neither have I. Clara did one trip as a fill-in, once, so she's our pro."

"I do know the *Journey*, even though I haven't performed aboard her," Charlie said.

"Of course you do. Your dad is just about the most famous thing about the trip," Alexi said with a smile.

Charlie nodded, lowering her head. She hadn't said a

word to Ethan or Jude about the ghost in Albion Corley's office. When they'd come in and found her there, she'd told them she'd just wanted a look around and left it at that, still busy trying to process what the ghost had told her about her father.

The two men had discussed the case in the car, both of them convinced that Selma had been killed because someone assumed she knew something about Corley's murder. It would have been easy for Charlie to say something, but instead she'd sat in silence, unwilling to tell them even part of what she knew for fear they would sense that she was hiding something. She was anxious to see her father tomorrow, and after that she would decide what to do next.

Why had he lied to her? He'd said he'd barely known the victims.

"So here's the set list," Alexi said, breaking into Charlie's thoughts. "We're doing a mix of Confederate and Union songs. We'll do the old standbys, of course, 'Dixie' and 'The Battle Hymn of the Republic,' and then 'Bonnie Blue Flag,' 'Lorena,' 'The Yellow Rose of Texas,' 'Just Before the Battle,' 'When Johnny Comes Marching Home,' 'All the Pretty Little Horses,' 'The Southern Wagon'…probably a few more. You know all those, right? Clara and I had a chance to run through them, and we want to throw in some more harmonies, maybe create a medley of some lesser-known songs. Here's the thing. We pretty much came up with this whole thing on the spot, so we have to sound good without much of a chance to rehearse. You're good to go, right?"

"Remember who my dad is. I can do them in my

sleep," Charlie assured her. She tried to smile and listen and nod at appropriate moments as Alexi went on to explain more of the logistics as the three men got up and wandered off to talk near the front door.

She wasn't really listening, though; she was too worried about her father.

What she wanted to know wasn't what songs they were going to sing in what order. She wanted to know what Ethan, Jude and Clara's boyfriend, Thor, were talking about. If they had something on her dad and Ethan wasn't sharing that information, she was going to be furious. She knew she was being hypocritical, since she was withholding information herself, but she didn't care. This was about her *father*, for heaven's sake.

Suddenly she realized that, despite the late hour, Ethan was about to leave.

She stopped pretending she was paying attention to Alexi and Clara, excused herself and walked over to join the men.

"Where are you going?" she asked Ethan, letting suspicion creep into her tone, though she hadn't meant to.

He smiled. "I'm not plotting anything," he said, but the look he gave her made it clear that he hadn't forgotten she'd done some plotting of her own. "I'm just going to see my great-grandmother before we plunge into all of this tomorrow. And not to worry—she's a night owl, and I've let her know I'm on my way."

"I can go with you."

"That's all right, you'll be fine here. Jude and Thor will keep you safe."

"Like a pair of rottweilers," Jude said.

"Oh, no, I'm not worried," she said. "I'd just like to see your Tante Terese," she told Ethan, using the name all the children had called her. Afraid that wasn't going to be enough, she added, "Plus, my apartment is near her place in Treme, and I realized I wouldn't mind grabbing a few things."

He was hesitant, and she wondered if he was angrier than she'd realized. Then he shrugged.

"Sure. Let's go." He looked at the other two men, and they nodded. Without a word being said, she knew they'd just agreed to lock up and stay vigilant.

Ethan continued to be distant, politely opening the car door for her but driving in silence. Charlie broke that silence. "How is Tante Terese?" she asked. Ethan's great-grandmother had been like a strange goddess when she came to visit St. Francisville. Her mother had been the granddaughter of a slave. Her father had been a sailor who had swept through New Orleans, then been killed at the tail end of World War I. Tante Terese would reach her hundredth birthday at the end of the year. She was a natural-born storyteller, and the kind of babysitter who never had to raise her voice, and yet every child obeyed her. Word was Tante Terese was a voodoo priestess and could see what they were doing when she wasn't even looking at them.

"Remarkable," Ethan said. He glanced her way and smiled. "She still doesn't look a day over sixty."

They arrived at her Treme neighborhood, just the other side of the French Quarter, off Rampart. Her home was a little whitewashed cottage built in the late 1800s. Her backyard was huge, and since one of her late husband's nieces owned a carriage company, she kept and cared for some of the aging mules when they retired from taking tourists around the city.

It was nearly midnight, but when they arrived, they heard her call to them from the back. They walked around to the stables, where Terese was patting the neck of a mule whose halter bore a nameplate that said Lafayette.

She quickly hugged her great-grandson, then turned to Charlie.

"Why, child, you've grown up just as beautiful as I knew you would. Still sweet as can be, too, I imagine. You were a lovely child, and so polite every time I'd visit your mama and papa. I'm so happy you've come to see me. I was just asking Ethan about you. I heard about the bad things happening up your way. Will it never end? Anyway, I've finished saying good-night to Lafayette here, so come on in. I have tea ready to go." Terese slipped an arm around Charlie's shoulders and said, "I had to have one of the kids show me how to watch you on that YouTube thing, but my, my, I loved it when I did. Always knew you were going to be a performer, Charlie. I remember how you used to tap-dance all around the kitchen when you were just a wee thing."

Charlie smiled, glancing over at Ethan. It was almost impossible to believe Terese's age. She was still straight as a stick and nearly six feet tall, making Charlie feel short, though she was a respectable five-ten herself.

"I'm so glad you brought Charlie by, Ethan. You know, Charlie, you're not even a stone's throw from me in the

Quarter. Now that you know where I am, you've got to come by more often."

"I will," Charlie said.

"Ethan, get the tea, please, and bring it into the parlor, will you?" Terese asked, then took Charlie's arm. "Come on, let's sit."

As soon as they were settled on the couch, Terese leaned toward Charlie, her amber eyes concerned. "You doing okay, Charlie?"

"Yes, yes, fine."

"I know you've got it, child, got it rich, the sight. Ever since you were a girl. But it can be a hard road, helping the dead. Hard to hear what they have to say sometimes. I see it around you now, you know. It's a shadow. They need you now, Charlie, but you have to take care, you hear?"

"You know, Tante," Ethan said, coming in with the silver tea tray, "I *am* here to help."

"And a good strong man you've become, too, but there's something about Charlie right now. They'll be seeking you out, dear," she said to Charlie. "Has Mr. Corley shown himself to you, or Mr. Hickory?"

Charlie shook her head.

"Well, I can feel it. Someone is going to be talking to you."

Ethan smiled at her, setting the tray down and pouring the tea. "Maybe, Tante, if you've got an in with anyone, you could ask them to speak to me."

"We all see Anson McKee, Tante Terese," Charlie told her. "Just as we did years ago."

Terese nodded and sipped her tea. "Yes, he's strong.

He watches over the area. He was there the day the war stopped, and he was there when they turned the *Journey* over to the Union with all their sick and wounded aboard. I believe he tries to watch over the two of you."

"He does," Ethan said. "Did you ever see him, Tante?"

Terese smiled and nodded, leaning back comfortably. "I never did live in St. Francisville. New Orleans has always been my home. Except, of course, after the hurricane, when they made me head out to California for a month or so. Went with your folks, Ethan, and it was a nice vacation, but this—this is my home. But years ago I was up in St. Francisville visiting, and I saw him there, in the graveyard. He walked right over to me, put his hand on my cheek and smiled, and I felt…peaceful. There was something so kind and good in his smile. You heed him. When he talks to you or tries to show you the way, you heed his directions, you hear?"

They both nodded.

Then Terese sighed and looked at Ethan. "I forgot one of those fool pills the doctor says I have to take for my heart. They're on the kitchen counter, Ethan. Would you mind?"

"Not at all," Ethan said, and rose, leaving them alone together again.

Terese leaned forward and spoke softly to Charlie. "Don't you worry none, Charlie. I know your papa, and he didn't do any of this. I know you're scared, but you have to tell the truth about everything you see, everything you hear. The truth at every turn is what is going to help bring this to an end. Do you understand?"

She spoke quickly and was already leaning back against the pillows again before Ethan returned.

She thanked him and took the container, then shook out a pill. "That snarly old Doc Berlin. He says I have to take these pills and not depend on any of my old cures. Well, I take his pills, but when he gives me a hard time, I say, 'Hey, Doc, what are you worried about? That I'm going to die young?' Ah, well. Never hurts, the man did study hard." She grinned at Charlie. "It's tough sometimes when you knew your doctor when he was in knee britches."

Charlie laughed softly. Terese turned the conversation to family, and they stayed a while longer. It wasn't until they were leaving that Terese spoke to her pointedly again, this time including Ethan.

"Charlie, remember, there's truth—and then there's what people perceive. You take care, extreme care. I've a feeling in these old bones. People might think you know what you don't. Never trust in what you see, always look below and realize what others see is never the same, you hear? And, Ethan, you watch out for her— watch out good. You both understand me?"

Charlie was surprised by the chill that went through her. Terese wasn't trying to scare her, but as the old woman gripped her hand, she felt a cold seep into her blood. "I'll be careful, Tante Terese, I promise," she said.

Terese wagged a finger at Ethan. "And you watch over her, watch over her with every second of your life now, son."

"I swear," Ethan promised. "Now, go back inside and—"

"Oh, hush, I'll watch you into the car. I'm fine right here. This has been my house, my place in the world, forever. You're staying at your folks' place, right?"

"Yes, ma'am," Ethan said.

"Good, good." Terese smiled. "It's so good to finally see the two of you together."

Charlie felt a flush rise to her cheeks. "Oh, we're not..."

"We're just working on..."

"No, no, I wanted Ethan to... A dead man spoke to me, and..."

"We're going on the *Journey* as part of my investigation," Ethan finished, sounding almost apologetic.

Terese smiled. "As I said, good to see the two of you together. Ethan, you get on back to your folks' house now. They want me to move in there with them. One day, maybe. Not yet. I'm still strong and kicking. Now, get. You have a full day tomorrow."

Ethan kissed her cheek, and Charlie did the same.

When they headed out to the car, Charlie still felt the same chill in her bones—and the hot flush in her cheeks.

But she was also smiling awkwardly.

"What?" Ethan asked.

"She's the only person I've ever known who could put you in your place so perfectly," Charlie said.

"What? I don't need to be put in my place!" he said.

Charlie just smiled, but then the smile vanished as she realized that she was afraid. Of something. She didn't know what. She also felt a strange nervousness, as if electricity were zinging along her nerves.

Terese knew. She always could read people. She knew how Charlie felt about Ethan.

But as for Ethan and what *he* felt...

She'd forgotten that she'd said she had to go to her own place until, just minutes later, he turned on to Dauphine.

"Here we are, so let's go get your things," he said.

She thought about what Terese had said to her about lying.

But this was not the time.

"I'll only be a minute," she said. "You can wait here, and I'll be right back."

"I'll go in with you."

Of course he was. She was apparently never going anywhere alone again.

"Okay. That's me to the left. Though I'm sure you already know that."

He shrugged. "Charlie, your address isn't secret. It's listed online and in the white pages."

"And even if it wasn't, you would have known it anyway, right?"

"Probably. I *am* the FBI, after all."

Both front doors opened on to Dauphine, with the building forming a U around the courtyard.

The front door led into a hall; the parlor and dining room were to the left, and a stairway on the right led up to the second story.

"Um, make yourself at home," she said. "I'll be right down."

She was glad she'd left everything neat, and she knew she had nothing to be ashamed of in the way she'd decorated the place. It was filled with art, much of it done by local friends who displayed their work in Jackson Square. She had one friend who did wonderful charcoal sketches of famous actors and actresses, several of which were displayed on one parlor wall. As she hurried up the stairs, she figured she would grab a few more jeans and shirts, since she'd packed mainly casual dresses.

She had to get something else, too.

She dug into a drawer and had just slipped her quarry into her pocket when she turned around and was surprised to find that Ethan had followed her upstairs and was standing in the doorway.

"So you really did need more clothes," he said.

"Of course."

"I thought you just wanted to be with me."

She hesitated, then threw a pair of jeans on the bed. "I really did want to see Terese," she said.

"What else is real, Charlie?" he asked her.

She stood still, looking at him, then shook her head and said softly, "No matter what things look like, I know my father. And he didn't kill anyone."

He nodded and walked into her room.

She was really glad she hadn't left it trashed.

She stared as he stepped closer, watching her. Studying her.

And then he came straight over and drew her into his arms. His eyes barely met hers before he bent and kissed her, his mouth a seduction, the firm pressure of the kiss so unexpected that for a moment the sensations it aroused rippled through her, too strong for her even to think straight.

She didn't pull away.

Instead she savored the kiss as his tongue parted her lips and warmth flooded through her in a rush that felt as powerful as the Mississippi. His hand cupped her cheek, and she wound her arms around his neck, returning touch for touch. She felt as if something, too long held back, had ripped free in a turbulent explosion. She didn't want to think, she wanted to explore his mouth as he did hers, let the hot liquid fire of the kiss consume them.

And then, breathless and torn, they pulled back at the same time, but they didn't break the embrace.

"Sorry," he said softly.

She shook her head. "No…no… I'm an idiot. I've gone all these years remembering what I felt for you. It's just…"

"You have the right to close the door, walk away. Maybe you should. I don't think you ever understood how hard it was for me when I was the one who walked away. Maybe you *should* walk away, for your own sanity, or for…"

She laughed, loving everything she saw in his eyes. "For revenge? Honestly, Ethan, I think we're both too old for that. But I'm afraid. I've had a life. I mean, I didn't join a cloister or anything, but… I just never found anyone like you."

He smiled and smoothed a stray strand of hair from her face. "I never found anyone remotely like you, either," he breathed.

For a long moment they simply stood there. Charlie

realized she was shaking. She had wanted him, dreamed about him, for years, and now...

Now he was holding her. Now he had kissed her.

And then he let go of her and stepped back. "We have to go," he said huskily. "We have to get back. We're in the middle of a murder investigation. And while I'm sure my coworkers would understand, they'll be calling out every agent in New Orleans if we don't get back soon."

"Yeah," Charlie said, glad she still had a voice.

She grabbed some clothes, tossed them into a tote bag and then started to brush past him to reach the door.

He pulled her back.

One more kiss. Deep, sensual, provocative—and filled with promise.

She returned that kiss with vital hunger and need...

And a promise of her own.

Dreams did come true. Even in the middle of a nightmare.

Ethan felt his phone buzzing in his pocket as they headed back; he picked it up quickly. As he'd expected, it was Jude.

"Sorry, I should have called," he answered, glancing at Charlie. "We're headed back now."

"Great. We'll wait until you're in, then lock the place down. Luckily your parents have a good alarm system."

"They have an FBI agent for a son," Ethan said, then added a quick goodbye and hung up.

After Ethan parked, he hurried around the car to open the passenger door. When and where he'd grown up, it was the thing to do—and it was a hard habit to break, even though it offended some women he'd come across.

Charlie wasn't offended—she'd grown up in the same place at the same time, after all—but she didn't move, either.

She looked up at him, something unreadable in her eyes. "I have to tell you the truth," she said softly.

"That you did go behind my back to arrange your little undercover stunt on the *Journey*?" he asked.

She shook her head. "I mean, yes, I wanted to do that, because Anson McKee pointed to the river, and I'm sure he meant that's where we'll find the answer. But, no, that's not what I meant."

"Okay, what *did* you mean?"

She turned to look at him, blue eyes tormented. "I saw Selma Rodriguez."

"I thought you might have. You had that deer-in-the-headlights look in your eyes when we came into the office. I figured you'd say something when you were ready," he said. "So...?"

"She said Corley mentioned meeting my father—Dad was good friends with both Farrell and Albion," Charlie said, then quickly added, "My father had nothing to do with this. I don't care what it looks like. My dad...my dad is a good man, a man who would help anyone. He's not a killer."

"Look, it's natural that you don't like hearing anything that implicates your father. Yes, he's an ass to me sometimes. And the evidence is really shaking me, but in my heart I still don't believe he did it—and that has nothing to do with the fact that he's your father. So don't worry, okay?"

She smiled. "Good," she said softly. She looked at the house, and color flooded her cheeks. "So...where am I sleeping?"

"Well, I *was* trying to take things slow," he said.

"Yes, exactly."

"But even so, I was kind of hoping you'd sleep in my room. It's not terribly exciting. I was out of the house when my folks moved to New Orleans, so none of my old *Sports Illustrated* and heavy-metal band posters are on the wall, but my mom did buy me a really comfortable bed."

Charlie looked at him and laughed. "This is what you call taking things slow?"

"We *were* slow. We left your place and came here."

At last Charlie smiled, so he offered his hand and she stepped out of the car. "Got to check in with Jude and Thor first," he told her as they headed to the front door.

That was going to be easy enough to do, seeing as Jude opened the door as they reached it. "Glad you're back. It's always good to know everyone is accounted for."

"What's going on here?" Ethan asked Jude.

"I was just making coffee. Want some?" Jude offered.

"Sure."

"I guess I'll go on up," Charlie murmured.

He refrained from telling her where his room was and potentially embarrassing her in front of Jude. She would figure it out.

"Thor, Alexi and Clara have already gone up," Jude

said. "I'll hang down here until Thor comes down. You can have the six o'clock watch. Work for you?" he asked, looking at Ethan.

"Sounds good," Ethan said, following him into the kitchen.

"Anything new?" he asked Jude. "You talk to Jackson or anyone?"

Jude nodded, pouring coffee and handing Ethan a cup. "Jackson has spoken with the *Journey* management. They're feeling pretty stressed, can't believe another of their ships might be involved in a murder. They're happy to cooperate with us in any way. *Journey* security—a small, four-man force—has been alerted to our presence. There are only going to be 402 people aboard, including crew and entertainment."

"I can't imagine this killer is a casual cruiser."

"No, I'm pretty sure what's happening is happening in port. Which doesn't clear Jonathan Moreau."

"Yes, and I believe, based on the implications of what Charlie said, that Albion Corley was planning to see him."

"You know that because…?"

"Charlie saw Selma Rodriguez."

"I had a feeling. I'm glad she was ready to tell you. She has to learn to trust us. And she will."

"Yeah," Ethan said, rinsing out his cup and setting it in the drainer. "I guess I'll go up, then. Good night."

"Good night." Then, after a moment, Jude said, "Hey, Ethan."

"Yeah?"

"I don't know Jonathan Moreau, but you do. Charlie

does. And if you're sure he didn't do this, that's enough for us to be looking at why someone thought they could make use of him when setting up the murders."

"Thanks. And, yeah, I'm sure," Ethan said.

He left Jude in the kitchen and started up the stairs. He realized his heart was pounding as if he were a kid again. All he had to do was think about Charlie, and it seemed he was kinetic with electricity.

She might not even be there; she could have changed her mind.

It was a big house. She might have found a different room.

His bedroom door was closed. A good sign?

He paused, knocking on the door.

"Ethan?"

He barely heard her whisper, and he was almost as quiet when he answered, "Yes."

"Come in."

He walked into his room, quickly shutting the door behind him.

She was there, very much there. It was like a replay from a decade ago.

A beautiful, unbelievable replay.

She was stretched out on his bed, chestnut hair spreading over the pillows. She was propped up on one elbow, facing the door, naked and waiting for him, just as she had been a decade ago. For a moment she appeared to be the absolute height of sensual sophistication, and then she said nervously, "I thought I'd better make sure it was you. I mean, I had a friend who did something like this once. There was a knock...and she told the UPS man to come in."

"No, it's me," he said huskily.

"I see," she said softly. "And if you walk out that door this time, you'll never get this chance again."

Without turning away, Ethan groped behind him to lock the door.

"I'm not going anywhere," he told her.

"Then," she said, "you might want to come over here, because I'm actually feeling just a little bit ridiculous. I'm not really good at this kind of thing. I developed a complex at a young age."

"Good," he said.

"Good?"

"I realize I'm being selfish, but I'm glad to know you've never done this for anyone but me."

He spotted a pile of brightly colored packets on the nightstand. One label caught his attention. It said Tickler.

He looked from the pile to Charlie and couldn't help but smile broadly.

"And you got those where?"

"The condom commercial," she said gravely. "I've heard they're very pleasurable, though I haven't had a chance to try them out yet. But..."

"I'm glad you waited for me."

He strode to the bed, kicking off his shoes as he went, sliding his Glock from his waistband, then setting the gun in its small holster on the bedside table.

Screw the rest of his clothes. He'd deal with them as soon as he had a chance to touch her.

"I mean, what the hell. You don't know for yourself until you try something, right?"

Tugging at his shirttails, he eased down beside her, pulling her up and into his arms. "You'll never understand," he murmured. Her scent was seductive in the most primal way. It wasn't her perfume, not her soap or shampoo, but the deep natural scent of her flesh. He whispered unintelligibly against her lips and her throat, then began to struggle in earnest with his clothing. She kissed him in return and joined him in the struggle with buttons and fabric. "You'll never understand... The hardest thing, the most decent thing, I ever did in my life was walk away."

"I *do* understand," she told him, which made him pull back and search her eyes.

"I *do* understand," she repeated. "I'm just glad you didn't do it again."

"No chance," he whispered, his words muffled against her flesh. "No chance."

They kissed deeply, Ethan trying not to take his lips off her flesh as he worked to divest himself of the last of his clothes.

They laughed at first, until she slid his trousers and briefs down and brushed his erection. Urgency burst through him as if he'd been lit on fire. Their eyes met again, and they fell into another hot kiss.

His clothes gone at last, he kissed the length of her, ardent, desperate, tasting her with lips and tongue. She writhed against him, touching him, nipping his shoulder and along his throat.

Finally and yet simultaneously too quickly, he was

over her and then in her, and his need was immeasurable. He had waited a decade, and now the release of his pent-up desire was making him nearly insane. His body was torn between agony and ecstasy, as if he was about to erupt like a Chinese rocket on New Year's, but he fought the desperation screaming inside him.

He had to take her with him.

His eyes remained locked with hers as they kissed, then broke away before kissing again. Suddenly she swallowed back a cry, and he did the same, and then waiting was no longer possible. He climaxed in violent spasms that ripped through him, muscles, blood and bone, and in that same moment he felt her tighten around him and let go of her own control.

They lay together afterward, breathing heavily, until Charlie said at last, "Ten years in the making…"

He rolled closer to her, smoothing back a wild lock of her hair, and asked, "And after all that time, how was it?" When she didn't answer, he smiled. "A little scary, huh? You go so long. You live with memories of what might have been but never was. And you wonder if you've put someone on a pedestal, and whether, if the dream should come true, would it really be…the dream."

"Better than the dream," she said softly. "That is, for me. Unless it wasn't…for you?"

"My imagination could never have conceived of anything so wonderful," he told her.

She rolled against him, arms around his neck, and kissed him.

And then it all began again. Kisses. The eroticism of naked flesh against naked flesh...

Somewhere in there, they slept. And then it was his time to keep watch. None of them expected any trouble at the house, but it never hurt to be vigilant.

He dressed and went down to the parlor, leaving Charlie sound asleep in his bed. Thor had brought up the news on his computer *and* made fresh coffee. Ethan decided Thor might be his new best friend. The other agent went up for a few more hours of sleep, while Ethan settled down to read email until his watch ended when everyone got up for breakfast.

He didn't think he'd ever felt so alive. More awake, alert or determined.

Or more in love.

After one night.

Then again, it had been one night that had followed ten years of a haunting dream that had played constantly in the back of his mind, always there, always a part of his life, no matter how he'd tried to lose it to the mists of memory.

10

"How could you lie to me?" Charlie demanded. She was finally alone with her father on board the *Journey*, and she was furious.

The passengers from the previous cruise had all gone ashore. The passengers for the coming week were starting to board now. That left her plenty of time to talk to her father, and now she was sitting on the small sofa in his cabin while he paced the floor.

He had started off being stern and playing the father card. What was she doing? Taking part in the investigation was dangerous, and she was an actress, not a cop. It was all Ethan Delaney's fault, he insisted, and he had no right to drag her into danger again.

Charlie had refused to cave, though, and she'd quickly turned the discussion around.

"Why did you lie to me?" she asked, breaking into his tirade. "You said you hardly knew the men who were killed, and it wasn't even a smart lie. Half the world knows you were friends with both of them. Did you think we wouldn't find out?"

"Yes, I knew them both. I didn't deny that. And I

guess you could say we were friends, but you don't understand," her father said. He was such a good speaker that he was usually eloquent under any pressure, but now he was waving his hands around in frustration, starting to speak, then stopping abruptly before starting up again.

"I'm *trying* to understand," Charlie said, "but you're not giving me anything to go on."

"We supported each other. We supported each other at…" he said.

"At what?"

Her father stared at her and slowly let out a breath. "At anything in life," he said softly. Then he quickly added, "Not anything bad, but if one of us asked the others to keep a secret, or if we asked for help…"

"So you *were* friends," she said accusingly.

"More than that," Jonathan admitted.

She gasped suddenly. "Masons. You were members of the same lodge."

"Charlie, I can't even say that! You know what we do. We raise money for children's hospitals, for cancer… good things. Only good things."

"Dad, I know that. I was a Rainbow Girl, remember?" she reminded him. The women's division of the Masons was called the Order of the Eastern Star, and the girls' division was the International Order of the Rainbow for Girls. Growing up, she'd been a Rainbow Girl in her father's lodge. She'd never seen the Masons involved in anything that wasn't completely aboveboard and good for the community.

"Dad, I would defend the Masons in every way—

unless they get in the way of justice. If someone in your lodge did this, then—"

"No, Charlie!" he interrupted. "That's just it—no one in the lodge did this. I'm certain of that. I know those men. We're close—we're brothers, in a way. The thing is, if I'd admitted how well I knew the victims…well, I would have been in jeopardy of divulging things to the authorities that were told to me in confidence."

"Dad, if what you know could lead to the capture of a killer…"

"That's just it. What I know would look to some people like motive, but that's not the case at all."

Incredibly frustrated, Charlie stood and faced him, hands on her hips. "Dad! You don't know what help your information could be because you haven't shared it with the authorities. Don't you understand? Everything we learn is leading to you!"

Her father lowered his head. "Ethan told you that, didn't he?"

"No, not Ethan. Detective Laurent, and probably others. And…" She paused, taking a deep breath before speaking again. "Dad, I saw the dead woman. Selma Rodriguez. She said Albion Corley had talked about going out to meet you."

"You saw Selma."

"Yes," she said quietly. He didn't see the dead, but he knew and accepted that she did.

He nodded. "I have no idea why anyone killed that poor woman."

"But you do know why someone might have killed Albion Corley and Farrell Hickory?"

He hesitated. "Dad," Charlie said firmly.

"Farrell was thinking about getting married again."

"Why would someone kill him for wanting to marry again?" Charlie asked, perplexed.

Her father was silent.

"Dad."

"Okay, okay. Farrell was in love with Albion's cousin Shelley. Albion knew about it, and he wanted to see me because he wanted to see what I thought was the best way to go about the wedding. And I was quiet for two reasons—what I knew was told to me in confidence, and I wouldn't have wanted the cops to get the wrong idea. I was in it to help Farrell and Shelley. They thought I'd know the best way to go about doing things."

"The best way to go about the wedding?" Charlie said, incredulous.

"Charlie, we can make laws, but a lot of people are still prejudiced."

"He was afraid because Farrell was white and his cousin was black?"

"He wasn't afraid, exactly. He just wanted to do everything right so both families would be on board once Farrell went public with the news. They've been keeping it quiet. He didn't really expect there to be a problem, but just the idea that Farrell was getting married again was going to be news to everyone."

"Was that really what Farrell and Albion were fighting about on the *Journey*? Nothing about history at all?" Charlie asked.

"No, the fight was over what really happened that day, and the supporting documentation just isn't there."

Charlie fell back on the sofa, perplexed. "Do you think someone out there…? Do you think it might have been a hate crime?"

"No, and that's why I omitted the truth about how well I knew the men."

"Omitting the truth is lying!"

"I'm sorry, Charlene, I really am. But I was afraid if I said any of this, the police would be so busy looking in the wrong direction that they wouldn't look in the right one."

"Dad, how can you be certain this *isn't* the right direction?"

"Because no one knew. No one but Albion, Shelley, Farrell and me. I guess someone else could have overheard something and figured it out, but it just doesn't seem like it could matter."

"Oh, Dad, of course it could matter," Charlie said. "You have to tell Ethan everything you know."

"Ethan!" he exploded. "Ethan nearly got you killed once and—"

"He saved my life. I would have been a sitting duck if he hadn't been there."

Jonathan turned away. "He should have gotten you out of there and told the police everything down at the station. He shouldn't have kept you there where you were nearly killed."

"But I wasn't, and that's because he tackled the killer. He saved my life."

Her father fell silent.

Charlie stood and hugged him. "Dad, get used to Ethan. He's going to be around."

He groaned. "Oh, Charlie, no. You aren't right for each other. I could see the way you looked at him back then, and I was afraid, and I don't feel any better about you two now."

"Why? Dad, Ethan is a good man."

"He scares me," Jonathan said. "He scares the hell out of me, because… Charlie, I love you. I'm your father, and I want you to be safe."

"You have to talk to him and tell him what you know," she said flatly, then glanced at her watch. "And I have to go find Alexi and Clara to start rehearsing."

"You shouldn't be here."

"Just a few days ago you *wanted* me here."

"But now I'm afraid."

"Dad…"

"They killed that woman in Baton Rouge, Charlie. They killed her just because she knew Albion. I'm afraid. I'm afraid they'll think you know something you don't."

"Who are 'they,' Dad, and what on earth could they think I know? You're the one with information that could help solve this case. If you know anything else at all…"

"I don't."

"Talk to Ethan, Dad."

His shoulders seemed to slump. "You shouldn't be here. You should have gone up to DC or Virginia or wherever your friends' new theater is."

"I love you, Dad," Charlie said, and kissed his cheek. "But that's not going to happen."

Then she hurried out and down the hall. She should

have met Alexi and Clara in the main restaurant ten minutes ago. They had a lot to go over.

But she had to talk to Ethan first. He had to get Jude and Thor, and the three of them needed to talk to her father—but first she had to be sure he understood that even though her father had lied, he was guilty of nothing more than trying to protect his friends. He was a good man.

Just as Albion Corley and Farrell Hickory had been good men.

She suddenly realized she was afraid, but not for herself.

For her father.

Ethan had been through as much of the ship as he could in an hour, escorted by the captain, a man named Timothy Banks. Banks was the perfect image of a riverboat captain, if Ethan had ever seen one. He was about fifty-five, tall, straight as an arrow, with a full head of white hair and a fine white beard-and-mustache combo to match.

He would have looked at home guiding the *Journey* all those years ago when she'd changed hands during the course of the war.

He loved the *Journey,* so he'd been happy to take Ethan on a quick stroll from deck to deck—the Main Deck, the New Orleans Deck, the Louisiana Deck, the Mississippi or Observation Deck, the Promenade and the Sun Deck. There were small inside staterooms on two of the decks, including the Main Deck, and those were given over to the crew and entertainment staff. The Eagle View dining room, the main onboard restaurant, was also on the Main Deck, and that was where Charlie would be performing every night with Alexi and Clara.

The gym, the pool, rows of lounge chairs and a small but excellent bar/restaurant were, naturally, located on the Sun Deck, while all the other decks above the waterline offered promenades, smaller and less crowded than those on the Promenade Deck. The Pilot House was also located on the Sun Deck.

As far as cruise ships went, the *Journey* was on the smaller side, but between passengers and crew, she still carried about five hundred people.

Captain Banks told Ethan that even though they were on the river and within easy reach of many fine hospitals, they had a ship's doctor, Gerard Amerind, two nurses and a small but state-of-the-art infirmary. It wasn't located on the Main Deck, where the infirmary had been located during the war. Of course, back then they'd needed a larger facility, since most of the men on the ship had been ill or injured. Today the infirmary could be found on the Sun Deck, where Ethan's tour ended.

From there, he and Banks could look out at the other ships currently in port. They were also high enough to stare out over the river and the crescent curve that made up New Orleans, the tall buildings of the Central Business District and even the tops of the old Spanish- and French-style buildings in the Quarter. If they turned around, they could see into the Celtic American terminal, crowded now with passengers eager and excited to embark on the cruise.

"Bad business, huh?" Captain Banks said, shaking

his head. "Don't know what you think you can learn from being on the *Journey*. I wish to God I could help you, though."

"What do you remember about the reenactment? Did you notice anyone who seemed to be harboring a grudge against either of the murdered men?"

"There was that one little spat I'm sure you already know about, but Jonathan stepped in and it was over quick."

"Did you know all the reenactors?"

"Good Lord, no! I've had occasion to meet a few of them here and there, but I seldom have time to watch any of the programming, much less leave the ship when we're in port. Every once in a while I meet up with a friend somewhere along the way. But I've captained this river-boat along the Mississippi six years now, and mostly I use any 'free' time to look out over the water and finish up the obligatory paperwork."

"Did you know Albion Corley or Farrell Hickory, or, by any chance, a woman named Selma Rodriguez?"

The captain took a long look at Ethan. "I met Corley and Hickory once at a combined function of the lodges."

"The lodges?"

"Masonic lodges. We were doing a benefit to help re-build one of the local schools. It's over a decade since Katrina, but there's still work to be done."

"So you *did* know them?"

"In passing. Enough so that we greeted one another the day of the program. I watched them that night, chatting up Wall Street types and oil barons, convincing them to open up their purse strings. I remember they said they were both involved in animal rescue after the big oil spill, too. They were right on the front lines, helping wash off all those birds and such. Hands-on men, they were, not just talkers. Now, as for Selma Rodriguez..." He paused, looking perplexed as he stared at Ethan. "I know that name. I'm just not sure why."

"She was murdered in Baton Rouge."

"Poor woman. That must be why I'd heard her name. The world can be a cruel place." He shook his head, as if at a loss to understand how such things happened. Then he looked at Ethan again. "Is there a relationship between her murder and Corley's and Hickory's?"

"I don't know. She worked for the college where Corley taught."

"Was she a reenactor, too?"

"No, but she and Corley were friendly."

"I see." The captain shook his head. "I'm sorry I haven't been any help, but if I can assist you in any way during the cruise, just let me know."

"Thank you."

Banks offered him a firm handshake, then headed off to make sure everything was ready for the arriving passengers.

Even though Banks hadn't told him anything to move his investigation forward, Ethan had found the tour extremely helpful. Now he knew where to find just about anything on the ship. He was glad that the Belles' cabins, and their rehearsal and performance spaces, would be close together. Easier to keep an eye on them that way.

There was a nine-man security staff aboard the ship—three per eight-hour shift—and that was reassuring, too.

When Banks had told him about them, he had emphasized his belief that the ship was a safe space. "Whatever's going on," Banks had told him, "it's not going on here, not on the *Journey*." He'd let out a deep sigh, a striking figure with his white hair and beard, and impeccable period-style captain's uniform.

Ethan had assured him that no one was targeting the *Journey*; they were simply trying to find out more about the day the two victims had been aboard.

"Seems to me you ought to be interviewing people in St. Francisville," Banks had said.

"Trust me, the police are on that," Ethan had assured him.

Ethan's thoughts were interrupted when his phone started ringing.

"Ethan, hi."

It was Charlie, and she sounded a little tense.

"Is anything wrong?"

"No, no...but you need to talk to my dad. Without accusing him of anything. Without...being hostile."

"Charlie, I'm not hostile to your dad. Your dad is hostile to me. I can't change that, but I still have to do my job."

"I know, I know. Anyway, he knows I'm talking to you. He has information. He's not guilty of anything except being a friend, but...talk to him, Ethan. There might be something to this that goes beyond the film connection. Please, just listen to him. Now I have to run and find Alexi and Clara so we can put our show together."

"You're alone?" he asked her. "You were with Jude and Clara last time I saw you."

"I ran out to see my dad before rehearsal, no big deal."

"Charlie, do me a favor. I'm not trying to be over-protective, but don't be alone, okay? Hurry up and join the others."

"All right, I'm almost there. Don't worry. I'll text you the minute I arrive," she promised.

"Thanks. Where's your father?"

"In his cabin."

"All right, I'm on my way."

He rang off, but before he went to find Jonathan's cabin, he headed to the main dining room to make sure she arrived safely. He got her text when he was halfway there, but he wanted to see firsthand that she was safe.

He didn't go in, just made sure she really was there and safely surrounded by friends. Jude saw him and nodded. Ethan nodded back and slipped away, glad the Krewe had his back.

It was easy, working with friends. As far as their vocal abilities went, they were well suited to perform to-gether. Alexi was a talented pianist, and she could adapt anytime a singer made a mistake. Clara had a pure, clear soprano, while Charlie was an alto. Alexi couldn't hit the highest notes, but had the broadest range of the three of them. As they went through the songs, Charlie created bits of dialogue to segue between songs, since they were mixing North and South.

She also planned to throw in bits of history that wouldn't step on her father's lectures.

They would share vocal duties on some songs, like "Dixie," when they even planned to encourage the audience to join in. Other songs would be solos. Clara had claimed "The Battle Hymn of the Republic" as her own, and Alexi had done the same with "Bonnie Blue Flag." As they made their set lists—allowing a half hour each night for requests—Charlie realized that she was having fun. She loved working anyway, and it was great to be back with Alexi and Clara.

For a little while she even forgot why she was there.

Then she glanced over to the table where Jude was sitting and enjoying the show, and it all came crashing back.

Because enjoying the show wasn't the only thing he was doing. He was watching over them. He was their bodyguard.

As much as he might appear to be simply enjoying himself, he was watching…

Watching every entrance to the dining room, the kitchen doors…

It was good to feel safe.

It was also unnerving.

Especially when she thought about the red band of blood circling Selma Rodriguez, a woman murdered just because she might have known something about Albion Corley.

Jonathan wasn't exactly hostile, but he was definitely cold. He let Ethan in and told him without preamble that Charlie had said he had to tell Ethan everything he knew, which he proceeded to do.

"Jonathan, you should have told us this right away. It would put a different spin on the investigation," Ethan said.

"No, that's just it," Jonathan said emphatically. "No one would have had any objection to the wedding. But the thing is, no one did know. That was my whole point. I didn't want you investigating this as a hate crime. There's something else going on, dammit. Something we're not seeing."

"Now I know they were both Masons—like you."

Jonathan exploded. "Oh, no! Don't you go there! They try to blame everything on the Masons, from Jack the Ripper to government conspiracies. Yes, George Washington was a Mason, and so were half the founding fathers. All we do is work for children's charities, for cancer research... We help people."

"If you don't want me to go there, then think. Can you think of anything else? Anything else that connected them? And maybe could relate to Selma Rodriguez, too?"

Jonathan sat, groaned and buried his face in his hands. Then he looked at Ethan and sighed. "I *have* thought. They were good men, not druggies, womanizers or gamblers. They did charity work, supported good causes. I'm sorry. I wish I could help, but I honestly don't know a thing."

"Actually, I think you *have* helped me," Ethan told him.

"How?"

"By reminding me about their charity work. Can you tell me what committees they were on, what causes they were involved with lately? Because if this didn't happen because of Shelley Corley, there has to be something else."

"Their charity efforts are all public record. They'll be easy for you to find." He met Ethan's eyes. "So you believe me, that their deaths had nothing to do with Shelley?"

"If no one knew, no. We'll have to talk to Shelley just to cover all our bases. And I need to know if Farrell Hickory spoke with his son about this."

Jonathan laughed. "Shelley is fifty. She and Farrell were not going to start procreating. Farrell's boy didn't need to worry about a new half brother and having to share the family fortune. That boy's intelligent. He'd know that."

"Yeah. I'm sure he would," Ethan said. "Jonathan, I need to know everything you can think of about Farrell and Albion."

"They were my friends. Good friends, both of them. We were lodge brothers. They were passionate about the environment, but they also understood business. They believed that business—the oil business, in particular— and environmentalists could work for the common good. They loved being reenactors. I don't know what else I can tell you."

"Thank you," Ethan said, and offered Jonathan his hand.

Jonathan held out his own and then shook his head. "You're putting Charlie into the path of danger again."

"Mr. Moreau, I've never put Charlie into the path of danger. I found her tied to a tombstone and freed her.

We didn't know that a killer was going to show up. And now I'm here because Charlie specifically asked to have me assigned to this case. I intend to do everything humanly possible to get to the bottom of this—and I will protect Charlie with my life."

"That may not be good enough," Jonathan told him flatly. "What if you *can't* catch the killer?"

"Trust me, I'll catch him. I intend to investigate everyone even tangentially involved with those men, and you might as well know that means you, too."

"You know I didn't kill those men."

"I *don't* believe you did, no. But you *did* lie to us."

Jonathan said nothing as Ethan turned to leave the room. He was startled when Jonathan spoke again.

"Are you sleeping with my daughter?"

Ethan froze, his back to the man.

Sleeping? Well, technically, yes. But when it came to Jonathan's real question, did one night count?

He turned around and met Jonathan's eyes. "I care deeply for Charlie, and I have since the night I found her in the graveyard. But we haven't seen one another in a very long time."

"I didn't ask you if you cared about her. I asked if you were sleeping with her."

"We're in the same cabin."

Moreau nodded, and to Ethan's surprise, he actually looked relieved. Had he been misreading the man? Curious, he said, "I hope that doesn't upset you."

"To be honest, at the moment I find it reassuring. I may not approve of my daughter's taste in men, but under the circumstances, since she refuses to leave the area, she's safest in your company."

"And I intend to keep her that way," Ethan said, and left.

His first action was to put through a call to Jackson Crow; he wanted Jackson to get someone to track down Shelley Corley. They needed to speak with her. The woman hadn't—to the best of his knowledge—called the cops looking for information when Farrell Hickory had been killed.

Strange, if she was planning on marrying him.

On the other hand, no one had known about the wedding plans, so people might have wondered what her interest was.

But he wouldn't know the real story until he talked to her, and Jackson had the resources to locate her quickly and maybe even set up a meeting.

"You don't want to say anything to Detective Laurent about this yet?" Jackson asked Ethan, after he'd explained the situation.

"I'd like to speak with her first, find out how committed they really were and if she knows anything that could help us."

Jackson agreed, and after ending the call, Ethan was satisfied that they'd made a good start on finding out the full story of Farrell's secret proposal.

And then he wondered if Charlie's father had talked to her about their conversation and, if so, exactly what he'd said.

They'd been rehearsing for a while when a lean, gray-haired man in a beige suit entered the main dining room and approached the stage. Before he got even halfway there, Jude was on his feet and staring down intimidatingly at the man, who Charlie thought looked vaguely familiar.

"Ricky Simpson—entertainment director," Alexi whispered quickly.

"Oh, right," Charlie murmured.

"Ricky, great to see you," Alexi said. "You remember Clara, and you must have met Charlie somewhere along the line. And this is Jude McCoy."

"Great to see you, too," Simpson said, smiling. "I have to admit, I was a little surprised when management booked you for this cruise at the last minute, but you'll be glad to hear you seem to have been quite the draw. We advertised your appearance on several travel sites, and the remaining cabins were reserved just last night. This being a history-focused cruise, I just need to know. Your stories *are* accurate, right?"

"Unless they're legend, and then we say so," Charlie said.

Simpson grinned. "You really are your father's daughter. I heard you as I was coming in. You sound great. The passengers are going to love you. And you can do run-throughs in the mornings, after breakfast. Then—"

"We know," Alexi said. "Once we're out of port, this dining room needs to be clear by eleven for the lunch setup. We report here each evening by five for the first dinner shift, and we finish up at approximately ten each night."

"Exactly," Simpson said. "Alexi and Clara, delighted to work with you again. Charlie, I look forward to getting to know you better. I saw one of your commercials recently, but you're even more talented than I knew."

"Thank you," Charlie said, wondering which one he'd seen. She'd made enough money to live for a year on the condom commercial she'd shot, but it certainly did come back to haunt her. She hadn't had to do anything remotely sexual and had been fully clothed for the entire thirty seconds. Still, the mere mention of condoms seemed to make people smirk.

Simpson looked over at Jude. "I truly pray you're not expecting trouble. I understand you were involved in some difficulties that plagued one of our sister ships?"

Charlie saw the slight tension in Jude's polite smile. "I believe that my colleagues and I were part of ending those difficulties. We don't expect any trouble during the cruise. We're simply here to learn anything we can that might help us solve two—possibly three—murders."

"My crew all know you're FBI. Too many people were aware of your presence in St. Francisville for that to be a secret."

"Not a problem," Jude said.

"Well, then…" Simpson paused and smiled. "Truth is, I'm here to kick you out. They need to prepare the room, since the passengers are beginning to board. The Sun Deck buffet is open, though, and we encourage the entertainment staff to mingle with the guests. In fact, I'll be up there myself in a little while."

He gave them a wave and left just as a number of men and women in tailored uniforms with the word *Journey* embroidered on their pockets walked in.

"Guess it's time for us to move," Clara said. "Sun Deck?"

"Thor is already up there, and I'm betting Ethan has joined him by now," Jude said. "The captain was showing Ethan around earlier, while Thor was talking to the ship's doctor. We can trade notes at the buffet."

As they left, Charlie looked back as the waitstaff moved around the room, efficiently getting it ready for guests.

Jude lingered with her.

She shook her head, looking at him. "I hope there really is something to be discovered on board. I can't imagine any of the dining staff would have seen or heard anything. I mean, the programming took place on deck, right? They would all have been busy down here or wherever."

He nodded.

"But Ricky Simpson…he and the entertainment staff— including the other tour guides—could have been on deck."

"And," he said, "they could be on the Sun Deck right now. Shall we go up?"

She nodded and started walking, then hesitated and turned back again. For a moment it seemed as if the day went away, as if a gray miasma fell over the room. She heard coughing and moaning, and where only a moment ago there had been a busy crowd of employees, only a few men and women, doctors and nurses, were moving about the room. The floor, though, was covered in men, some lying on pallets, others seated, all of them wrapped in bandages and the tatters of their uniforms, both the blue and the gray. Rickety tables held bowls of water, and most of that water was red. She blinked, but the vision remained, and she wondered if what she was seeing replayed daily, like long-gone soldiers living out their last minutes on the battlefield. They were clearly unaware of her or anyone else.

She reached out to grab Jude's arm, but he had already moved into the hall, and she could vaguely hear him talking to Alexi and Clara.

Suddenly one of the men—a doctor, she thought—turned to look at her, aware of her even as the scene went on around him. He saluted her and then went back to his duties.

"Charlie?" Clara said.

"Coming," she said, and quickly joined her friends in the hall.

A dish dropped and shattered, followed by laughter. Drawn by the sound, Charlie looked back through the doorway.

The window to the past had disappeared.

But memories of the long-dead man who had paused to look at her remained. He'd realized she was there.

Did he know something? Anything? Could he help her?

If he could, she knew he would find her.

She shivered slightly. These days the *Journey* might be a beautifully restored riverboat.

But her past, Charlie knew, had been bathed in blood.

11

The *Journey* was leaving port.

Ethan saw Charlie standing at the rail, watching the river. A quick glance assured him she wasn't alone. Clara, Alexi and Jude were only a few feet away. Thor had been planning to meet with the ship's doctor earlier, but the man hadn't shown, so Thor had chatted with the nurses instead. The doctor still hadn't arrived by the time Thor had to leave to join the others.

The wind caught Charlie's hair and swept it back. Her profile was so perfect, caught in the golden light of the setting sun. The Algiers district was across the river, and as they left port, they could see the riverfront by the French Quarter, the steeple of St. Louis Cathedral rising high. Ethan strode over to her, aware the ship was now filled with passengers crowding the rail here on the top deck as they set out.

"Isn't it beautiful?" Charlie said to him. "I understand why my father's chosen to work on a ship. Of course, he didn't start until after I left for college and my mom died. Before that he'd taught in Baton Rouge and gave tours there and at various plantations. But he loves this."

She paused, looking at him. "Speaking of my dad… How did it go?"

"Great. He thinks you have deplorable taste in men, but since you can't have a giant German shepherd on board, he seems to think I'm the next best thing. In fact, he pretty much gave me his approval to sleep with you."

"I'm sorry," she said, laughing. "But…really? Dad gave you his approval? I'll believe that when I see it." She turned serious. "But I guess you being able to joke about it means he wasn't too hostile?"

"No, actually, we had an almost pleasant conversation."

"Well, good. And what do you think about what he told you?"

"I think I need to speak to Shelley Corley and find out if anyone else had even an inkling of what was going on between her and Farrell."

Charlie looked worried. "I'm not trying to pretend bigots don't exist, but I honestly don't think the killer's a racist who was mad because a white man and a black man were friends."

"Charlie, I agree. I think we're looking for someone who had a very personal grudge against both victims, a grudge that had nothing to do with racial prejudice but might still involve the engagement."

"But why kill Selma?" she asked. "Albion was friendly with her, but I doubt she knew anything about his personal life."

"I don't know the answer to that, not yet. But I'm certain she died because she knew him."

Just then Thor walked up and joined them. "It's beautiful here—very different from where I come from." He leaned against the rail. "I talked with the two nurses. A number of the reenactors wound up in the infirmary. Two wasp stings, one gash that needed stitches—another reenactor didn't know his right from his left—and a case of poison ivy acquired ashore. They didn't remember the names, but they're going to get the records for me. Probably won't mean anything, but…" He shrugged. "I still need to talk to the doctor. Apparently he's up here on deck somewhere."

"I think that's him," Clara said, and pointed across the deck. "I saw his picture on the Meet Your Crew bulletin board by guest services."

A man in a white uniform, complete with cap, was talking to a pair of young women. He was tall and blond and suntanned, lean, probably about forty-five or fifty.

"We can find out," Ethan said and walked over to the man. He excused himself to the women and said something to the man, who shook hands and then accompanied Ethan to join them at the rail.

He was indeed Dr. Gerard Amerind—"Gerry to my friends"—and he said he hoped they would all be his friends.

After the others introduced themselves, Ethan cut right to the chase and asked, "So, what do you remember from the day of the special reenactment?"

"What do I remember?" Amerind asked. He snorted. "Grown men getting hurt in ridiculous ways. First, two of them disturbed a wasps' nest. Could have been worse if they hadn't been the only ones stupid enough to try getting rid of it. Then there was an idiot guy who got confused between right and left, and cut one of his fellow reenactors. That guy needed stitches. Another idiot got into poison ivy before he came aboard."

"Your nurses told me about all of them," Thor said politely.

Amerind let out a sigh. "They're great nurses, though they'd be even better if they weren't jumping out of their skins all the time. They're convinced the ship is haunted."

"What respectable ship isn't?" Clara asked with a smile.

Amerind didn't seem to hear her. He looked perplexed, as if he had just thought of something. He looked at them and said uneasily, "There was another man. He came in after the reenactment... Well, he didn't come in, exactly. He was older, tall, a very dignified-looking African American. He was seated at one of the deck tables, near the infirmary. He looked flushed and he was out of breath. Given his age, I immediately wondered about his heart, but when I offered my assistance, he said he'd be fine in a minute. I'd heard him arguing with a couple just before I walked by and saw him, so I assumed that he'd gotten a bit upset, and his blood pressure had risen. He wasn't in any immediate danger, so there wasn't much I could do. But I did ask Mindy—Nurse Gunderson—if she'd bring him some water, which she did. He was one of the men who was killed, wasn't he?"

"Possibly," Ethan said. "It does sound like Albion Corley. He was a very striking man."

"Noble," Amerind said thoughtfully. "That's what

came to mind. And he had a beautiful speaking voice, deep, rich, very clear."

"Like a professor," Charlie murmured.

"Yes, exactly."

"Do you have any idea who he was arguing with? He'd had an argument with someone earlier when the performance was being set up," Ethan said. "You said you overheard him arguing with a couple. Could the man have been the same one he'd argued with on deck?"

"It definitely wasn't the same man he'd argued with earlier. I wasn't out on the deck at the time, but we all heard about it. No, it wasn't the same man he'd argued with before the reenactment."

"How can you be so sure when you didn't witness either argument?" Ethan asked.

"Because I was on deck for the reenactment, and when it ended the other man had to leave right away. People were talking about the argument, and someone pointed him out. Later I saw him saying goodbye to people. You can ask Jonathan Moreau and Captain Banks, because he talked to both of them before he left. Our entertainment director, Ricky Simpson, said the guy had put off some kind of business to be there for the event and had to leave right away to take care of it. So it couldn't have been him. He was gone."

"But the other reenactors were still around, right?" Ethan asked.

"Yes. Most of them, anyway. I can't swear they all hung around."

"If I showed you pictures of them, do you think you could tell us who stuck around?"

Amerind sighed. "I could try. A lot of them had beards and mustaches I don't think belonged to them. Naturally, that is. Beards may be in these days, but not with the sideburns a lot of them had. One of the women was still here, too."

"Pretty, blonde, petite?" Charlie asked.

"Yes! She played a nurse."

"Jennie McPherson," Charlie said. She knew, of course, that Jennie had been involved in the reenactment.

"I don't know her name," Amerind said. "But if you have pictures, I'm happy to look at them and try to identify those who were still aboard, if you think it would help."

"Thank you. I'll drop by the infirmary with the pictures later," Ethan said.

"Just let us know when you'll be in," Thor added politely.

"I'm in any time someone needs me. I have a small cabin behind the infirmary. There's a red bell, so if one of the nurses isn't on duty, just ring it. As it happens, I should be in now. We're out on the water. Anyone prone to seasickness will be turning green soon. They call her the Mighty Mississippi for a reason. And this old girl can rock and roll quite a bit. Excuse me, gentlemen. Ladies."

With a broad smile, he left them.

"So Corley argued with someone else," Thor said thoughtfully, looking at Ethan.

"A man, so it can't have been Jennie. But she could've been somewhere nearby. I mean, we've heard about a couple. Jennie's the makeup artist on our film," Charlie explained quickly to Thor. "Not that she could kill anyone anyway. She's as tiny as a flea."

"It does seem unlikely that she shoved a bayonet into anyone," Ethan admitted.

"And it wasn't my father," Charlie said, looking him straight in the eye. "Dr. Amerind knows my father, so he would have recognized his voice."

Charlie was right, though; knowing Jonathan, Ethan had never suspected him, even when circumstantial evidence had pointed in his direction.

Even so, Ethan didn't think Charlie was going to be happy anyway once they finally discovered the truth.

They had grown up in a small world, and he was very afraid that someone in that small world would prove to be their killer.

The *Journey* was beautiful. There was something truly magical about taking a riverboat up the Mississippi, Charlie thought. The coastline filled with views of bayou country, sweeping landscapes, homes large and small, high bluffs and low shores, was stunning. The tremendous power of the river made itself felt beneath them and seemed to hum in time to the *Journey*'s engines.

The main dining room didn't open until eleven, for lunch, and then it closed at three before opening again at five for dinner. Breakfast was available in-room or could be enjoyed on the Sun Deck.

At four thirty the Southern Belles were in the dining room, getting ready for the diners who'd chosen the early seating.

They had enough material to cover seven nights with

very little repetition, since they would be playing to the same diners every night, though when they were in port many of the passengers would choose to dine on shore. By land it was just a little over two hundred miles from New Orleans to Vicksburg, the farthest point in their journey, so they spent a fair amount of time in each port. But the Eagle View was open every night, since some passengers preferred to dine aboard ship, so there was entertainment every night, too.

The first sitting brought in most of the older diners and families, which included children of varying ages. Jonathan had alerted them to the age range before they started and supplied them with a number of Civil War–era toys, such as cup-and-ball games—getting the damned ball in the cup was a lot harder than it looked, Charlie had discovered—metal "detangle" puzzles, cloth dolls, tin soldiers and more. As Jonathan helped them prepare, Charlie found her heart swelling with love for her father.

"I'll be here," he promised them. "Shout if you need help. But you won't."

They opened with one of their medleys—the only songs they would repeat to open their show each night. After three songs, Charlie spoke, explaining the importance of the Mississippi River during the war. "Counting everything from major battles to skirmishes to small confrontations, there were nearly ten thousand engagements during the four years of the war. The loss of life on the battlefield was only a part of the tragedy our greatest internal conflict created. There was pain on the home front, as well," Charlie said, introducing their next song. "Sometimes brother was forced to fight against

brother when they chose to enlist on different sides."
While most of their songs were from the period, one had
been written by Irving Gordon in the twentieth century.
"Two Brothers," often known as "One Wore Blue and
One Wore Gray," was heartbreakingly beautiful and
often thought to have been taken from an old folk song.

They took a break and invited the children up to play,
then sang some more. They were thrilled to see how
well their act was received. Charlie was particularly
happy to see her father nodding his approval.

Charlie was enjoying herself. She had missed this
kind of creative expression, just three friends making
music together and sharing it with an appreciative audience.

Things began to change as the second seating drew
to a close.

As the diners were enjoying their dessert and Charlie
was singing a sad ballad, "Home Sweet Home," a song be-
loved by soldiers both North and South, she realized that
reality was being overwritten right in front of her eyes.

It wasn't that their living passengers disappeared, but
rather that a gentle gray mist settled over the room and
filled it with the sick and the injured from the long distant war.

Charlie saw the man she was certain had been a doctor sitting in the front, tears streaming down his cheeks.
Her throat tightened, and she nearly missed a note. There
was an aura of sadness mingled with hope in the room
that was almost palpable.

The song ended. She was rewarded with thunderous
applause. The mist lifted, and she was just a woman on

a dais in the twenty-first century, surrounded by her friends.

Alexi and Clara came forward, and the three of them linked hands and bowed. The diners began to flood out. It was late. The next day they would be at Oak Alley, and many were eager to see the famed plantation and spend the day roaming the beautiful estate.

"My God," Clara breathed, and Charlie turned to look at her. She'd known that Alexi saw things, but she hadn't realized Clara could, too. Then she remembered that Clara had recently been through a brush with death. Perhaps that had brought about the change? There was more that connected them than they had wanted to admit until they were left in a position where they had no choice.

"You saw them, too?" Charlie asked.

Both women nodded, but neither spoke. Jonathan was hurrying toward them, a huge smile on his face. "You were amazing!" he congratulated them.

Charlie hugged her father, then saw Ethan was nearby, as well. Earlier only Thor had been watching over them. She'd known that Ethan and Jude had been working the ship, striking up conversations with anyone who might know something that could help them.

But now Ethan was here. And she loved the way he was looking at her, with so much pride.

He nodded respectfully to her father as he walked up to her, pausing to hug Clara and Alexi first. To her surprise, her father suddenly said, "Man, sorry I've been a jerk. Ethan, go kiss her. It's hard for a man to let his little girl go, but…she's grown up, and I need to accept that."

"Despite my bad taste in men?" Charlie said, grinning at her dad.

He shrugged. "You could do worse, I'm sure." He grinned back at her.

Ethan stepped forward. She slid into his arms, and when he kissed her, for a moment she wasn't aware of anything around them. She couldn't mourn the time that had passed with them apart, because now they were together, and this was real. She didn't give a damn who knew or who saw it. She grinned and rose up on her toes to kiss him again.

She wanted a lot more.

"All right, all right, that's enough," her father said.

Laughing, and a little breathless, she stepped back. Ethan was grinning, as well. Charlie assumed he was happy that Jonathan seemed to have accepted him at last. She certainly was.

"We need to get out of here so the staff can get everything set up for tomorrow," Alexi said.

"I would love to buy all of you a drink on the Sun Deck," Jonathan said. "Coffee, tea or the nightcap of your choice."

"Dad, I thought they didn't bill you here?" Charlie said.

"So I'm cheap. I'd still enjoy spending some time with the bunch of you. I'd like to hear more about your investigation," he said, "and see if I can help in any way."

"Not a bad idea to hang out for a little while," Thor said, slipping an arm around Clara's shoulders. "Together," he added.

"Let's go," Jude said.

As they left, Ethan slipped his arm around Charlie's waist and whispered softly, "You're shockingly sexy in period attire."

"Despite the Victorians' repressive attitudes toward sex, they still found a way to dress to entice," she said, then laughed. "Good thing we have our supply of colorful condoms, though. I don't mind the dress or even the corset, but I draw the line at Civil War condoms. A sheep's bladder is not my idea of birth control. I certainly wouldn't trust them to protect against STDs, although if they did, I don't suppose people were terribly bright about it, seeing as syphilis and gonorrhea were running rampant in both armies."

"I had no idea you were so knowledgeable about the sexier side of history," Ethan said, pulling her closer.

"I learned a lot making that commercial. STDs are still ruining lives."

She wasn't whispering, and Clara turned around and joined their conversation. "I know. Young people need to watch out."

"Young people?" Ethan said. "I read about a retiree community that's had the largest concentration of STDs in the DC area for years."

"I guess we never lose the need for love—or sex."

Jude joined in then. "I suggest you don't share that tidbit with the family dinner crowd."

"Probably not a good idea," Ethan agreed. "Now let's go have that drink."

Ethan and his fellow agents appeared to be having a

good time, Charlie thought. They were enjoying their time aboard the *Journey*.

But at the same time, they clearly lived and breathed their work. There were eighty-plus crew aboard, and she knew they would find a way to meet them all this week, and find out anything they'd seen or heard.

Charlie paused just as they reached the door and turned to look back at the room. At first all she saw were crew members clearing tables and others following in their wake to reset them for the morning. Then the clatter of plates faded away, and she saw the room as she had seen it before, cloaked in gray mist.

Men, the wounded and the sick, lay on their pallets on the floor. She saw makeshift operating tables scattered with bloody surgeons' tools. And then she spotted the doctor just as he turned to look at her again.

He offered her a sad smile and saluted. She smiled in return.

She knew she would see him again and hoped they would learn more from the dead than they had learned so far from the living.

12

It was, Ethan thought, quite an incredible thing—cruising the Mississippi on the *Journey*.

He knew the places they visited so well, from New Orleans to Vicksburg. He'd grown up in St. Francisville, and from there he'd come to know Baton Rouge, Natchez and Vicksburg. Then he'd gone to college in New Orleans and fallen in love with the flavor of the city.

This was all familiar territory, but he'd never seen it from the water before—and certainly not while sleeping beside Charlie every night.

It would be far too easy to forget that they were trying to catch a killer.

He glanced at the bedside table. His Glock, loaded, was still within easy reach. The door, he knew, was bolted. His fellow agents were asleep just down the hallway.

Even so, he couldn't let himself become too comfortable.

They weren't expecting trouble on the *Journey*, of course, but he knew bad things could happen anywhere, as Jude and Thor had learned firsthand all too recently, facing deranged serial killers. That was all part of the job, of course, but the Celtic American connection had him on edge. Those killers had been sociopaths or possibly psychopaths—he left all that for the psychiatrists—though, and he didn't think they were dealing with that kind of crazy now. His gut told him that Albion Corley and Farrell Hickory had been killed out of necessity—necessity as the killer saw it, anyway—and then Selma Rodriguez had been killed for pretty much the same reason: because of something she knew.

But what the hell was that something?

He didn't believe the killer had gone after the two men out of some twistedly violent objection to a mixed marriage. The world had come a long way, but racists did still exist, and plenty of them were violent. He just didn't feel that that explanation fit. If nothing else, how would it have led to a reason to kill Selma?

No, the motive for the original killings lay elsewhere, and she had known something about it—or the killer believed she did.

As he lay there thinking, Charlie edged against him. He felt the warmth of her body, the sleekness of her bare skin. He winced slightly and swallowed; just her movement aroused him.

It was still early.

He slid his fingers provocatively down the length of her spine to the curve of her buttocks. She moved closer and nestled against him, and then he felt her fingers trail down his chest and below, and he knew that she was awake, too.

They made love. It was a hell of a good way for a man

to start the morning—especially since he was on the ship, because most of the time he'd be working.

The killer remained at large. But he had come to believe that Charlie—and Confederate Captain Anson McKee—was right. The key to solving this case was here on the *Journey.*

They lay curled together after their lovemaking, but finally Ethan admitted to himself that he needed to get started on the day. The ship was large, and there were still a lot of staff to talk to, plus they needed to research whether any of the current passengers had also been aboard for the special reenactment. They planned to split up today. He and Charlie would attend Jonathan's first lecture of the day, then stay aboard, along with Jude; Thor would follow Jonathan to Oak Alley. Alexi and Clara would stay aboard, as well, to prepare for tonight's shows, but they would be available if he needed to call on them for help with anything.

"Do you know what's strange?" Charlie murmured against his chest.

"Frankly, there's a lot in this world that's strange."

She laughed softly at that. "No, I mean with what we know. A man and a woman arguing with Albion. I think we need to know more about that. Maybe it doesn't have anything to do with the murders, but I still think there's a connection to the *Journey,* and maybe to the Masons, too. We keep getting led in all kinds of directions, but we still don't know what anything means."

"To be honest, your father could have given us a bit more direction earlier."

She rose on an elbow and shook her head vehemently.

"My father kept quiet out of respect for a confidence of a personal nature, and he didn't want to point the investigation in the wrong direction. He didn't 'lie' for any reason other than to protect his friends and Shelley Corley."

"I agree," Ethan said. "But it was still important that he tell us everything. Most murders have a clear motive. Love, hate, greed. I don't think this is a case of love, and hatred doesn't really fit, either, given what we know of the two men who I believe were the only intended victims. That makes greed seem likely. But greed over what? To answer that, we need to talk to Shelley Corley. I'm hoping we find out more from her."

"When will that be?"

"Later today. Jackson located her in Baton Rouge and put a call through to her. I was going to have Jude or Thor go and speak with her, but she said she'd drive down. Once she arrives, I'll go ashore to meet with her as soon as I know Thor or Jude is here to…"

"To watch over the Southern Belles?"

"I'm sorry, but I think it's important."

"I have no argument with that!" Charlie assured him. "I'm rather fond of living." She smiled. "More so now than ever," she added softly, then kissed him.

He groaned and jumped out of bed. "Shower. Cold," he said huskily.

"At the time that Oak Alley was built, the sugar industry was booming. All along the Mississippi River, plantations were being carved out along the shore. Some of these were relatively small, and many have been lost to the ravages of time. Oak Alley was left to the Oak Alley Foundation by Mrs. Josephine Stewart, who bought the place with her husband, Andrew, in 1925. They were among the first people to realize the importance of the past, to restore such a historic home, and to preserve her for generations to come. She is a living, breathing piece of the past. Today she hosts weddings, photo shoots, even concerts. She is as much a part of today as she is a memory of days long gone. When you're not cruising aboard the *Journey*, you can rent a cottage and stay on the property." Jonathan smiled. "Since this is our first full day out of New Orleans, I'm going to try to give you a picture of what the area was like from the end of the 1850s through the tragedy of the Civil War, at the end of which we became—though not without difficulties—what we are today, one country, united and proud."

"The South shall rise again!" a teenager shouted.

"Son, whatever you may think, today's South is united with the whole of our great country in a battle against terrorism—domestic and foreign—no matter how crazy some of our politicians seem to be."

His remark brought laughter from the crowd.

"Trust me," Jonathan continued. "I'm from this great state of Louisiana, and I love her with all my heart, but here's what's important—the political situation at the beginning of the Civil War. So thank you, because you've led me right to the topic I have planned for this lecture, before we head out on today's 'journey' of discovery to Oak Alley."

Hovering in the background, Charlie smiled. Damn, her father was good. He could turn any heckler around.

"To understand that time, the men leading our states and our country, to understand why the South seceded and why so many men fought and died, we have to go back not only over a hundred and fifty years to the start of the Civil War but to 1776 and the birth of this country. Thomas Jefferson, in writing the Declaration of Independence, though a slave owner himself, wanted to see slavery abolished and wanted those words in his document. But he was also desperately trying to make thirteen separate colonies—thirteen separate entities—agree on one document. The country was designed to be a *loose* union of states. A man's loyalty was to his state before it was to the union.

"So to understand, you have to put yourself in the frame of mind that existed as 1861 rolled around. As I said, a man's loyalty was to his state, but what many people don't know is that not every Southerner was pro-slavery. In fact, one of the greatest generals our country ever produced, Robert E. Lee, was very vocally against secession. The man who would become the first and only president of the Confederate States of America, Jefferson Davis, served as Secretary of War for Franklin Pierce and gave speeches against secession in both the North and in the South."

"I heard that many of the most powerful politicians and generals of the day were best friends, that they'd served together in the White House and fought side by side in the Mexican-American War," a man offered.

"Very true. Many of them had gone to West Point together. I think one of the most heartbreaking details of the war has to be Robert E. Lee's decision to say no when he was asked by Lincoln to lead the Northern armies. Had he accepted that assignment, the war might have been much shorter, though we'll never know for sure, of course. But Lee was a passionate Virginian, Davis a passionate Mississippian, and in keeping with the mind-set of their day, they cast their lot with their states. Once you understand this, you can see why so many of the men fighting on opposite sides were good friends.

"In some cases even family members fought against each other, if some lived in one state and some in another. Mary Todd Lincoln's people were from Kentucky, a border state, so not only did she live with the heartache of being on the opposite side from much of her family, but she had gossips and journalists accusing her of being a traitor.

"And, yes, slavery and its importance to the Southern economy was key among the rights the South was defending. But let's move on to Louisiana and *The Day the War Stopped*, the day when the *Journey* was handed over to the Union, along with the ill and injured Union men who were aboard her. Around 620,000 men died in the Civil War, but, it should be noted, two-thirds of them were lost to disease rather than directly in battle."

"Was this where they gave the ship over to the Union?" someone asked.

"No, the ship was farther north that day. From the beginning of the war, commanders on both sides knew that controlling the Mississippi was paramount to winning the war. But all along, the fight really was for control of the river, not to decimate the area, and it's to that strategy that we owe the fact that Oak Alley still stands, that and the later efforts of the Stewart family, who, as I said, were among the first to see the value in restoring our historic homes and plantations."

"How old is it?" someone asked.

"Oak Alley was completed around 1839," Jonathan said. "The property was originally called Bon Sejour and was purchased by Valcour Aime in 1830. Aime was known as the Sugar King, and he was immensely wealthy. In 1836 he traded the property to his brother-in-law Jacques Roman and the house was soon begun—built entirely by slave labor. The house was not damaged during the fighting, but the economy plummeted after the war, Jacques died, his widow spent heavily, and the family lost the property in 1866. It was auctioned off, but the new owners failed to keep it up, and the property fell into disrepair until it was purchased by the Stewarts."

Charlie watched her father and thought that he was a better showman than she might ever be herself, despite her years of drama school. It wasn't the words he spoke; it was all in the rise and fall of his voice, and the quick way he responded to questions or turned a heckler around.

"At Oak Alley you'll learn not only how both the rich and their slaves lived during the great sugar years, but all the details of the running of the house and plantation. So now, if you're ready, the buses are waiting to take us to the plantation. I'll be talking to you again once we arrive, and I'll be available throughout the day for any questions. If I can't answer them, we'll find someone who can. And since you'll need to eat lunch while we're there, I should mention that the restaurant serves the best shrimp po'boy I've ever had."

A kid in front started waving his hand and asked, "Aren't we just learning what bad people did?"

"What we're learning is history, and history is created of both good and bad deeds carried out by people who are mostly a mix of good and bad themselves. As a philosopher named George Santayana once said, 'Those who cannot remember the past are condemned to repeat it.' History happened. We can't change it, only learn from it. And they weren't necessarily bad people, they came from a different time. Hopefully, every year that we live, we all learn to become better people ourselves."

Charlie smiled at her father as he looked up suddenly and saw her. He smiled back, then nodded at Ethan, who was standing right behind her.

She lowered her head. She wasn't sure her father actually liked Ethan any better. He was just glad Ethan had law-enforcement training, carried a gun and was there to protect her.

As her father turned to lead the guests off the boat, she saw Thor join him. Apparently Jude would be staying behind and would take over guard duties when Ethan went ashore later.

As she and Ethan left the room, Alexi joined them. "Wanna run through tonight's set and then head up on deck for a leisurely lunch?" she asked. "Maybe Ricky can join us."

Clara and Jude met them as they headed to the Main Deck and the Eagle View dining room, where Alexi promptly went behind the piano and pulled out their set lists, while the two men walked over to the side of the room and started talking.

Charlie gave her attention to Alexi, but as she listened, she couldn't help looking expectantly around the dining room. But there was nothing to be seen, just empty tables waiting to be filled.

By the living.

"It's odd," Alexi said, looking at her.

"What's odd?"

Alexi leaned toward her and Clara, though the only other two people in the room were Ethan and Jude, who were still deep in private conversation.

Still, Charlie knew, the walls might have ears. "What's odd?" she repeated.

"This room," Alexi said softly. "According to the experts in these things, there are two kinds of hauntings. There are residual hauntings, where, say, soldiers fight the same battle over and over again. And then there are active hauntings, like the ones we've all had opportunity to experience. This room seems as if it's the site of a residual haunting. The men here…lying sick and injured as they did all those years ago, when more than half of them eventually died. But there's that one man who looks like a doctor. He keeps looking at you, Charlie."

"I know," Charlie said.

"I think he wants to talk to you, but it seems like he's afraid, maybe because you're always surrounded by other people."

"I'm not sure why a ghost would be afraid," Clara put in.

"We need to find a way for him to talk to you," Alexi said.

"I agree," Clara said. "But we can't leave you alone."

"Maybe if you're around but not too near..." Charlie murmured.

"We'll work on it," Alexi said. "Okay, first up...begin with the medley." She kept talking, riffling through her sheet music.

Charlie looked around the room again, hoping to see the doctor materialize.

Talk to me, please, talk to me, she thought.

But the room remained empty, so she returned her attention to their practice for the evening's performance.

She thought how lucky she was to have such good friends. They'd both been through hell very recently—and on cruise ships, no less.

But they were here now, for her.

She turned around and saw that Ethan and Jude had settled at a table.

Even Ethan was back.

For her.

And then, as she watched, the ghostly doctor materialized right behind Ethan. Once again, he caught her eyes.

Then he raised a hand in a solemn salute.

When it came time to head upstairs for lunch, Ethan brought the files containing photos, including some of Chance Morgan's, of people who had been aboard the *Journey* before Corley and Hickory had been murdered.

He left Jude to watch over the Southern Belles and

enjoy lunch, and he headed straight to the infirmary. He hadn't seen Dr. Amerind flirting with passengers at the Sun Deck buffet, so he had to assume the doctor was in his quarters or seeing a patient.

Two attractive young women in nautically themed nurse's uniforms, a blonde named Mindy Gunderson and a brunette named Haley Howell, greeted him as soon as he entered the infirmary.

Haley explained that Dr. Amerind was in with Mrs. Vineland, a frequent passenger. She suffered from motion sickness but cruised aboard the *Journey* time and again anyway. She simply liked the ambience of the riverboat and the various excursions available when they were in port.

Ethan noticed that she had a chart in her hand; she had obviously been about to join Dr. Amerind and Mrs. Vineland.

"I assume you were both here the day of the big reenactment, right?" he asked pleasantly.

"Of course," Mindy said. "We're under contract, so we don't have a choice. At least the reenactment was something a little bit different."

"You don't enjoy the shipboard programming?" he asked.

"There are only so many lectures about history a girl can take," Haley said. "The best is when we're in port in New Orleans."

"We get a week off the ship once a month—fill-in nurses, waiting for full-time jobs with the cruise line, come on. Time for us to have fun," Mindy said, and winked. "I mean," she added solemnly, "we're purer than the driven snow while we're aboard."

"No drinking allowed, and I have no problem with that. We never know when we might be needed," Haley explained.

"Then you'll make good witnesses," Ethan said.

"Witnesses?" Haley gasped. "Does this have something to do with those two reenactors who were murdered? But why? It's not like they were killed here on the ship."

"No, they weren't," Ethan agreed. "But we're trying to piece together everything that was going on in their lives before they were killed, in case there's a clue in there somewhere."

"But you can't blame the *Journey* for what happened!" Haley said, clearly upset.

"No one blames the ship. We're just trying to find any hint that could lead us to their killer," Ethan said. "Dr. Amerind told me two people were arguing with Albion Corley up on deck. A man and a woman. I have pictures. Would you mind taking a minute so I can show them to you? I'm trying to figure out who might have been arguing with Mr. Corley."

"No prob," Haley said, and then flushed. "Oh, if you don't mind a slight delay. One of us is supposed to be in with the doctor when he has a patient, so he's waiting for me."

"I'm happy to hang out till you're free," Ethan told her.

"I can help you right now," Mindy said, and smiled at him. "You're really a Fed? That's a big deal, huh?"

"Not so much," he told her, and laid the pictures out

on the check-in counter, first shots of Albion Corley
and Farrell Hickory.

"Those are the dead men, right?" Mindy said, looking up at him.

He nodded. "I have pictures of some of the other
people who were there. Can you tell me if you remember any of them, especially if you saw them with Professor Corley when he was here on the deck after the
program?"

"I can try. We were half watching, half working and,
honestly, kind of bored," she said, wincing apologeti-
cally.

"That's all right. I appreciate anything you can tell
me."

He laid out more pictures, these of Brad and Mike
Thornton, George Gonzales, Barry Seymour, Luke Mayfield, Jennie McPherson, Jimmy Smith and Grant Ferguson.

She looked up at him, pleased with herself. "I saw
them all!" she said.

"After the reenactment was over?"

"Not these two—" She pointed to the Thornton brothers. "But this chick," she said, pausing to point to Jennie. "I had a long talk with her after. She was playing
a nurse. She was really nice and even did my makeup
before we left port."

"She's a makeup artist," Ethan said. "And the others?"

"Those men, yes." She pointed at the pictures of
George, Barry, Luke, Jimmy and Grant. She zeroed in
on Grant. "Very distinguished, said he's an accountant,
but I've seen him in some commercials. I didn't see him

talking to Mr. Corley, though. He was talking to a passenger, and he looked pretty tense and kind of annoyed. And this guy... He was cute." She pointed to Jimmy's picture. "He knocked into me on his way to do something, and when he apologized, for a minute I thought he was going to ask for my number. He didn't, though. He just looked at me kind of funny. I'm sorry he didn't ask. He really was cute." She looked more closely at the pictures of George, Barry and Luke. "I don't remember much about them, but these guys hung around for a while before we sailed, too. These two," she said, indicating Barry and Luke, "were talking to each other. One wanted to hang around, and the other wanted to get going. I forget which was which, though. And this guy..." she said, indicating George. "He just looked hungry. The reenactors were welcome to eat at the buffet, so that's probably what he did."

An older woman whose skin appeared to be a pale shade of green came out to the small triage area and smiled at them. "I feel much better already!" she said to Mindy, then turned to Ethan. "I'm sorry—did I keep you waiting? You certainly look healthy to me."

"You didn't keep me waiting at all, Mrs. Vineland," Ethan said.

"Hmmph," she murmured, glancing back at Dr. Amerind. "How does he know my name?"

"I'm Ethan Delaney, Mrs. Vineland," Ethan said.

"He's with the FBI," Haley added.

"That explains it. Big Brother is watching. No wonder you knew my name."

"Mrs. Vineland, trust me, Big Brother is too busy

elsewhere to tell me your name," Ethan said, smiling
at her. "I know your name because someone mentioned
that Dr. Amerind was in with you."

"Oh. Well, this is small and intimate, as cruising goes.
We're very friendly on the *Journey*," she said, as if she
had joined the ranks of the employees. "You may call
me Mildred. And I'll call you Ethan. No Agent Delaney for me."

"That will be fine, Mrs. Vineland," he said.

"Mildred."

"Sorry, I grew up around here and had it drummed
into me not to be too familiar with women I didn't know
well. I'll do my best to remember to call you Mildred."

She smiled, satisfied. "Lovely. I'm off to get some
toast. I'm actually quite hungry now."

"Stay topside to eat. That will help," Dr. Amerind
told her.

"Whatever you say, Gerard," Mildred said, and waved.
"Pleased to meet you, Ethan."

"You, too—Mildred."

Once she was gone, the doctor turned to Ethan. "You
brought your pictures?"

"Yes, and Mindy has already been very helpful. I'm
just wondering if you saw any of these people around
once the reenactment was over."

Gerard Amerind stared carefully at the pictures, with
Haley looking over his shoulder. "I remember this woman.
She played a nurse."

"Jennie McPherson," Ethan said.

"She's tiny, but she has a temper. Now that I think
about it, I'm pretty sure she was the one arguing with

Mr. Corley on deck. I didn't see her, of course, but it's the voice. I can't be a hundred percent sure, but I think it was her." He pulled the pictures of Brad and Mike. "I saw them leave, but the others, they all hung around. There was some talk about a movie they were all making."

"Yes, they're filming up in St. Francisville," Ethan said.

"I'd talk to that little blonde if I were you," Dr. Amerind said. "She was definitely upset about something. Very pretty, but also very upset."

"Want to come ashore for a brief excursion?" Ethan asked.

Charlie was perched on the bed in her small cabin, going through DC-area housing brochures with Alexi and Clara. Alexi and Jude were set. Jude had snagged a great rent-to-own property near the Krewe offices in Northern Virginia. Clara and Thor were in a short-term rental but looking for something more permanent. Clara had told Charlie it was actually a difficult search because everyone kept trying to make it so easy. "There are about thirty-five agents working out of the office now—not to mention the tech department!—and they're all giving Thor leads, which makes for dozens of places for us to look at. Thing is, we have to have space and I'd like a yard—we have a husky."

Charlie had just laughed at that. Of course, they had a husky. Thor was from Alaska.

Then Ethan had knocked and identified himself, and they'd opened the door. Charlie felt as if they were being a bit overcautious, but plenty of people were killed in broad daylight, so there was no point taking chances.

Charlie was curious as to where he wanted to take her. They were docked at Oak Alley, which she'd seen plenty of times before, but the truth was that she would be happy to go anywhere with him, so she said, "Sure."

"We'll be back in an hour or so—plenty of time for you to set up for tonight's show," Ethan said, adding quietly, "We're going to see Shelley Corley."

"Poor woman," Alexi said. "First, she lost a cousin, and then she lost her fiancé."

Ethan nodded. "We'll be as sensitive as possible, but the truth is, when you've lost someone you love, you do want justice for them."

"I worry about myself. I think I might flat-out want vengeance," Alexi said. "Not nice, not right, but…true."

After a quick promise to see them in plenty of time to get set up to greet the early dinner seating, Charlie joined Ethan, and they left the ship. On shore, she saw a woman standing beside a Chevy sedan. Ethan must have told her whom to look for, because she waved as soon as she saw them.

Shelley Corley was about fifty and was also one of the most attractive women Charlie had ever seen. Her skin was a beautiful café au lait color, her hair was dark, and her eyes were a true amber. She was dressed in a pale blue business suit and a large sun hat in a matching shade. Her features were strong and arresting, and though she smiled as she greeted them and shook hands, her smile was grim.

"When Special Agent Crow spoke with me this morning…well, I realized immediately I needed to speak with you. I want to help in any way possible. There's a small place down the road where we can talk, past Oak Alley and just on the other side of Laura Plantation."

"I think I know the place you're talking about," Ethan said. "Thank you for picking us up."

Shelley nodded and got into her car. Charlie immediately took the backseat, allowing Ethan the front.

As they drove, they discussed the *Journey*, the historic plantations they would be passing, even the weather. Once they were seated inside the small mom-and-pop coffee shop that was their destination, Shelley quickly went into high gear.

"When Albion was found murdered, I thought my heart broke in two," she said. "Then, when Farrell was killed…well, I felt like whatever was left of my heart had been shattered completely. I don't say that for pity, because I'm strong, and I'm going to be fine. Albion had never married, and he had no children of his own, but I'm a widow—I went back to my maiden name—and I have two daughters. They both live in California now, but they came home quickly to be with me. And I have cousins and nephews and nieces, friends. I'm surrounded by those who love me. I don't need anyone's pity."

"I would never offer pity, but you do have my deepest sympathy," Ethan said. "I have to ask, though… Did anyone else know about you and Farrell?"

"Well," Shelley said, looking toward Charlie, "your father knew, of course." She turned back to Ethan. "But otherwise, no. I hadn't even told my daughters. When n was killed, I had to wonder if it was a hate crime.

But when Farrell was killed, too, I didn't see how it could be. No, what I believe is that they somehow crossed someone." She turned to Charlie again, and reached for her hand. "You found Farrell," she said softly.

"Yes," Charlie said.

"Thank you. Otherwise he might have lain there for a very long time."

"I'm just hoping that finding him sooner was also better, that it will make it easier to catch the killer," Charlie said.

Shelley nodded. "I just know whoever did it, he didn't do it because of Farrell and me. And I can't believe one of our friends would have had anything against Farrell or Albion. Our friends are professors, musicians, actors and painters, all professions that tend to skew very liberal." She paused for a moment. "You have to understand, they were both good men. I can't think of anything they were involved in that would have upset anybody, especially not upsetting them enough to commit murder." She sighed. "I honestly have no clue why they were targeted, but I brought you a list of the causes they were involved with—names and addresses and everything."

"This is going to be very helpful, Ms. Corley. I can't thank you enough," Ethan told her.

She smiled. "You're welcome. I didn't know what else to do. I called the police and asked about Albion's body, because I need to plan his funeral. They're not releasing him yet, though. Or Farrell. With Farrell... Well, I'll be attending that funeral, naturally. But his son will be planning it, and his body won't be released to me."

"I'm so sorry," Charlie murmured.

"As I said, I'm fine. I have a great support system. But thank you. Just find out who killed them. And don't worry, I'm not going to go to the police. If I did, they'd just start questioning my family. Or Farrell's son. And if there's one thing I'm certain of, it's that no one in our families did this."

Shelley's certainty reminded Charlie of her own certainty of her father's innocence.

Suddenly Shelley turned to her. "I know it must be difficult to talk about, so I apologize for asking, but how did you find Farrell, Ms. Moreau?"

Charlie was taken by surprise. "I— We had been filming in the area. I was looking for missing props."

Shelley studied her, as if trying to decide whether to believe her explanation or not. Finally she smiled. "You're a lovely young woman, and I'm so sorry for what you've been through here. And your father's a fine man. I never knew him well, but I know my cousin and Farrell thought very highly of him."

"Thank you," Charlie said, and smiled herself. "I rather like him myself."

"Albion said your mom has been gone a while."

"Yes."

"But her family, so they say, had a...feel for the dead."

Charlie looked at Ethan. He shrugged to let her know she didn't have to answer. But before she had a chance to even think of how to answer, Shelley spoke again.

"Has either of them, Farrell or Albion, spoken to you? Come to you in, say, a dream?"

"I'm so sorry, no," Charlie said, and glanced at Ethan again.

"If they do," Shelley whispered, "will you listen?"

"Of course," Charlie promised. "Ethan…?"

Shelley turned and looked at Ethan. "So that's how it is. They speak to you, too. I guess what they say is true. Your unit *is* special. The Krewe of Hunters, isn't that what they call you? I googled some of their past cases. I doubted any government agency would go beyond the obvious, but I seem to have been wrong, and that gives me hope you'll find the man who killed Farrell and Albion."

"We're committed to that," Ethan assured her.

"Yes, we are," Charlie said.

Shelley patted her hand, as if satisfied, then looked at Ethan. "I hope you'll talk to the charities on that list I gave you. There's a no-kill animal shelter. One that focuses on historic preservation and another that's trying to regulate the number of oil rigs in the Gulf, even one dedicated to saving a single historic church in Baton Rouge. I hope you meant it when you said the list will help you."

"It will, Ms. Corley," Ethan told her. "You can count on it."

"Please, call me anytime you need me," she said, producing cards and handing one to each of them. "I teach piano and voice, so you shouldn't have any trouble reaching me." She studied Charlie again. "If one of them is still here in spirit form, Ms. Moreau, he'll find you. If you let him."

Charlie nodded. "I hope so, Ms. Corley."

She wasn't just saying the words, either. She really did hope. She was accustomed to seeing the dead, and both Farrell and Albion had been good men. She hoped they'd both found peace, but if one of them did appear to her, it would only be to help, and that could only be a positive thing.

And yet a strange fear filled her.

She remembered being a small child, holding her father's hand by the church, seeing several men walking around in their uniforms.

Men no one else saw.

Except her father. He had known. Known she was seeing the dead. And he had told her, "Fear the living, Charlie. Because the living are the only ones who can hurt you."

She had understood then, and she still considered those words to live by.

Someone out there had killed three people. And that person was still out there.

She looked at Ethan and caught him studying her.

She tried to smile back at him as they left the little café, his arm lying comfortable across her shoulders.

She couldn't help but wonder if he'd felt the same strange twist of fear.

13

Ethan met with Thor Erikson and Jude McCoy at four thirty, while the Southern Belles went into their preparation mode for the evening. Thor told him he'd enjoyed seeing Oak Alley, along with the trip "next door" to Laura, a Creole plantation, in contrast to an "English" plantation. Jonathan Moreau had left the houses tours to the on-site guides, and Thor had enjoyed listening to them as much as he'd enjoyed listening to Jonathan. He hadn't learned anything useful, but on the plus side, nothing bad had happened to Jonathan.

Ethan was glad that Charlie hadn't realized yet that her father might be in danger; he was glad nothing had happened—and that Thor had enjoyed listening to Jonathan. In turn, Ethan shared the conversation he'd had with Shelley. He'd already emailed them the list she'd given him of the various charitable groups Albion and Farrell had worked with. He'd also sent the list off to Angela at headquarters, so she could use the Bureau's more powerful databases and resources.

For boots on the ground investigation, he'd divided up the list, and they would each take responsibility for

a few. Thor and Ethan were going to check into an organization called Doggone It, which was dedicated to
turning every shelter in the country into a no-kill facility. They happened to have an office in Natchez, so
they could drop in the following day. The two of them
were also going to tackle Sane Energy, an organization
that fought to regulate where and when oil rigs were set
up in the Gulf, and what kind of piping was allowed to
be laid along the riverfront. Their head office was in
Vicksburg, the next stop after Natchez.

Jude would watch over the Southern Belles and see
what he could learn from the crew.

Dinnertime rolled around, and Alexi, Clara and Charlie began their second-night set.

That night, after the opening medley, they began the
unique part of the set list with a little-known ballad, "My
Love in My Arms to Move No More."

Jonathan joined them as the meal was served, and
he watched the women with a look of pride and pleasure on his face.

Charlie told a story that night about two men who
had been friends but had served on opposite sides during the war. The Union soldier had been badly injured
and left for dead on the battlefield. His friend found
him, but rather than let him be taken prisoner, he took
the chance of being shot as a traitor himself and spirited
the wounded man to the home of another old friend, a
Confederate who had already lost his only son in the
war. A physician, he saved the life of the Union soldier
and hid him until the war's end. Charlie ended by tell-

ing the rapt audience where to look to find more information on the men and their lives.

As she finished, she looked over at Jonathan, since storytelling—especially historical storytelling—was his forte. He smiled broadly and nodded his approval, and Charlie smiled back. Ethan could tell how much it mattered to her that she had pleased her father.

Just as the performance was ending, his cell phone vibrated in his pocket. He excused himself and headed out on deck to answer. It was Randy Laurent.

"I'm getting nowhere here," Randy said. "I hope you're having better luck."

"Nothing yet," Ethan told him, which wasn't really a lie, since he didn't have anything solid. He told Randy he was planning to investigate the various groups Corley and Hickory had been involved with. "All quiet there? No other..."

"No other murders?" Randy asked him drily. "No, thank God."

"Keep me posted."

"Will do—and you do the same, please."

"You got it."

They rang off, and Ethan headed back toward the dining room. He arrived just in time for the final song, but as he entered, he felt something shift in the atmosphere.

A smoky mist seemed to sift into the Eagle View dining room.

The living diners were still there, but now they had been joined by the dead. Soldiers in tattered uniforms of blue and gray and butternut, identified by the insignias of the infantry, cavalry, artillery and the navy.

They were heedless then of the living, except for an occasional shiver as a server moved through one of them.

They were staring at the small raised stage, completely focused on Charlie, as she sang another mournful ballad.

He stayed where he was, standing in the doorway. He noticed one man in particular who had hunkered down right in front of Charlie. The ghost wore a shirt with rolled-up sleeves, a vest and an apron—an apron smeared with blood. He was, Ethan thought, a doctor—the doctor who had acknowledged Charlie before, the ghost she'd talked about.

Ethan's heart felt heavy in his chest as he looked out over the room. On the one hand, he was sorry for the burden the men carried. On the other, he was touched to see that none of them seemed to be aware whether they were North or South, that they should be enemies. In this room they were just men, injured, ill, and possibly dying soon, aware only that they'd left families behind, loved ones they might never see again.

Charlie finished the song. Applause erupted. The mist faded away.

And with it went the dead who had filled the room only moments before.

Except for one.

The doctor.

Ethan wished that he could keep the living from moving, from talking. They'd already driven the other ghosts away, and he found himself striding forward, wondering if he couldn't somehow reach the doctor, urge him to stay.

Too late.

The Belles were bowing, and the diners were rising, filing out. He couldn't reach the doctor quickly enough.

But he could see Charlie.

She smiled and waved to the audience, then walked toward the doctor, her hand outstretched.

The doctor, too, reached out, touched her hand.

And then he was gone, and Charlie was reaching out to nothing more than air.

Charlie had to wonder if it was wrong of her to find moments of such deep pleasure and happiness when three people had been murdered, and their killer was still out there somewhere. But she couldn't help herself.

Ethan was back.

And they were together, just as she'd hoped they would be all those years ago.

It was as if a decade had never separated them. Their connection was something deep and rich, something that had played in their minds throughout the years, something stronger than anything they'd actually shared all those years ago.

Of course, theirs had been a strange relationship back then. They had known one another, but they had been three years apart, a vast gulf at the time, because he'd been legal age, a college man, and she had still been in high school, nowhere near her eighteenth birthday. But after the events in the graveyard, there had been hours spent with the police, a lot of time when they'd waited, alone together, to give another statement to yet another officer or the prosecuting attorney. There had been another bond between them, too. They had both seen the ghost of the Confederate cavalry officer; they both saw the dead and sometimes even communicated with them.

There hadn't been anything sexual between them—not that she hadn't tried—and yet it still seemed to her she'd never shared a more intimate relationship with anyone than she'd shared with him that night.

And now...

It was heavenly to lie with him, sleep with him, touch him, tease, laugh. To be naked next to the heat of his body, slip a hand over his flesh and feel him grow instantly aroused as he turned to her. To make love as naturally as if they'd been together forever. There were things he did that shouldn't have been so erotic, so suggestive. The way he kissed and teased her fingertips with his lips and tongue. The way he placed a kiss behind her ear, then trailed more kisses down her nape...

Then there were the other incredible things he did, things that were so extremely intimate she could hardly think of them without feeling herself flush with heat, so far beyond seductive that she could scarcely breathe as he did them....

And there was just lying there beside him, feeling him breathe, hearing the sound of his heartbeat.

But the murders continually hovered over them, and late that night, as they lay together, cooling and sated, he turned to her.

"You're pretty close to Jimmy Smith, huh?" he said.

There was nothing accusing in his question, no jealousy in his tone. Just curiosity.

"I am. He's kind of like the brother I never had."

"Never more than that?" Again, there was no jealousy or accusation in his tone. She had the sense he just felt he needed to know. Ten years had passed. Others had come and gone in their lives. This was almost like a fact-finding mission, but only the future truly mattered.

"No, it was never anything more. We were both only kids, so that drew us together. And he was a member of the Gargoyles, the boys' organization that was like a brother club to that stupid Cherub thing I was going to join years ago, that I was pledging for that night," she told him, turning to look into his eyes. "We went to Tulane together, too. Our last year of school, he was one of five roommates I lived with. We all pooled our resources to rent a big old place in the Garden District." She frowned, suddenly worried about his question. "You don't think that Jimmy Smith could be involved— Wait! You do. You're convinced that the film crew had something to do with the murders."

"I don't particularly suspect Jimmy. But, yes. You know I'm investigating the film crew."

"Shelley thinks it's someone involved with one of the organizations Corley and Hickory were involved with. That's what she seemed to be saying, anyway."

"I know."

"Trust me, Jimmy is innocent. He's a great guy." She hesitated. "He *was* with the group who tied me to the tombstone that night, but he kept trying to talk the others into letting me go. And after everything, after the police, after the trial, after everything that went on, he spent years apologizing to me. He even quit the club he was in—he said they were nothing but a bunch of jerks."

"People grow up. They see how tough life is. They change."

"We all change, and, yes, most of us get tougher. But we don't suddenly become homicidal. Certainly not Jimmy," she said.

He was quiet. She could sense that he wasn't convinced but simply didn't want to argue with her, and that scared her.

Not that she could entirely blame him.

If someone didn't know Jimmy the way she did, he might well look like a viable suspect.

"You don't know Jimmy. He could never murder anyone," she said with complete certainty.

He propped himself up on an elbow and looked at her seriously. "Okay, so it's not your father—we agree on that, although he lied and there are factors that point in his direction, to the point that I'd guess the police probably still consider him a suspect. So…who? For the sake of argument, let's say it *is* someone working on the film." He put up a hand to stop her when she started to protest. "Though I can't be absolutely positive, I tend to put Brad and Mike Thornton in the innocent pool. Certainly neither one of them threw a knife at you, because they were both with me, though, of course, either one of them could have conspired with someone else. We never found the knife, and no prop knives are missing, as far as we know. That would leave Jennie McPherson—"

"Jennie? You can't be serious."

"Unlikely, I agree. Then there are the tech guys—George, Luke, Barry—and then the actors and extras, Harry and Blane, Grant. So you tell me—which one of them do you think might be involved?"

"None of them!" Charlie protested. "It's someone else. It's got to be. You really *do* think it's someone else from the film, don't you? Why? Why are you so sure?"

"No reason—other than proximity and logic," he said in a flat tone. "Charlie, the bayonet that killed the men was most likely the one that disappeared from props. The same is probably true of the knife that was thrown at you," he explained. "We know people from the film were closer to both Corley and Hickory than they wanted to admit. And we know people other than Hickory were in some kind of a confrontation with Albion Corley on the *Journey* before he was killed. And, yes, we know about Shelley now, too, and I'm not forgetting that both men were heavily involved in charities and environmental issues."

"So that could point to someone else," Charlie suggested. "You don't understand what it's like in the movie business. People are focused on their own careers, and that's their only interest."

"Charlie, I don't care what anyone does for a living or even if being an actor becomes not just what someone does but who that someone *is*. There's always another interest out there. And when someone isn't bat-shit crazy—my own term, by the way, nothing official—the motive generally comes down to love, hate or money. Sure, there's spur-of-the-moment murder, carried out in a fit of emotion. But these murders were planned carefully. We have to find out why, and I'm sorry, but what evidence we have so far points to it being someone you know."

She nodded slowly and rose. "Natchez," she said simply. "See what you find out in Natchez." And then she headed into the bathroom to shower and get ready for the day. She felt awkward, as if they'd just had their first argument as a real couple.

He followed her. In a few minutes she felt the argument was over.

Yes, definitely.

They were very good at making up.

Ethan stood on the dock with Thor, listening as Jonathan talked about the excursion he would be leading later that day. There were numerous shore excursions on offer, but he would be taking a group to explore several of the various nearby Civil War sites, as well as the city of Natchez itself.

Once he had finished and the buses were loaded, Ethan and Jude would head into town and the offices of Doggone It.

"Natchez is the county seat of—and only major city in—Adams County, Mississippi," Jonathan said, his deep, rich voice commanding attention without trying. "She sits nice and high on a bluff, as you can see. Natchez is ninety miles south of the Mississippi state capital of Jackson and eighty-five miles north of Baton Rouge. At one time Natchez was both the capital of Mississippi and one of the most important cities in the South. The local planters engineered new breeds of cotton, and at one point she had the highest per capita income of any city in the United States—pre–Civil War, of course. The French established Fort Rosalie in 1716, and the area became known as the Natchez colony, named for the Native American tribe that lived in the area. History is rarely peaceful, however, and many French colonists were slain by the Natchez tribe and vice versa. After the Seven Years War, the French ceded the colony to the British. Meanwhile, other local tribes took in the remnants of the Natchez, though today their descendants have reorganized under the Natchez name. So, French, British—and then Spanish/American. This is because a treaty gave it to America, but the Spanish had helped the Americans, and they had their fingers in the pie, trying to keep control as long as they could. Eventually the Americans gained the upper hand, but today visitors to the city are greeted by a uniquely charming combination of Spanish, French, British and American architecture and culture.

"But I'm skipping ahead. In the nineteenth century Natchez flourished, with her share of great plantations, just as there are throughout the South. But, as I explained yesterday, everyone knew control of the river was crucial once the Civil War began. New Orleans fell in 1862, and Natchez surrendered soon after, thus sparing herself the destruction of war and ensuring the safety of so much of what you'll see today. I've just simplified about three hundred years of history, but I'll go into more depth as the day goes on."

Jonathan looked straight at Ethan as he directed his people to their buses. Ethan met his eyes in return, and

Jonathan nodded, as if to say he felt free to do his job, knowing *they* were on the job, as well.

Thor had called ahead for a rental car, and it was waiting for them as they went ashore. "You drive," he said, tossing Ethan the keys. "I'm from the land of ice and snow. Driving in all this heat might be the death of me."

Ethan grinned as he caught the keys in midair. Thor was not only smart, he was the size of a Norse god. Definitely a good man to have at his back.

They heard their destination before they saw it; Doggone It was located on several acres just beyond the city limits.

The bays, howls, yips and barks of what Ethan estimated to be a couple hundred dogs filled the air as they neared the compound.

"I've got to commend the group's dedication," Thor said. "No animal will be destroyed. It's a hell of a good goal."

They entered a tiled and absolutely spotless reception area and were greeted by a young woman with the words *Kathryn, Doggone It Dog-Loving Volunteer* embroidered on the pocket of her shirt. She ushered them into an office for their scheduled meeting with William C. Hayworth, director of the charity.

Hayworth shook their hands and offered them seats in front of his desk. The man's office was filled with pictures of dogs—all kinds of dogs—posing with the volunteers who had helped them back to health or into forever homes.

"This is a great cause," Thor told Hayworth.

The man beamed. "Thank you. I understand this visit isn't social, that it has something to do with Mr. Hickory and Mr. Corley, so how can I help you? They were wonderful men, a big part of the work we do here. I admit I'm more than a little curious as to why you're enjoying a Mississippi cruise instead of scouring every street in St. Francisville for clues."

"The parish has an excellent detective handling the investigation there," Ethan said. "Detective Randall Laurent. He's following every local lead. But because we suspect that the men were killed because of something to do with the many interests and activities they shared, that means we need to look farther afield than St. Francisville."

"You think their work saving dogs got them killed?" Hayworth asked incredulously.

"Not saving dogs per se, but maybe doing something in the course of that work that upset someone else deeply enough to kill them," Thor said.

Hayworth shook his head. "I knew them both well, and I can't think of any reason why someone would have held their work here against them. They were both comfortable financially but not rich. What made them invaluable to our mission was their energy. Albion Corley encouraged his students to volunteer here, and several have continued their efforts even after graduation. And Hickory…he took in older dogs with not much time left but who needed some love. They both donated money, of course, but it was their encouragement to others to give both money and effort that helped us the most." He sighed. "I just don't see how any of that could have gotten them killed."

"We don't know that it did. We're still investigating

all angles. Mr. Corley and Mr. Hickory were involved in a number of causes," Ethan said. "Still, we have to ask. Did you ever see them argue with anyone around here? Do you have any neighbors who are against you having your facility here? Do you know if the victims ever fought with anyone on behalf of this place?"

Hayworth shook his head, clearly at a loss. "My neighbors are a dairy farm and a fellow who raises goats for cheese. Our dogs have never once gotten out or caused an incident with either one. We're friends. We all belong to the Masonic lodge together."

Ethan glanced at Thor.

"Are you aware if either Corley or Hickory had any difficulties with anyone at the lodge?" Thor asked.

Hayworth looked annoyed at that. "Oh, please! I'm so tired of seeing Masons portrayed as conspiracists and killers in the movies. Neither one was a member of my lodge here." He hesitated, thoughtful. "Come to think of it, I did run into both men recently at one of our 'Walk the dog for the dogs' functions, and they were pretty upset about something that was going on."

"Did you hear the specifics of what they were arguing about?" Thor asked.

Hayworth shook his head. "They weren't arguing, or not with each other, anyway. They said they were going to hold firm, and they'd take it as high in the courts as they could go. But what it was about, I don't know. When I asked, Albion just said they'd be happy to fill me in as soon as it was all settled."

Ethan asked him if he could remember anything else, but he couldn't, so the agents gave him their cards, telling him to call them directly if he should think of anything.

When they were leaving, a slim young woman entered with a huge male husky tugging at the leash while she futilely asked him to heel. She might as well have been asking him to jump over the moon, for all the attention the dog was paying her. He started baying and jumping, nearly taking her down.

"Hey, fella," Thor said, moving forward, grabbing the leash and rescuing the woman. "Sit. *Sit.*"

To Ethan's combined surprise and amusement, the dog immediately obeyed.

"Thank you," the woman said. "He's beautiful, but he's so big. I have to bring him back. I just can't keep him."

Hayworth came hurrying out of his office. He looked distressed. "Oh, no," he murmured.

"I'm sorry, Mr. Hayworth, so sorry. But I just can't keep Loki," she said.

Hayworth looked genuinely distressed. "Of course, I understand. Loki is… I just don't know what we're going to do." He noticed that Ethan and Thor were still there. "This is our third return on Loki. Every time he comes back it gets harder for us to place him."

"Mr. Hayworth, don't worry. If you can hold on to Loki until we've solved this case and I can head back home, I'll take him," Thor said.

Hayworth looked at him with combined surprise and gratitude. "You're not just saying that?"

"I'll be back for him, I promise. I'm from Alaska. Huskies are my breed. In fact, if you'd like, I'll be happy to see him back to his kennel, get to know him a little bit more," Thor said.

"Thank you. You have no idea how much of a relief all this is," Hayworth said, then pointed. "This way."

Thor followed him, leading Loki.

When they returned, Hayworth was talking away about all Loki's wonderful qualities. Thor met Ethan's eyes and nodded toward the door to indicate that they could leave.

"What are you? A dog whisperer?" Ethan asked him once they were out of earshot.

Thor grinned. "My sister and her husband raise huskies. I've always been good with them, and I already have one husky at home, so what's one more?"

"I'm glad. That's a beautiful dog." As they reached the car Ethan turned the conversation back to the case. "Did Hayworth remember anything more that might help us?" he asked.

"I think so," Thor said. "I'm hoping tomorrow will tell us more. There's a lot of oil up my way, so I've seen it before, the constant conflict between energy and the environment. We need energy to live, but we also need to preserve the environment. A lot of people on both sides get heated up about it. But heated up enough to kill? Maybe. A lot depends on money, the way it does for pretty much anything else. So I'm hoping we'll learn more when we get to Vicksburg and talk to the Sane Energy people."

"So how does Hayworth figure into it?"

"While we were walking Loki back, he remembered hearing our vics talking more than once about the environment and the river. He said they knew they had to tackle some pretty difficult people on the issue, and they had to get others—including the courts—involved. Hayworth thinks that's what they were talking about at that dog-walk thing, and that they were planning on meeting someone in particular who might be able to help them."

"Did he say who?"

Thor glanced at him unhappily. "You're not going to like this," he said. "Jonathan Moreau."

Jude McCoy was sitting in the Eagle View dining room and watching the Southern Belles rehearse their performance for that evening. At first Charlie thought he must get bored, viewing them day after day, but then she realized that he was getting paid to watch his girlfriend do what she loved and was probably completely happy with his assignment.

He seemed laid-back, completely relaxed, as he sat there, but when she looked closely, she could see how aware he was of every move they made and every staff member coming and going through the dining room doors.

His watchfulness made her feel safe, and she had to admit, after the incident with the knife, safe was a really good feeling, even though she didn't expect anything to happen aboard ship.

When they finished the rehearsal, they headed to lunch. The day was beautiful and, even better, uneventful. Ethan checked in with Jude at one point to say they were heading back and would be there in plenty of time for the second dinner seating.

After lunch, Jude and Alexi walked Charlie to her

cabin. Jude waited until she was inside, told her to lock the door and reminded her that they were right next door.

Charlie thanked him. She was glad for the escort, but she was also still convinced nothing was going to happen to her while she was aboard the *Journey*.

She'd stepped into the shower when she heard the sound. It was faint, not as if someone was knocking at the bathroom door, but rather as if they were brushing something against it.

She turned off the water and listened. The sound had stopped, but unease was racing through her system.

She clenched her teeth, picturing her cell phone where it lay on the bed. Mental note—she mocked herself— remember to bring cell phone into the bathroom next time.

There was nothing else, no other sound. She waited, listening, for what seemed like forever. Finally, wrapped in a towel, she drew a deep breath, opened the door and stepped into the cabin. There was no one there. She wondered what the hell she had heard—or if she had actually heard anything at all.

Feeling unnerved and extremely vulnerable in her towel, Charlie dressed quickly.

As soon as she had clothes on, she picked up her phone to give Clara a call. Thor was on shore with Ethan, so Clara would be alone, too. Charlie felt a bit silly, but even so, she could ask Clara to open the door and watch the hall so she could run the few feet to her friend's cabin.

But she never dialed, because suddenly she heard the strange brushing sound again, this time against her cabin door. For a few seconds fear, primal and paralyzing, ripped through her.

Pulling herself together, she moved carefully to the door to look out the peephole.

And then she saw him.

He hadn't knocked because he couldn't knock. And he couldn't knock because he was a ghost.

It was the doctor from the dining room.

Charlie was sure she didn't really need to open the door for him, but she opened it anyway. He was from a long-ago era. In his day, a man would never enter a lady's cabin without an invitation. Actually, given that she was there alone, he was probably uncomfortable about entering at all.

And yet...

He'd been around for generations. He must have seen about everything by now.

None of that mattered, of course. What mattered was what he could tell her.

She quickly opened the door. "Come in, please," she said.

He entered, and she swiftly closed and locked the door, then indicated the chair at the dressing table. "Thank you for coming. Please, have a seat."

"Thank you, miss," he said politely.

"I've seen you every night," she told him, taking a seat herself. "I was hoping you would speak with me."

"Yes," he said softly, a slight crackle in his voice.

He was so quiet that she was certain no one else would be able to hear him, even if they were standing outside in the hall with their ear against the door.

"Two men were murdered," she said. "I believe it either had something to do with the recent reenactment here or that the killer was aboard that day and maybe even learned something that made him realize murder was his only option."

"They were good men," the doctor said somberly. "Very good men. I watched the reenactment, and I particularly watched them. I was proud of the job they did. That was an important day but also a hard one." He appeared to wince. "Apologies for not introducing myself sooner. I'm Captain Ellsworth Derue, miss. United States Medical Corps. I was aboard when the Johnny Rebs held the boat. They were decent to me and gave me what they had to treat the men. I was proud of the reenactment because it told the story well, and because all those involved that day were good men, didn't matter what color they wore—or what color they *were*."

Charlie wasn't sure how to reply. "I'm glad," she said softly. "And also so sorry for all those who died in the war and on this ship."

"You have to understand, we all—whichever side we fought on—thought we were patriots."

"I do understand," Charlie said. "My father—"

"Your father is Jonathan Moreau. We've watched him many times, with a great deal of pride," Captain Derue said.

Charlie smiled. "Thank you."

"But I regret to tell you, he is somehow involved in this," Captain Derue said gravely.

Charlie froze. No. She didn't care who tried to tell

her that her father was involved, they were wrong. She knew him. He was not a murderer.

"He didn't kill anyone," she said at last, her voice brittle.

"No, he is no killer. But he was here on the *Journey*, and they were talking about him…the soon-to-be-dead men, Corley and Hickory. They were trying to figure something out. They kept saying, 'Jonathan will know.' They planned to meet with him and ask for his help."

"Do you think he's even aware of what he knows?" Charlie asked. "Of how dangerous it seems to be?"

"That I don't know. But he needs to be careful. Others were nearby when the two men were speaking and might have overheard. Later your father talked with Albion Corley up on the Sun Deck, and not long afterward the small blonde woman showed up and had an argument with Professor Corley. There were others from the reenactment nearby, as well."

"Who? Do you know who?" she asked urgently.

He shook his head. "I know your father because he is always on the ship. I knew Mr. Hickory and Mr. Corley because I was there when they argued, and your father spoke their names when he stepped in. I don't know the names of any of the others. One couple talked about taking care of their children. Does that help you identify them?"

"So they were a couple in real life?" Charlie asked, then winced inwardly at the insensitivity of the term.

He nodded. "She was about five-and-a-half feet and blonde, and her husband was over six feet tall and weighed at least two hundred pounds."

She gasped. He'd just described Nancy and Todd Camp.

Charlie reached out—she still hadn't gotten the hang of *not* doing so—and her hand passed through the tenuous image of his, and yet she was certain that he'd felt the warmth and appreciation in her touch.

"Thank you. I need to talk to my father. If he hasn't realized what he knows, maybe I can help him figure it out."

"Be careful. I fear for him, just as I fear for you."

She smiled. "I'm safe. I have three government agents looking after me—and I think I have you and the others, as well."

He nodded gravely.

"I wish there was a way to thank you," she said.

He smiled. "Sing 'Lorelei,'" he told her. "And that duet mixing 'When Johnny Comes Marching Home' with 'Dixie.' Please. For all the friends I lost, North and South. For those, like me, who died of disease, praying for the war to end."

He stood, ready to leave her.

She stood as well, and said, "Thank you, Captain."

She didn't need to open the door again. He simply dissipated into the air.

Charlie sank down on the bed, suddenly weak. She glanced at her watch, anxious now for the excursion in Natchez to be over and for her father to return to the ship.

She desperately needed to talk to him.

Alone.

14

As they boarded the ship, Ethan called Jude to tell him they were back. Jude assured him that everything was fine. Charlie was in her cabin next door to his, and he'd called to check on her not five minutes ago. He was about to go get her, then walk her, Alexi and Clara to the dining room.

Ethan briefed Jude on what they had learned and told him that he would wait on deck for Jonathan Moreau to return.

He'd been waiting for what felt like hours when the tour buses finally began to pull up by the dock. In a few minutes he saw Jonathan Moreau—followed by a string of what he could only call fans—approach the ship.

Ethan had to give the man credit; he never seemed to notice the admiration in the eyes of his listeners, nor did he pay any extra attention when an attractive woman was especially in awe. His excitement was all for the history he passed on.

As he reached the deck, Jonathan noticed Ethan—and Ethan's expression. He excused himself to the group and approached Ethan.

"What now?" Jonathan asked flatly.

"You tell me. What are you still not telling us?" Ethan said.

"What are you talking about?" Jonathan demanded. "If I knew anything—especially since I know my name keeps coming up in your investigation—wouldn't I tell you? Good people have been killed. If I could help in any way, don't you think I would?"

"I'd like to believe that, yes."

"Then what the hell are you talking about?"

"I'm talking about Doggone It," Ethan said.

Jonathan stared at him, then shook his head. "What about it? It's an organization promoting no-kill shelters. I send them a check for twenty dollars every month. How did I hear about it? At my Masonic lodge. A number of my lodge brothers are into saving animals. People who like to save animals don't usually kill humans—who are animals, too, after all."

"I was at their headquarters this morning," Ethan said.

"I hope you left a healthy check."

"I spoke with Mr. Hayworth."

Jonathan continued to stare at him, but Ethan simply waited patiently for him to crack and say something.

"I don't know the name," Jonathan said. "I've never actually visited the place."

"All right. How about Sane Energy?"

Jonathan frowned. "I help them out from time to time, yes."

"Doing what?"

"Trying to get people to talk to one another."

"Were Hickory and Corley some of the people who need to talk?"

"I don't know. Maybe. There's a company called Gideon Oil. Sane Energy has been reaching out to them, hoping to discuss a potential win-win solution. There are several engineers in my lodge who say there's a safer, albeit more expensive, way to lay oil lines along the river from the Gulf of Mexico. There was talk about arranging a sit-down between members of Sane Energy and the management of Gideon Oil."

"Why didn't you mention this?"

"Because it didn't occur to me to mention it! Sane Energy has hundreds of members, and I don't even know anyone at Gideon Oil. I assumed they had someone with better connections setting it up."

"Hickory and Corley were passionate about Sane Energy's cause, and word is they intended to use you as a negotiator." He was guessing, of course. But, if he sounded definite enough, he might be able to draw out the truth.

"If they were, I knew nothing about it. But you can easily find out tomorrow. The head office of Sane Energy is in Vicksburg. Use your badge to make people there talk to you. Ask *them* what *they* know. If Hickory and Corley wanted to involve me, maybe they told the top people at Sane Energy. They certainly didn't tell *me*."

"How could you not know if your friends had plans for you?"

"I'm passionate about one thing, Ethan. History. Other than that, I help out my friends when they ask. But I swear to you, no one had asked me about this. So, yes, I lied at first. I lied to you. And, God help me, I lied to my daughter. But I did it to protect a confidence. Now you know the truth, and the truth is that both murdered men were my friends, and I would do anything possible to help find their killer. If it has something to do with Gideon Oil, that's news to me. So go to Sane Energy tomorrow and—"

He broke off, looking at Ethan and shaking his head. "You already planned on going to Sane Energy tomorrow, didn't you?"

"Yes, I did. We did."

Jonathan stared at him. "Then excuse me. I'd like to shower and change and go hear my daughter sing."

As Jonathan walked away Ethan glanced at his watch. The second dinner seating was due to begin shortly.

He headed to the Eagle View.

She waited until the second seating, but then, as she had promised, Charlie saw to it that they sang both songs Captain Ellsworth Derue had requested. And, as she expected, she looked out over the dining room and saw them all—the ghosts of the soldiers who had died so long ago—filling the room. They were like double-exposed film, moving silently among the diners who still lived and breathed.

She caught Alexi looking at her, and they exchanged a smile. She realized Alexi understood how much this moment spent singing just for the shades of the dead meant to her. She wasn't sure if happiness was something the dead could still feel, but she had to believe they could, because based on the sense of peace she felt in that moment, she and her friends had indeed made these men happy.

She saw Ethan in the audience, too, sitting with Jude and Thor. He looked grave, and something in her heart sank.

She saw her father, as well. He was sitting by himself, and he smiled at her each time he caught her looking his way.

But when he didn't notice her watching him, he looked irritated, even upset.

At length, the evening came to an end. Her father came up to kiss her and congratulate them all. He was quick to leave, though, which disturbed Charlie—especially since she still needed to talk to him alone.

She left the dining room with Ethan and the others, pausing to look back at Ellsworth Derue. He saluted her with a nod, as if promising that he would be there for her if and when she needed him.

It was late, so they all said good-night and headed for their cabins.

Ethan seemed preoccupied as they got ready for bed. He didn't ask her about the ship's long-dead doctor, though she was sure he must have seen Derue and all the rest of the ghosts.

She didn't say anything, not that she wanted to lie, but because she wanted to talk to her father first. Instead she asked him about the animal shelter.

"Thor's going to get a new husky."

"Well, he *is* an Alaskan, and I think Clara told me they already have one husky, his dog that he brought with him when he moved down to Krewe headquarters," she said. "What else?"

He looked at her. "The head of Doggone It, Mr. Hayworth, told me that both Corley and Hickory were passionate about something going on at Sane Energy. Apparently the two of them were talking about a man they planned to ask to set up a meeting with one of the oil companies for them."

"Who?"

"Your father."

She had no idea what to say, so all she could manage was "Oh…"

"I talked to him. He said he knew there was talk about setting up some kind of meeting, but no one had approached him yet. He said he didn't even know that Albion and Farrell would be the two men doing the talking."

"I'm sure he's telling the truth." When he didn't respond, she let out a sigh and sank down on the bed. "So I have something to share," she said.

"What's that?" he asked as he shrugged out of his jacket, took his holster and gun from his waistband and set them by the bed.

"The doctor paid me a visit today," she said softly.

"The ship's doctor?" he asked.

"Yes. His name is Captain Ellsworth Derue," she said. "He thought both Farrell and Albion were good men, and he adores my father. He saw people talking and arguing with Corley. Saw them, Ethan. And he actually heard Albion and Farrell talking about a 'situation' and saying they wanted to talk to my father."

"I see."

"No, you don't see. They died before they could talk to him. Dammit, Ethan, my father is not a murderer!"

"No, I don't believe he is. But he *has* held back important information."

"What did he hold back that would have changed anything? Yes, Farrell Hickory was going to marry Shelley Corley, and he kept that confidence, but it doesn't matter. No one involved in the investigation believes that it was a hate crime."

"That's true, but the way an investigation works, you often have to find out what things weren't before you can find out what they were. If your father had just been open about what he knew—"

"Your friend Laurent might have arrested him!" Charlie snapped.

"Charlie, I don't want to fight about your father."

"Then quit acting as if he's a criminal."

He let out an explosive sound, finished taking off his shirt and walked over to check the door and turn out the lights. She didn't move. When he slid into the bed to join her, she said, "My father is not a criminal."

"Charlie, I'm not treating him like a criminal. I'm just trying to find out everything he knows."

She fell silent, and for a few minutes, neither of them moved, neither of them spoke.

Then she scooted toward him and curled up on his chest and said, "Want to hear something great my father taught me when I asked him why he and my mom never seemed to fight? Might be clichéd, and I'm sure you've heard similar, but it's all so true!"

"What?" he asked her.

"My dad told me that he and my mom never went to bed angry."

"He can be a very sage man," Ethan said.

And then he took her into his arms. For a while, the world was sensation, the scent and feel of him, the wonder of making love—with someone you truly loved.

But then she lay in the darkness again. Even held by him, even close…she was worried. And she knew the worry would stay with her—until they discovered the truth.

"Vicksburg, Mississippi," Jonathan said. "All of you heading to the National Military Park with me, let's talk about Vicksburg. 'Vicksburg is the key.' Who knows who said that?" he asked the group.

"President Lincoln?" a teen asked.

"Bingo! And do you know what President Jefferson Davis of the Confederacy had to say?" Jonathan asked.

"Something like 'up yours'?" another teen asked.

"He might have thought it," Jonathan said, smiling, "but what Davis actually said was, 'Vicksburg is the nail head that holds the South's two halves together.' So you can see that, for both presidents, the Vicksburg campaign was one of the most important in the war. The siege of Vicksburg lasted from May 18th to July the 4th of 1863. It was the last major stronghold of the Confederacy on the Mississippi River. Of course, something else was going on at the same time. Anyone know what else happened from July 1st through the 3rd in 1863?"

"Gettysburg!" several people called out simultaneously.

"Exactly. So, the Fourth of July—Independence Day—

proved to be a pretty good day for President Lincoln, wouldn't you say?"

There was a chorus of agreement. Jonathan went on to talk about logistics and how the campaign was part of the "Anaconda" plan to put a stranglehold on the Confederacy.

Ethan stood with Jude and watched until Jonathan, leading scores of passengers, headed off to board the buses that would take them to the National Military Park.

Thor was staying on the boat with the Belles, leaving Jude to accompany Ethan today. "You want to drive?" Jude asked now.

"Don't care—we both know the way around here," Ethan said.

"I'll drive. You seem pissed off, not a great mood for getting behind the wheel."

In the car, Jude said, "I just don't believe Jonathan Moreau is guilty."

"I don't believe it, either," Ethan said. "I know the man, and he isn't a killer. What I don't understand is why he hasn't been more forthcoming. He knew about Shelley. He knew at least something of what Corley and Hickory were up to. Selma Rodriguez was almost certainly killed because of something she knew—and she knew Corley was going to see Jonathan."

"Careful. It sounds like you're laying her death at Jonathan's feet," Jude said shrewdly.

"I'm not. I believe the killer thought she knew more than that Corley was going to meet with Jonathan. That's not a reason to kill. There has to be more. Perhaps the killer thought Selma knew *why* Corley wanted the meeting."

"Let's hope we can find out," Jude said.

The Sane Energy office was small, nothing like the sprawling property belonging to Doggone It. Of course, they didn't need that much space, either. They saw a man seated at a desk when they entered. He quickly rose, sized them up and smiled. "Hello, welcome," he said with a definite Mississippi accent, deep and rich and rolling. "I assume you're Special Agents Delaney and McCoy? I received a call from your office yesterday, so I made a point of being here today. I'm Frank Lorenzo, president, though I'm not sure how much the title means. We're an all-volunteer organization, and I'm usually at work at this time. But under the circumstances, I'm happy to miss a day of work. How can I help you?"

"We'd like to understand what was going on, what Mr. Corley and Mr. Hickory were so upset about," Ethan said.

"Gideon Oil," Lorenzo said flatly and firmly. "They're laying an oil pipeline along the Mississippi. The states are in on it—Louisiana and Mississippi, that is. They've given their approval. But we've had engineers create models that show that there's an alternative, a safer alternative. The hitch is, our alternative plan is more expensive, so their shareholders won't make their fortune as quickly as they were promised. Here, let me show you."

He led them to the back of the office where several 3-D models had been set up.

"Construction will take longer and the equipment will be pricier, so you're looking at more money, for sure. But we think we have a good argument for long-term benefits with no downside, so in the end the payout to the shareholders will be higher. Setting up a meeting has been next to impossible, however. They're constantly putting us off. A lot of us have been talking about what we should do, but Albion and Farrell…they were rabid on the subject. They were ready to take it to both state legislatures. And I believe," Lorenzo said, meeting their eyes, "that they might have succeeded in getting the pipeline stopped and our plan instituted."

"Why didn't you inform the authorities about this?" Ethan asked. "This could be motive for murder."

Lorenzo appeared to be truly perplexed. "Well, for one thing, they hadn't done anything yet. And playing hardball was their last resort. They believed they had the right man to try to set up friendly negotiations with Gideon Oil. Anyway, from what I've heard, their deaths had something to do with a Civil War reenactment they were in."

"We're investigating every angle, Mr. Lorenzo," Jude said.

"I had no idea I'd have anything at all helpful to say. Not until I got that call from Agent Hawkins yesterday, saying you'd be in and asking me to give you any information I could," Lorenzo said. He seemed to be growing defensive. That wasn't going to help.

"Mr. Lorenzo, we're not accusing you of anything, and we're very grateful you took the time to see us today," Ethan said.

The man appeared to be somewhat mollified.

"Can you give us the names of anyone at Gideon Oil

who might have been involved in the negotiations?" Jude asked.

Lorenzo shook his head. "That's just it—we hadn't even talked to anyone yet. Albion and Farrell were going to talk to Jonathan Moreau about opening negotiations with Gideon Oil. Everyone respects him, and no one doubts his knowledge of and respect for the South, which makes everyone willing to listen to him. But it never got that far, because they never talked to him. You know, I talked to both Farrell and Albion…" He paused, as if he'd lost his breath for a minute. "I talked to them both before they were killed. Awful. One dead the first day, and not a day later, the second."

"I don't suppose you have the name of the CEO of Gideon Oil? Save us looking it up?" Jude said.

Lorenzo laughed drily. "Sure. Gideon. Saul Gideon. His family's been big oil forever."

They spoke for a few moments longer; Lorenzo gave them copies of his files on Gideon Oil and the river project. They studied the models again, and then it was time to leave.

When they were driving back, Jude looked over at Ethan and said, "There's one thing that argues against the murders being tied to the whole Sane Energy-Gideon Oil situation."

"I can think of two, actually. First, the fact that they hadn't even begun setting up negotiations, and second, the fact that the deaths of two men wouldn't really change anything," Ethan said.

"Yeah."

"I'm wondering about something else, too," Ethan

said. "As in, why were the two of them dressed up in their uniforms if their plan was to meet up with Moreau to ask him about being a negotiator?"

"It would make more sense to think they had a date with that photographer, Chance Morgan," Jude said. "Except he had an alibi."

"Kind of brings you back to the movie people," Ethan said.

"Which brings us back to what the hell motive could any of them have to kill those two men, much less Selma Rodriguez. Unless we *are* back to a hate crime."

"I just don't see it. But we can find out from Gideon Oil if any overtures were made toward them, maybe something they didn't know about at Sane Energy," Ethan said.

"Greed. Always a motive for murder."

"Call Jackson. Ask him to ask Angela to look into what's going on at Gideon Oil."

"I'm on it."

"And tomorrow the *Journey* is back in St. Francisville. At the very least, we'll have a chance to drop in on the movie set again."

That night Ethan didn't come to either show, leaving Charlie to worry about what was going on. Thor, Jude, Alexi and Clara all walked with her to her door, saw her safely inside, then separated and headed to their own cabins.

Ethan was waiting for her in the room, pictures spread out on the bed. Charlie walked over to where he sat studying them.

She saw with a shock that they were photos of the entire cast and crew of Brad's movie. Only her own picture was missing.

"No luck at Gideon Oil?" she asked him.

He looked up at her. "No. Are we feeling frustrated? Yes. HQ is working on finding out if any private communications were exchanged between Gideon and Sane Energy."

"And you're focused back on the movie crew."

"People don't usually dress up in Civil War uniforms to meet up with oil barons."

Charlie perched on the edge of the bed. "That's true, but…"

Her voice trailed off as she heard that strange brushing sound at the door again.

She raced over to open it, but Ethan was there in a flash, stopping her with her hand on the knob. "Charlie, you can't just open the door."

"It's him, Captain Derue," she explained.

"You have a ghost that knocks?"

"He's a Southern boy. He would never just walk into a woman's room."

Nevertheless, Ethan put his body between her and the door, then looked through the peephole to see the ghost.

"Come in," he said, finally opening the door.

"Captain Derue, this is Ethan Delaney," Charlie said as the ghost entered. "Ethan works for the FBI, the Federal Bureau of Investigation. Ethan, Captain Derue. He died of disease while tending to both Union and Confederate soldiers."

Captain Derue nodded. "Mr. Delaney," he said, his husky voice low but still clearly audible.

"Captain, thank you for your help," Ethan said.

"I wish that I could do more," the captain said, staring intently at Ethan. "You might be a descendant of my cousin, sir."

"Your cousin?" Ethan said.

Captain Derue nodded. "We were torn apart, sir, by the travails of the war. My mother's sister married in St. Francisville, while my own mother married a man from Boston. For many years my cousin and I saw one another frequently. Both our fathers were military men. They fought together in Mexico, but then South Carolina seceded from the Union, and the war began. He went with his state, and I went with mine. We met again here in the bloody hell of shelling that went on during the Port Hudson campaign."

"Anson McKee," Ethan said. "He was your cousin, wasn't he?"

The captain nodded. "Yes, and you look just like him."

"He does," Charlie agreed.

The captain turned sharply to look at her. "You've— you've seen Anson?"

"We've both seen him," Ethan said. "He's there by Grace Church, outside St. Francisville. He's helped us several times."

"He saved my life," Charlie told him.

"What I wouldn't give to see Anson," Derue said.

"We'll be in St. Francisville tomorrow, but the *Journey* stops there every week," Charlie said.

"I haven't stepped off the ship since…since I died aboard her," Captain Derue said softly.

"You must! Come with us tomorrow. I'm sure we can find him," Charlie said enthusiastically.

"I can't leave the men," the captain said. "They were entrusted to my care."

"And they'll be fine if you leave them for just a little while," Charlie said.

The captain nodded, then glanced toward the bed. He saw the pictures there and walked over to look down at them. "Her," he said, pointing to the shot of Jennie McPherson. "She's the one I told you about yesterday. She was arguing with Albion, and then…" He paused and turned to Charlie. "Then she went to speak with your father. I had forgotten that."

Ethan and Charlie looked at each other quickly. Charlie had wondered if the argument had been with Nancy and Todd Camp.

Captain Derue looked at the pictures again. "Yes, many of these people were here. I remember all of these men," he said, and pointed to the pictures of Jimmy Smith, Luke Mayfield, Barry Seymour and George Gonzales. "I remember them all." He straightened. "It has grown late. I will leave you to sleep, but I would be most grateful if I might accompany you ashore tomorrow."

"Of course," Ethan said. "We'll be with friends, but they're all…safe. They've seen you, just as Charlie and I have."

Captain Derue nodded. "I have seen them, I think,

and I have noticed that they can see me and the men.
Thank you, and good evening."

He saluted and turned. Once again, he didn't bother
with the door but simply vanished.

"Jennie's name does keep coming up," Charlie said.
"But she's not even from St. Francisville, plus she's all
of five feet and ninety pounds. I can't see her lifting an
Enfield or wielding a bayonet, even if I could think of
why she'd want to."

"It will all make sense somehow," Ethan murmured.
"We'll find out tomorrow. For now..." He stopped,
shrugged and quickly cleared the photos off the bed, then
smiled at her. "Time for bed, so we can make an early
start in the morning."

She was surprised when he swept her into his arms.
"Seize the night—that's what they say, isn't it?"

"Seize the night," she agreed.

And so they did, letting Charlie forget, at least for
a little while, how much she was dreading tomorrow
and the possible discovery that one of her friends was
a killer.

The plan was that they would all go ashore in St.
Francisville. Alexi wasn't worried that they wouldn't
have a chance to rehearse. They already had a set list
and knew all the songs well, so they would be fine.

Jude and Thor were going to go talk to Randy Laurent, who was expecting them. He was glum, having
talked to half the people in town without discovering
anything new.

Jackson Crow had contacted the CEO of Gideon Oil,

Saul Gideon, and he had agreed to meet with them at his office in Baton Rouge the following day, although he'd made a point of saying he wasn't sure what help he could possibly give them. He'd said he hadn't even been approached by anyone from Sane Energy, but would have had no problem considering a new plan. And since he owned 51 percent of the company, the final decision on which method to go with would have been his.

They hadn't spoken with Jonathan yet. Ethan had purposely delayed that morning, so by the time he and Charlie were ready to head ashore, Jonathan and his tour group were already gone. He wanted to observe Jonathan in St. Francisville. In fact, he was hoping to get Jonathan onto the film set, which might be possible, since he would be talking at Grace Episcopal Church, and it shouldn't be too hard to sidetrack him afterward.

Alexi and Clara were going to hang out at Mrs. Mama's Café. It was public and safe, and they just might overhear something useful.

The six of them met on deck before heading ashore, but they waited until pretty much everyone who was leaving the ship for the day was gone. When the deck was virtually empty, they saw Captain Ellsworth Derue coming toward them. They nodded to acknowledge his presence, since talking to thin air would have looked suspicious to the few people who were still around.

Derue was smiling broadly, and Ethan thought he was the happiest ghost he had ever encountered.

If nothing else, Ethan imagined there weren't that many occasions when anyone acknowledged him at all, much less six people at one time.

Once they were off the ship, they claimed their rental cars and split up. Captain Ellsworth Derue accompanied Ethan and Charlie as they headed toward the bluff by Grace Church, where the film crew were still working on some last "rising ghost" shots. They'd spent the last several days, while Charlie was unavailable, working with Harry Grayson, Blane Pica and the ghosts, getting new angles on the climactic scene of the ghosts destroying the oil-company exec and the crooked senator. Ethan thought it was ironic they were now looking into Gideon Oil's potential involvement in three real-life murders.

"This is a movie set?" Captain Derue asked as they arrived. He was familiar with movies from his time on the ship and was keenly interested not only in the filming itself but in everything behind the scenes: the catering tent, the dressing rooms and especially the crates of props, so many of which could have come directly from his own past.

"Yes, this is it," Charlie said.

"Interesting," Captain Derue said. "And the reenactors will be here?" he asked.

"Many of them," Ethan assured him. "From here, we'll walk over to Grace Church and see if we can't find Anson McKee."

"Thank you." His words were heartfelt.

Charlie might have been gone for a month rather than only a few days, she was greeted so warmly by Brad, Mike, the crew and the actors on call, not only Blane and Harry, but Jimmy and Grant Ferguson, who were also part of the "rising" scenes.

"Charlie, any chance you have time for one scene?"

Brad asked her. "Your costume's here, and I just want to shoot you getting up after the ghosts have saved you— over by the old graves on this side of the churchyard."

She glanced at Ethan. He nodded. "Sure. We have a few hours," he said.

Ethan kept his eye on the dressing room while she changed, chatted with the other actors to pass the time.

"I'm so sick of being filthy," Jimmy said. "And people think an actor's life is all glamour."

"We do get to sit in the shade and sip mineral water," Grant said.

"Want to join us?" Jimmy asked Ethan.

"No, I think I'll wander down to watch the filming," Ethan told them.

"Have fun," Jimmy said cheerfully, heading for the catering tent.

Charlie came out of the dressing room, transformed into a modern young professional in her office attire. Brad, Mike, Luke—hauling his microphones, headphones and other equipment—and Jennie—makeup box in hand—walked with her over to the spot where Brad had chosen to shoot. Everyone but Charlie was completely unaware that they'd been joined by Captain Ellsworth Derue.

From his vantage point a short distance from the church, Ethan could see both the filming and Jonathan standing near the church and speaking to a crowd.

He noticed that Jennie frequently looked over in Jonathan's direction.

The filming went off without a hitch. There was nothing for Charlie to see as she got up from the ground where she'd fallen, but Brad painted the picture with words as she looked around her. She was terrified when she first saw the ghosts, but then she realized they were there to protect her, that they would save her from the evil *living* men who were chasing her. Once they'd captured a satisfactory take, Brad had Luke set up a new scene marker and called for silence on the set. Charlie had been set up with a mic, and now she thanked the ghosts who were supposedly surrounding her, though once again she was on her own, talking to the air. When the scene was completed to Brad's satisfaction, he called "Cut!" and went over and kissed Charlie on the cheek, and told her she was brilliant.

While Charlie was busy talking with Brad, Ethan strolled over to where Jennie was standing.

"Not only did you know Corley and Hickory," he said softly and without preamble, "you knew them pretty well."

She flushed and looked at him. "Not really. We were all involved in an organization called Sane Energy. They wanted to try to talk to some oil-company bigwig about changing an oil pipeline, and I thought it was a good idea."

"You claimed you barely knew them."

She sighed and looked at him. "Okay, I knew them a little more than 'barely,' but it's not like we were buddies or something. And I didn't want to get involved, because what if that made me a target? I don't know who killed them or why, I swear."

"Okay, let's leave that for now and talk about the fact that you talked to Albion Corley on the *Journey* the day of the reenactment, and then you rushed to talk with Jonathan Moreau. Why did you need to talk to Jonathan if not to tell him what you must have known, that Albion and Farrell wanted his help with their plan?"

Jennie shook her head. "Yes, that's why I wanted to talk to him, but I didn't get the chance to tell him anything. Someone was talking to him, asking him questions. People are always asking him questions. He left to set up his next lecture before I got a chance to talk to him."

Ethan had to be satisfied with that, because Brad and Charlie had stopped talking and were heading his way.

"Done for the day," Brad said happily. "We should all head to the café."

Ethan looked at his watch, surprised to see that it was already midafternoon, and they'd promised Derue a visit to the church. "Can't. Charlie has a show at five thirty," he said.

"Well, that sucks," Brad said.

"How about breakfast tomorrow?" Mike asked, walking up to join them. "The *Journey* stays in port until midmorning. We could do an early breakfast, say eightish? Maybe eight thirty."

"Sounds good," Ethan said.

"Sure," Charlie agreed.

"Still wish you could come with us now," Brad said.

"Me, too, but we'll see you in the morning," Charlie promised.

"Okay, then," Brad said. "Come on, Jennie. Let's go."

Jennie looked toward the church again, and Ethan followed her gaze. Jonathan and his group were gone.

Damn. He'd wanted to observe the man more closely while they were so near where Hickory's body had been buried.

Ethan and Charlie waited until the others were trekking back to their cars. Then he turned to Captain Derue, who had been waiting quietly, and said, "Let's head over to the church."

"So many lives..." Derue said quietly, looking off toward the graveyard.

Ethan took Charlie's hand. He squeezed it as they followed Derue toward the church.

They were almost there when they saw Anson. He materialized right in front of them, but he didn't even seem to notice Ethan and Charlie, only the ghost who was with them.

"Ells," he said in shock.

"Anson."

The two ghosts embraced warmly, and then they walked away and sat on an aboveground tomb, where they rested and talked.

Ethan knew he had to get Charlie back to the *Journey*, but there was no reason not to leave the two cousins there to catch up. Derue had plenty of time to find his own way back.

"Charlie and I are going to head back to the ship!" he called.

Anson McKee looked toward them for a moment, then lifted a hand and waved goodbye. Ellsworth smiled and did the same.

Ethan and Charlie turned and headed toward their rental car.

"That was beautiful," Charlie said.

"I always figured ghosts could find each other if they wanted to, but apparently I was wrong. I guess we'll never know all the answers, even if we do have the 'sight.' Not until we die ourselves, anyway."

"In that case, I hope I stay ignorant for a long time," Charlie said with a smile.

At the car, Ethan glanced at his watch. He was barely going to get Charlie back in time for her first performance.

"Don't forget I still have to change," she said, checking the time herself.

"I'll get you there."

He drove to the dock, aware of the time the whole way. When he reached the dock and the spot where he was supposed to leave the car, Charlie asked, "Do you really think a ninety-pound woman could be our killer?"

"What?"

"Jennie. I saw you talking to her, and from the look on her face, you weren't making casual conversation. You were questioning her, weren't you?"

"I was asking her about Sane Energy."

"Oh?"

"She admitted she knew Albion and Farrell better than she'd admitted before, said she was a member of Sane Energy, too. She did know that they wanted to set up a meeting with Gideon Oil."

That was the end of the conversation, because they had to produce their ship ID cards so they could board. Charlie was ready to run ahead without him, but he insisted on going with her.

"I'm going to check on the others, but I'll be back over to walk you up to the dining room."

"Just hurry, 'cause I'm running late."

"Okay, okay, just be sure to lock the door."

"Locking!" she called.

Ethan walked the two steps to Jude and Alexi's cabin, though he suspected they'd already gone up to the Eagle View. He had just raised his fist to knock on their door when he heard a startled scream from his own cabin.

Charlie!

15

Charlie stood still, staring in horror at the mirror above the sink.

You're next.

The words seemed to drip down the glass, and they looked like they were written in blood, but they couldn't have been. Could they?

Charlie backed away from the mirror.

She didn't even realize she had screamed until Ethan burst into the cabin and raced up behind her.

It was lipstick, just lipstick, she thought, and tried to reassure herself that this was a sick prank.

She felt Ethan's hands on her shoulders, firm and reassuring.

"Lipstick," he said. "Don't touch it. I'll get hold of Randy and have him send a forensics team. We may find something, fingerprints or…something."

"Is this…a joke? The printing looks like a kid's, and the message…it's like something from half the cheesy horror movies out there. But…how did someone get into our cabin?"

"We'll worry about that later," Ethan said. "Maybe someone 'borrowed' a master key from one of the maids. But joke or not, people are dead, and this isn't funny. Find your things, and we'll get you into one of the other cabins. You can change there while I wait for forensics to show up. The *Journey* doesn't leave St. Francisville until tomorrow morning, so we have plenty of time to get a handle on this."

"Okay," Charlie said. She turned and hurried to the closet, collecting her dress, shoes, corset and petticoat. She felt cold, and as if she was moving like a robot. But she was calm. No, she realized, she was *too* calm. She was almost numb.

Paradoxically, she was also angry. How dare some sicko sneak into her cabin and try to scare her this way?

She didn't think she would be able to sleep in here again. Yet where could she go? She was pretty sure the ship was at capacity.

Once she was ready to leave, she noticed that Ethan was just hanging up the phone, and when he took her arm and led her out, Jude was already out in the hallway and waiting for them next door.

Alexi was peeking out the doorway as Ethan tersely explained the situation to Jude.

"Might suggest we've been wrong and someone on the ship is our killer," Jude said.

"It might, but the ship has been at the dock in St. Francisville all day, too," Ethan said. "Someone could have sneaked aboard."

"I'll step out so you can go in and change," Jude said to Charlie, nodding toward the pile of clothing in her arms.

"Thanks," she said.

As soon as she closed the door, Alexi looked at Charlie questioningly.

"There was a message on the mirror, written in lipstick," Charlie explained. "It said 'You're next.'"

Alexi shook her head. "Something similar happened on the *Destiny*. My guess is it means someone thinks you're getting close."

"Why would they think *I'm* getting close?" Charlie asked.

Alexi looked at her grimly. "Because even though you don't realize it yet, you must know the killer," she said quietly. "And that scares him. Or her," she added.

"You think a woman could have done this? Wielded an Enfield with a bayonet attached?" Charlie said, slipping out of her clothes and into her costume. She turned so Alexi could tighten the corset. "Jennie McPherson's name keeps coming up, but she's about the size of a mouse."

"She might not have done the killing herself. There could be two or even more people involved," Alexi told her. "Women are willing to do strange things for the men they love—and vice versa, of course."

"Including kill?"

"Maybe," Alexi murmured.

There was a tap at the door, and after checking through the peephole, Alexi opened it to let Clara in.

The most effusive of their group, she threw her arms around Charlie. "You okay?" she asked.

Charlie nodded. "Oddly enough, though I admit I'm scared, I'm angry, too."

"Good. Angry is good," Clara said firmly. "Anyway, you guys ready to go? Jude is going to walk us to the dining room and stay with us. Ethan and Thor are going to wait for the forensics team and talk to Laurent when he gets here."

"It's a plan," Charlie murmured.

They headed out to the hall, where the three Krewe agents waited.

"Showtime," Alexi said.

"You going to be okay?" Ethan asked Charlie. "Alexi and Clara could go on without you."

"Don't be silly. I'm fine. And hopefully Captain Derue will be back, and his men are there. One of them might even have seen something. Besides, I'm not afraid of lipstick on a mirror."

Ethan smiled at her, a smile that was grim but admiring. She wished she deserved his admiration, but she really hadn't done anything other than not fall apart completely.

"I'll have a new cabin settled by the time you're finished with the second show," he promised.

As they walked down the hall, Charlie looked at her companions. "How hard would it have been for someone to have gotten on the ship?" she asked. "I mean, someone who isn't supposed to be here?"

"Well, security's not as tight as when you're traveling internationally," Jude said from where he was walking a few feet behind them.

"Tight?" Clara gave what sounded almost like an

unladylike snort. "They allow prospective cruisers on during the day. They supposedly scan IDs, but the procedure is pretty casual. I was down on the Promenade Deck the other day with Thor, and we could see how easy it was to come aboard. Of course, there's supposed to be a count at the end of the day. It makes sure everyone who got on is off, but…"

Charlie lowered her voice. "So it's conceivable someone from St. Francisville got on the *Journey* sometime during the day and went to my cabin to write that message?"

"Just about anything is conceivable," Alexi said.

"In this case, I'd say it goes beyond conceivable to quite possible," Clara added. "And it's not like they had to smuggle a weapon on. We're talking about a lipstick. No one would look twice." She slipped her arm around Charlie's shoulders. "But you've got nothing to worry about. You have us."

"All of us," Alexi added.

Charlie smiled, thinking about the friends who'd just vowed to protect her. A piano-bar hostess and a soprano with the voice of an angel. Not exactly a couple of Navy SEALs.

But she knew both of them had survived terrible ordeals to be where they were now, and even if they weren't gun-toting bodyguards themselves, they came with a pair of them. And then there was Ethan, of course. Her skin flushed at the thought of him.

"I'm tired of everything pointing at my father, who would certainly never hurt me. Or anyone else, for that matter. I'm angry, and I want to shake someone to get to the truth," Charlie said as they reached the dining room.

As soon as they entered, she saw that Captain Derue and his men were there. Every single one of them, from those who could stand to those who were too weak to rise from their sickbeds, saluted the four of them.

For a moment, they all stood dead still.

This was worth it. Whatever happened to her here aboard the *Journey*, this was worth it.

They saluted in return, then headed to the small stage to warm up.

Soon the diners began to file in. Charlie watched for Ethan and Thor, but they didn't appear.

Neither did her father.

Captain Derue was in front of the stage as they ended, watching as if mesmerized, applauding enthusiastically. As the diners headed out to allow the room to be set up for the second seating, he approached Charlie, looking clearly concerned.

"You're all right?" he inquired anxiously.

"Yes, thank you."

"Some of my men say they saw some of the same people on board today who were here the day of the re-enactment. The petite woman was one."

"Jennie? Jennie McPherson, the makeup artist you saw on set today?"

"Early, very early," the captain said. "The others... a bit later. There were three of them, and they went in different directions."

Charlie nodded, glancing around. A robust woman

in a long blue gown had cornered Alexi and Clara. Jude was on his phone.

She looked down as she spoke, trying to make sure—if she was being observed—that it didn't look like she was talking to herself.

"Captain, someone wrote a threat on the mirror in my cabin. They used lipstick so it would look like blood."

He looked at her gravely. "We're afraid for you. Me, my men—and Anson, too. He believes the killer may think you found the body of Farrell Hickory because you'd seen something that indicated where to look, perhaps that you've even seen the murderer himself."

"But I *didn't* see anything. I *couldn't* have seen anything. The evidence shows he was killed the night before I found him," Charlie said.

"Perhaps the killer thinks you know something else, then. It doesn't matter. You must be careful. Please, be very careful."

Charlie nodded solemnly. "I will be. Thank you."

He had faded away before she finished speaking, leaving her talking to the air.

"Charlie?"

She turned to see Alexi looking at her worriedly and walked over to lean on the piano so she could tell her about the captain's warning and what the men had seen.

"Wasn't Jennie on set today?" Alexi asked her.

"She was, but he said it was very early, so it could have been before she had to be on set. Do you think she wrote on my mirror? Ethan and I did go up top for breakfast," Charlie said. "I just can't see her having the strength to kill the men the way they were killed."

"Maybe she didn't kill them but did write on your mirror," Alexi suggested.

Clara moved over to the piano to join them. Jude was still on the phone, but he was watching them as he talked.

"I'm thinking about spending the night at my dad's house in St. Francisville," Charlie said, after they'd brought Clara up to speed. "I don't want to be in that cabin again. I don't know why, because I'm not actually afraid when I'm with Ethan, but I just feel it has been touched by something dirty, something evil. Silly, huh?"

"We can switch cabins," Alexi offered.

"That's too much trouble just because I'm being ridiculous. It's only about ten minutes from the ship to my house, and the *Journey* doesn't leave port until ten thirty. I don't think Ethan will mind if we stay at the house tonight."

"He won't mind doing anything that makes you feel safe."

Jude walked over to the piano, pocketing his phone. "Ethan and Thor have gone down to the station with Randy Laurent. They're going to enhance some of the ship's video surveillance footage and try to find out who might have been on the ship. I'm not sure when they'll be back."

"Charlie doesn't want to sleep in her cabin tonight," Alexi told him.

"Charlie and Ethan can have our cabin," Jude said.

"I already offered, but Charlie doesn't want to put us out," Alexi said.

"I kind of want to get off the ship tonight," Charlie said.

"Do we know how long Ethan and Thor are going to be?" Clara asked. "We could all go to Charlie's house and wait for them, even all spend the night there. Ethan and Thor could just meet us there whenever they finished."

"After your second set, we'll figure out what to do," Jude said.

"Have you seen my dad?" Charlie asked him.

"No, he hasn't come in here," Jude said.

"Would you see if you can find him?" Charlie asked. "I'm worried about him. He's always here for our shows."

"I'll send someone," Jude assured her.

"You could just run down to his cabin," Charlie said.

"Not on your life. No way am I leaving the three of you," Jude told her firmly. "I'm sure your dad is okay, but I *will* send someone. Meanwhile, I think your next set of people are coming in."

Jude smiled and walked over to the table where he planned to sit for the second show. Several diners approached the Belles before sitting down to ask them to reprise one song or another from a previous night.

Finally everyone was seated, and the trio launched into their opening medley, after which Charlie began the story of the *Journey* and how she'd changed hands several times between North and South.

"And now she's an Irish-American ship," Clara piped in, which got a laugh.

Once everyone settled down, Alexi began to play softly as Charlie talked. As she neared the end, she saw the ghosts of the men who had been on the *Journey* the day it changed hands for the final time.

As the show went on, Charlie kept looking over to where Jude was sitting. Several times he got up and moved to the doorway at the back of the room to speak on the phone.

Her father had yet to appear, and she found herself growing more and more restless.

When their last song was over, she dodged the fans approaching the stage to congratulate them and hurried over to Jude.

"My dad—"

"Your dad is fine. He's in his cabin, with the Do Not Disturb sign on the door, but I asked the steward to disturb him anyway, just to ask if he needed anything. He answered and said he was fine."

Charlie looked at Jude and shook her head. "He's not fine. I know my dad. He would have been here tonight if he were fine. Jude, please, we have to go to his cabin."

"Okay. Get Clara and Alexi. We'll go now," Jude told her.

The four of them hurried toward the exit. It wasn't an easy escape. People kept stopping them to ask questions or just pass on a compliment. The whole time, Charlie's fear for her father was growing. Maybe it was just as irrational as not wanting to sleep in her cabin, but rational or not, it was eating away at her insides.

Finally they were out of the dining room and heading down the hallway. Charlie saw the Do Not Disturb sign on her father's door and ignored it, hurrying ahead to pound on the door. There was no answer, not even when she called, "Dad? It's me, Charlie." She turned back to look at Jude. "We have to get in there!"

"Do you have a key to his cabin?"

"No, but—"

"Never mind, not if you're that worried."

Jude turned sideways and slammed his shoulder against the door, which splintered at the impact.

He proceeded to kick in what was left of it.

As he did, someone in the cabin screamed, high-pitched and startled.

Ethan, Thor and Randy sat head to head as they went over the video surveillance from the *Journey.* They ran through it several times in real time, then had the tech speed it up and slow it down, searching through the hundreds of people who'd come and gone that day.

"I don't see a single member of the movie crew," Randy said. "No one who could've left that message on the mirror!"

Ethan hadn't seen anyone, either. He leaned back, puzzled. The lipstick message hadn't been a joke; it had been a serious warning. And there was no reason for anyone to go after Charlie unless they were convinced she knew or had seen something that could put them at risk. Like Selma Rodriguez—who hadn't known anything at all.

Except that Albion Corley had planned on meeting with Jonathan Moreau.

"Ethan, it's possible someone paid someone else— maybe an employee on the *Journey*—to write that message. The *Journey* is old, but she's had her doors reconfigured for key cards, and key cards are the easiest thing in the world to duplicate," Thor pointed out.

"Yeah, it's possible," Ethan agreed, then leaned back, perplexed. "Why do people kill?" he murmured.

"Sometimes," Randy said, "I think they kill because

they're just rotten somewhere in their souls. Sometimes from hatred. Or love. Jealousy."

"Greed," Ethan said. "Greed's a big one. We're meeting with Saul Gideon, CEO of Gideon Oil, in Baton Rouge tomorrow. The guy isn't from Louisiana. He's a Texan. And he wasn't against meeting with the Sane Energy people. If his company made the change the Sane Energy people were going to propose, it would have cost them a great deal of money in the short term. But the meeting was never scheduled—no one even talked to Gideon about it—and we know, because HQ checked his whereabouts, that Saul Gideon didn't come here and bayonet two old friends in reproduction military uniforms." He turned to the tech. "Let's run the video one more time, please."

Ethan watched again and asked the tech to slow down when they hit late afternoon, right about the time the tour buses were returning to the *Journey*.

"There!" Ethan exclaimed.

"There, where?" Randy said, puzzled.

Thor pulled his chair closer and pointed at the screen. "I see it, Ethan. Officer Johnson, run back and slow it down there…right there. Go frame by frame."

"Start where that family of three goes through the checkpoint, and then there's a lull," Ethan said. "And then— There! Looks like a kid, but…"

"That's not a kid, that's a small woman," Thor said.

"And I know who it is," Ethan said flatly. "Jennie McPherson, who was supposedly on her way to have dinner at the café with a bunch of her coworkers when we last saw her." He stood up. "We have to get back to the ship."

As Thor and Randy rose, there was a tap on the door. Ethan opened it to reveal an officer standing in the hall.

"We've got a match on some of the prints we found in Charlene Moreau's cabin," he said.

Charlie couldn't have been more stunned to see the small blonde standing in her father's cabin than if Godzilla had been there.

Jennie McPherson looked both startled and horrified. She was staring at them like a deer caught in the headlights.

"What—what are you doing? Breaking into Jonathan's suite?" she demanded, her hand fluttering to her throat.

"What are *we* doing here?" Charlie demanded. "What the hell are *you* doing here? And where the hell is my father?"

Jennie looked truly surprised. "I thought he was with you."

"No, he's not with me," Charlie snapped and stepped forward aggressively. Jude caught her and pulled her back right before she could tackle the other woman. "I'm asking you one more time. Where's my father?"

"If he's not with you, I have no idea!" Jennie said.

"What are you doing here? And how did you get in my cabin? Why did you write on my mirror?"

"What are you talking about? I was never in your cabin, and I certainly didn't write anything on your mirror."

"What are you doing aboard this ship?" Jude asked evenly. "We can have you arrested for breaking and entering, you know."

"Breaking and entering?" Jennie gasped. "You're the one who broke the door down. I was just…waiting."

"How did you get in here? And why were you waiting? Waiting for what? My father? Why? Were you going to stab him in the heart?" Charlie asked.

"What? No!"

"Then why are you here?" Charlie demanded. "If you've hurt my father in any way I'll—"

"Hurt him? Are you crazy?" Jennie protested.

"Then…?" Jude asked.

"Oh, good Lord. Dammit, Charlie, I'm sleeping with him," Jennie said.

Charlie was actually stunned speechless for a minute. Finally she managed to say, "What?"

Jennie let out a sigh. "We didn't want to say anything to anyone yet, especially you. Your dad was worried what you would think. I mean, I'm only a few years older than you are. We're friends. I think we were friends, anyway, and I hope we still are. I wanted to tell you. It was ridiculous, two adults sneaking around to be together. I came aboard to…to see him for a few minutes. He…he gave me a key. He told me to come aboard as a visitor when I finished on set, then slip in and get some rest, and he'd see me when your show was over. I begged off going to the café with the crew and came here instead. Charlie, I swear, I'm crazy about your dad."

Charlie felt sick. "He said he was going up to watch the show?"

"Yes. He said he watched you every night, and did I mind," Jennie told her. "I told him of course I didn't. Charlie, you're everything to him. He didn't want you hurt, and he certainly didn't want you to end up blind-sided like this. He just wanted to be able to tell you in his own time."

Charlie just stared at Jennie, still stunned.

"When did you last see Jonathan?" Jude asked.

"Right before he gave his speech at the church. I saw him from the bluff and went over to say hi," she said. "He—he said he'd join me here as soon as the show ended. I didn't know what to do when that steward showed up, so I just made my voice really deep and said I was fine. And when you showed up, I figured if I just ignored you, you'd go away, but then I started to worry. Charlie, I care about him so much."

Jennie?

And her father?

But more important…

Where the hell *was* her father?

She turned to Jude. "We need to call Ethan and Randy and ship security and anyone else you can think of and…and I don't know what. Jude, something is wrong. I know it. We have to find my father!"

"Where would he go if he didn't come back to the ship?" he asked her.

She shook her head. "Nowhere, not if he said he'd be here. I know my dad. He'd be here if he could be. Something is wrong, something is really, really wrong."

"All right, I'll get you guys—except you, Jennie, you stay right here—back to our cabin, and then I'll make the calls. We'll get everyone on this. But, Charlie, you have to stay there where you'll be safe. In the cabin, door locked. And you can't leave, no matter what."

* * *

Ricky Simpson had been in bed when they started pounding on his door.

He'd gotten up quickly and opened it, then looked surprised to see Ethan, Thor and Randy standing in the hall staring at him. He immediately flushed and looked uncomfortable, though he managed to ask, "Hey, what's going on? Is there a problem?"

The three men pushed their way into the cabin. "Sit down," Ethan told him.

"Hey, you may be with the government, but I know my rights. You can't just bust in here and start pushing me around. I have my rights!" Ricky protested.

"There are a dozen charges I can haul you in on," Randy said, adding drily, "Being the local man, you know. We know you did it."

"Did what? What is this all about?" Simpson asked them.

He had to know, Ethan thought, though he was still doing a good job of faking ignorance.

"It's about a message. A threatening message left on Charlene Moreau's mirror. Written in lipstick."

"Lipstick! Has to be one of the dancers or, more likely, one of the other singers. Those girls, they can get pretty jealous, and when they get jealous, they get mean."

"Ricky, I think you have plenty of access to lipstick," Randy said.

"We think that message has something to do with the recent murders in the parish. And guess what?" Ethan said. "Your fingerprints popped up all over that bathroom."

"What?" Ricky demanded, looking stunned.

"Fingerprints, buddy, they gave you away," Randy told him.

"Well, of course they did! I've used that bathroom," Ricky said.

"You sneak into your performers' bathrooms for kicks or something?" Randy demanded.

"No!" Simpson protested. "Last cruise, Mandy Drake, the country singer, was in that room. She and I are old friends. I spent lots of time with her—and not the kind of time you're probably thinking, either. We're friends, old friends. I was one of the first people to hire her, years ago."

Ethan addressed Randy. "Could the cleaning staff on the *Journey* be that bad?"

"They'd have to be pretty bad," Randy said. "You can wipe down fingerprints with just about any kind of cloth. And on a mirror, with an ammonia cleaner... easy-peasey."

"Maybe the damned mirror wasn't dirty!" Ricky snapped. "Look, I'm the entertainment director, and—"

"I think he *was* the entertainment director," Thor said.

"*Was*, yeah, I'm going to say, that's the key word," Ethan agreed.

"Lawyer! I want a lawyer," Ricky said.

"I haven't charged you with anything yet," Randy told him.

"But—"

"Actually, no one but us knows we're here, Ricky. So

I don't think you should get a lawyer. I think you should just fess up, tell us the truth," Thor said.

"Depending on your story, we might not have to go to the cruise line and tell them what you did," Ethan said.

"It's your right to get a lawyer if you want one, and you don't have to say anything until you do," Randy said to Ricky, then looked at Ethan and Thor, and added, "We want this all legit and by the book if we go to court with this jerk. We don't want any evidence tossed out because we haven't followed due process."

"Petty mischief would be one thing, and not worth the taxpayers' money, as far as taking it to court," Thor said.

"Losing your job is bad," Ethan said. "Going to jail…"

"But I didn't do anything!" Ricky protested.

Ethan shrugged and looked over at Thor and Randy. "I say he's lying."

"Sounds like a lie to me, too," Randy said.

"I'm *not* lying," Ricky protested.

"Randy, you want to write up the report?" Ethan asked. "We're going to have to look deeper, involve the captain of the ship, the VP of entertainment for Celtic American…whatever it takes to get to the truth."

"I'm afraid I'll have to take you in, Mr. Simpson," Randy said. "Stand up, please. I don't want to hurt you putting on the cuffs. Of course, once we're down at the station, you'll be able to make a call, and get your attorney," Randy said.

Ricky Simpson did exactly what they'd hoped for.

He caved. "Wait, wait, wait. Okay, I did it. Frankly, I... well, I needed the money."

"The money?" Ethan asked him.

"Yeah, I was wandering around yesterday, by the church. I listen to Jonathan Moreau whenever I can. What that man knows about history could fill the ocean. I always learn something new."

"What about the money?" Ethan interrupted impatiently.

"Oh, well, there were a bunch of people coming and going, all in uniform—some Yankee, some Reb. I asked why, because I knew there was no reenactment yesterday. Somebody said they were all working on a movie. One of the guys came up to me—he's in the movie, same movie Charlene Moreau is the star of, I guess. Anyway, he wanted to prank her. Gave me fifty bucks just to slip in and write the message on the mirror. I thought he was just teasing her, replaying a scene from the movie or something."

"You went into someone else's cabin and wrote a threat on her mirror *as a prank*?" Randy asked, disbelieving.

"Who was the man? The one who paid you?" Ethan asked.

"I don't actually know his name, but he's in the movie, so you should be able to track him down."

"What did he look like?" Ethan asked.

"Like a Civil War soldier," Ricky said.

Ethan prayed for patience. "North? South? Was he young or old?"

"Um... I think it was a Confederate uniform, but I'm not sure. I'm not from around here, so I don't pay much

attention to all that North-South stuff. The guy was…
I don't know. Twenties, thirties, maybe even early forties. He had so much beard, who the hell could tell?"

"If you saw pictures, could you recognize him?"
Ethan asked.

"Sure. Maybe. Like I said, man, he had a lot of hair
on his face."

"Okay, where's the money? You still have the money?"
Ethan asked. He glanced over at Randy. It might be a
long shot, trying to get prints off the money, but it was
possible.

"The money?" Ricky said blankly.

"The fifty dollars, the money you were paid," Ethan
said, trying to contain his irritation.

"Oh, well, I told you. I needed it. I had to replace my
phone. I spent it in town. Got the new phone, though,"
he said happily.

Randy pointed a finger at him. "First thing in the morning, we're going into town. And you better hope we can
find that cash."

"Are you—are you going to arrest me?" Ricky asked.
"It was a prank, just a prank!"

Ethan turned away in disgust. Just then his phone
rang.

Jude was calling.

As always, Jude spoke tersely but calmly and cohe-
sively. Jonathan Moreau was missing. He ran through
the whole story of finding Jennie McPherson in Jonathan's cabin and everything she'd told them. He said
Charlie was beside herself, pretty much frantic, but she

was safe with Alexi and Clara in the cabin he and Alexi were sharing.

"I'm on my way," Ethan said. "And I'm still with Laurent. He'll get an APB out."

He turned around and gave Randy Laurent the same information he'd just received.

"You. Be here and be ready to go first thing in the morning," Randy snapped to Ricky.

"Yes, whatever you say. I'll be right here, I swear. But... I'm not under arrest?" Ricky asked. "And you're not...not going to tell the captain?"

Randy didn't answer. He, Ethan and Thor were already on their way out of the room.

"I'll start looking for Moreau on the top deck," Thor said. "Jude's already called security, right?"

Ethan nodded. "I've got to get to Charlie," he said.

"No problem. Everyone is on this, Ethan," Thor assured him.

Randy nodded his agreement and said, "I'll get the ground troops moving."

Ethan turned and headed for the stairs. He had to get to Charlie—fast. God knew what she might do if she feared her father was in danger.

"I need to change," Charlie said. "I have to get out of this corset. I need to go back to my cabin."

Jude walked her to her door, then made her stay behind him as he checked out the small room and even smaller bathroom.

"All clear," he said. "I'll be with Alexi and Clara, so

you call me when you're ready, and I'll come get you. Don't you dare leave here until then, got it?"

"Got it," she said, and he left. She locked the door behind him and hurried to strip out of her costume and put on jeans and a pullover. As she slipped the shirt over her head, her phone rang.

She grabbed it, hoping it was her father, ready to explain his delay.

The caller ID read Unknown Number, but she answered anyway.

"Charlie."

Just her name—and it sounded strange, as if someone was purposely disguising his voice.

"Who is this?"

"The man who has your father."

"What?"

Charlie sank down on the foot of the bed, her heart racing.

"We have your father. And we want to talk to you. You need to ditch the army of Feds you travel with. If you ever want to see your father alive again, that is."

"I'll do anything. But I have to know what you're talking about. You have him where? What do you want me to do?"

It would be stupid, stupid, stupid to do anything this man asked her to—especially ditch the Krewe, Charlie knew. But this guy and his cohorts had her father. If they got hold of her, too, they could just kill them both. But what else could she do? She had to play for time, keep her father alive.

"How do I know you really have my father?" she asked, trying to sound calm and reasonable.

"I think you know, but I'll text you proof. You've got an hour to get here."

"You're going to be caught. You know that, right? Murdering someone else isn't going to help the situation. They *will* get you."

"No, they won't. Once you come and get your father, you'll understand."

She wished she could recognize the voice. She should. Even changed, she should have recognized it.

"Besides," the man continued, "I'm already a murderer, so what difference will one more make? You come, Charlie, or he's dead."

"Come where?"

She was surprised by the laughter that followed. "I think you'll know where once I text you. And, Charlie, if we see a cop or one of your FBI buddies, if we see you with *anyone* else, your daddy's dead. I swear, I'll kill him, even if it means I'll be caught. I'll kill him just to get even with you for bringing me down, you got that? I mean it. If I'm going down, he'll go down with me. I hear or see anyone other than you, he's dead."

Then he clicked off, and she was left listening to nothing but the sound of her own breathing.

The phone buzzed again almost instantly. She'd received a picture.

It was of her father.

And he was tied to the same tombstone she'd been tied to once, long ago, in the unhallowed ground just beyond the Grace Church graveyard.

The picture showed Jonathan Moreau, bruised and securely bound, a man standing by his side, his face turned away from the camera.

The man held an Enfield rifle, the bayonet fixed, the point of the blade touching her father's chest just above his heart.

16

Television shows and B movies were filled with people who behaved irrationally, teenagers going off alone into the woods where a murderer walked and ending up dead themselves.

If she'd ever been asked if she would behave so stupidly, Charlie would have said no. Emphatically. In fact, she would have mocked the mere possibility.

But she'd never thought about what she would do when someone she loved was threatened.

Her father. Her whole world, for so much of her life!

If she survived the night—a big if—Ethan would probably never speak to her again.

But she had the picture. They weren't bluffing. They had her father.

And once she arrived, they would still have him. The big difference? They would have her, too.

But that didn't matter. She had to go. She had to do whatever was in her power to, if not save her father, at least buy time. But…

If she went to meet them with nothing, she would

be entirely at their mercy. She wasn't about to be *that* foolish.

She hesitated, looking at the bedside table where Ethan kept his gun at night. Of course it wasn't there. Hating herself for doing it, she dug into his travel pack. To her relief, at the very bottom, she found a second weapon in a holster. She thanked God her father had taught her how to shoot. His second gun was a Smith & Wesson Bodyguard revolver. She quickly checked that it was loaded, then she slipped it into her waistband and threw on a jacket.

There *was* one thing she could do, and she did it. She left the phone on her bed. Ethan would find it.

Very carefully, she cracked the door to her cabin.

Jude was waiting in the hall.

"Hey," she said. "Sorry, but can you give me another ten minutes?"

"Sure. Whatever you need."

Damn, he was going to stay in the hallway.

"Tell Alexi and Clara I'm fine, will you? I promise I'll call as soon as I'm ready."

"Will do."

She heard his cabin door close. Silently, she slipped out and hurried down the hallway and made her way to the security point where she could exit the ship. There was a man on duty, of course, so she couldn't just glide by unseen. No choice. She produced her *Journey* ID, smiled and told the guard—who knew her both as her father's daughter and one of the Southern Belles—that she needed something at her house. He smiled and let her through.

Easy enough so far.

The others would find the picture on her phone, then have no trouble discovering that she'd left the ship, and soon enough they would be behind her. But that was what she'd wanted, right? If she and her father were going to die, at least she was certain the Krewe would catch their killers.

Once off the ship, she panicked. There weren't a lot of cabs around at this hour, and she'd left her phone behind, so she couldn't call for one.

And the clock was ticking.

She hurried to one of the main hotels and had the doorman call her a cab. The driver informed her that it was late and Grace Church was closed until the morning, but she only thanked him for his concern and said she knew that, and it was okay.

He left her in front of the church.

For a moment she paused and stared up at the facade of the church, so beautiful in the moonlight.

"Charlie?"

She spun around, her heart in her throat. To her surprise, she saw Barry Seymour on the ground, propped against the fence that went around the graveyard to the church. Blood was dripping down his forehead.

"Barry!" she cried. "What happened to you?"

"I came out because we lost some props again," he said. "I stopped here to look at the church, like you just did, and suddenly someone hit me."

She hunkered down, trying to ascertain how badly he'd been injured.

"I'm okay, I just need to get out of here." He paused, looking at her. "I think it was Jimmy, but...why?"

"Jimmy?" she said, disbelieving.

Jimmy Smith? Her friend forever and ever?

"Are you sure?" she asked. "Barry, let me help you. I have to hurry—they have my father!"

"Your father? What?" He tried to stand but fell back, unable to get his feet under him. "I'd help you, but I can't quite…get up."

"I don't have my cell, Barry. Use yours. Call for help."

He nodded and pulled out his phone. "Why didn't I think of that? It's my head. I feel so dizzy. Watch out, okay? Watch out for Jimmy."

"I will." She was torn. "I have to find my dad, but… are you sure you're all right? Until help can get here?"

He nodded.

"Then I have to go." She suddenly remembered the caller's—Jimmy's?—warning. "Barry, this is important. Tell them no lights and no sirens. If Ji—if whoever it is knows they're coming, they'll kill my dad. Okay? Do you understand me?"

He nodded again, so Charlie left him to call for help and hurried past the graveyard toward unhallowed ground.

The trees and foliage grew denser, the shadows deeper, as she went, and she had to slow down, even though everything in her longed to run. Only thin strands of moonlight penetrated the darkness, but she knew where the grave was, knew exactly where to go.

She made her way carefully through brush and over tree roots. Then, in the distance, cloaked in shadow, she saw the gravestone and the man bound to it.

And from somewhere in the trees and the shadows and the darkness, she heard a voice.

She recognized it clearly.

"Charlie, how good of you to join us."

Ethan knew immediately that something was wrong. Jude was in the hallway, knocking on the door to the cabin Ethan and Charlie had shared.

"Charlie, you all right in there?"

Ethan stared at him, frowning, and stepped past him, sliding his key into the door. He pushed the door open and stepped inside, looked briefly around the small space and headed into the bathroom.

No Charlie.

"I stood out in the hall and watched. I was gone for about sixty seconds when she asked me to tell Clara and Alexi she was fine and just needed a few more minutes. Ethan, she purposely eluded me."

Fear streaked through Ethan like a violent stab of lightning. He wanted to jump on Jude, wanted to shake him. How could he have let Charlie outsmart him like that?

But he knew Charlie, too. Knew how good an actor she was. She had probably been able to make Jude think she was fine without breaking a sweat. But she would never do anything to put herself into actual danger, not when she had people to protect her. Would she?

"All right, she eluded you. So now we're looking for Jonathan *and* Charlie."

"I'll try her father's cabin, see if she went back there

to talk to Jennie McPherson for some reason. Maybe she thinks Jennie was lying, and she knows something."

"I'll head to the departure checkpoint, see if she's tried to leave the *Journey*," Ethan said.

"Call her," Jude suggested. "You never know."

Ethan pulled out his phone, and just as he finished punching in her number, his caller ID registered an unknown caller. While his phone connected to Charlie's, he answered the incoming call.

"Delaney," he said curtly.

"Ethan?"

It was a woman's voice, but not Charlie's.

"Yes? Who is this?"

"It's Nancy. Nancy Deauville Camp."

"Nancy, this isn't a good time." As he spoke, he heard a soft buzzing sound, a phone vibrating somewhere nearby.

In the room.

"Ethan, I know, I'm sorry. I'm closing up at Mrs. Mama's, and I just gave a cabdriver a last cup of coffee. We should have been closed, but he came just before I locked the door, and I felt sorry for him."

"Okay?"

Jude had found the ringing phone and held it up. It was Charlie's, and it had been lying on the bed.

"Nancy, I have to go."

"Sorry. Anyway, the driver just took someone who sounded like Charlie out to Grace Church. He was going on about crazy women wanting to go ghost hunting all alone, and I just wanted to call and make sure everything was okay."

As Nancy finished speaking, Jude showed Ethan Charlie's phone.

The last message she'd received was a picture.

A picture of her father.

Tied to a tombstone.

He barely managed to grunt out a thank-you to Nancy before he hung up.

"Let's go," he told Jude.

He was already headed out the cabin door.

He stopped short the second he stepped out into the hall. Ellsworth Derue was there. "Come on," he urged Ethan. "Hurry!"

"I'm way ahead of you," Ethan said softly.

"Charlie," Jonathan said when she reached him at a run. "Charlie, you shouldn't have come. Go, run—please, get out of here!"

"I can't, Dad," she said, bending down to study the ropes that bound him to the tombstone. They were tied tight—very tight—but she found an end and started working at the knot, which began to give. "Almost got it, Dad, almost got it," she murmured.

Too late. She heard a rustling, the killers in the bushes behind them, waiting to spring at her.

She turned and drew the Smith & Wesson from her waistband, then aimed it at the man coming toward them.

She'd known the voice, because she knew the man.

And it wasn't Jimmy.

It was Grant Ferguson. Another friend—or so she had thought.

He smiled at her. He was in full uniform, as if he'd

just finished filming. And he was carrying the Enfield, bayonet attached.

"Don't come any nearer," she warned.

"Why, look at you, Charlie, toting a big mean gun. I'd never have figured."

"Just because I don't particularly like guns doesn't mean I don't respect them and know how to use them," Charlie said, surprised that her voice was so cool and calm. "Why are you doing this?"

"Come on, don't play dumb. Your dad here was about to figure it out. And of course you did see me trying to cover up the corpse."

"What?" she asked.

"You were there, the day we filmed. Right when the ghost army was rising. I saw you look at me. I was shifting dirt around, trying to cover up the body more thoroughly. Sooner or later you'd remember what you saw and start wondering what I was doing."

"You idiot! She didn't know anything until you just went and told her," Jonathan said, tugging at the ropes. "None of us had a clue, so why the hell did you have to kill anyone in the first place?"

"Why? Because those two idiots would have ruined everything," Grant said. "I argued and argued with Albion. Told him he had to leave Gideon Oil alone and not propose that stupid new plan of his. I have money tied up with Gideon Oil and that pipeline. Everything, actually. And if old Saul Gideon had agreed to Sane Energy's proposed changes, well… I might've been dead and buried myself before I finally saw a return on my investment. So I got rid of Albion. Okay, in all honesty? I didn't intend to kill him. I lured him out to talk by telling him that we were looking to do some very special filming, and I needed to see him in uniform. So I was in uniform, too, and...well, he wouldn't listen. So he had to be dealt with. And I had no choice when old Farrell Hickory got suspicious and I had to kill him, too. Such an old fool—didn't even think to be afraid for himself."

Charlie held the gun steady on him. "Well, now you won't need money. I don't think there's much to buy in prison."

"Now who's the idiot? I'm not going to prison, Charlie."

"Okay, I'll just shoot you."

"No, you won't."

"Why not?"

"Because we were afraid you might try to pull something, maybe even bring a gun."

"We? You're working with Jimmy Smith? And, yes, I know about Jimmy, because he beat up Barry. But Barry's still alive, and he told me."

"Barry just pretended Jimmy had beat him up. Barry is fine. In fact, he's quite close and has been for a few minutes." He smiled, savoring the information he was about to deliver. "Right now Barry has a precision rifle aimed at your father. You might want to check for that little red laser dot on your dad's chest."

"So you want me to throw down my gun and let you shoot both of us?" Charlie said. "You're not going to let us go. I never saw a damned thing, but now that you've confessed, you have no choice but to kill us, do you? And what about that poor woman you killed in Baton

Rouge? Selma Rodriguez. She didn't deserve to die. She didn't know anything, either. And whether you kill us or not, the truth will come out. They're meeting with Saul Gideon tomorrow." She thought that what she'd said was true. She wasn't sure. But she'd learned from Ethan— sound like you know what you're talking about! "They'll start investigating all the shareholders, and they'll find you. They'll find you and arrest you, and you'll rot in prison. There's no way out."

"Charlie, drop the damned gun!" Grant roared furiously. "Shoot, Barry! Just shoot. Shoot the old man first. We'll let Charlie see her dad die."

"Don't shoot, Barry. I'm a crack shot and I will kill Grant," Charlie said, wondering if she'd managed to talk long enough for help to arrive. Everything depended on how quickly Ethan had found her phone.

"I don't give a damn if you shoot Grant. You and your father will still die, and I'll get off scot-free. I already called in about my 'injury' and blamed it on Jimmy Smith, saying he attacked me. Jimmy will look guilty as all hell—of just about everything," Barry said, pleased with himself. "That'll tie everything up neatly." He grinned. "Jimmy will be too dead to protest."

"What the fuck?" Grant demanded, spinning around. "You don't care if they shoot me?"

"Hey," Barry said. "I was there with you, trying to get those guys to back down. You killed them. I was there."

"You were just as involved with the stocks as I was. Bull! You're in this all the way."

"Hey, go ahead, Charlie. Yeah, Grant, they *should* shoot you—rather you than me. I'm not going down!"

Jonathan took that split second to show he'd finished what Charlie had started; he was free. He jumped up, forcing Charlie to the ground as Barry let out a shot. Charlie shifted out from under her father and fired, but she was off balance, and her shot went wild.

She and her father rolled desperately down a small slope in the old overgrown graveyard, and somehow the Smith & Wesson flew from her grasp. They came to a stop behind an old gravestone and took advantage of what little cover it provided. She looked around, seeking the gun she'd lost, but it was too dark, and she couldn't see where it had landed.

"Get up, but stay low," her father whispered. "Head for the trees and hide."

"The gun—" she began.

"No time, Charlie, just run."

She rose but remained hunched low behind the stone.

Shots rang out, but their pursuers seemed to be firing in the wrong direction.

"Where the hell are they?" Barry roared in the night.

"Run, Charlie, run hard," Jonathan urged.

"Dad, you—"

"I'll be right behind you."

Charlie ran. She heard another shot—and an explosion as a nearby gravestone burst into fragments.

Either Grant and Barry had gotten lucky, or they had figured out where she and her father had gone.

So she ran. Ran hard, into the trees. She heard Grant and Barry thrashing through the trees and brush behind her, close, so close.

A mist seemed to be rising. She was lost, no idea anymore where she should run.

But she could hear Barry and Grant coming up behind her, close, so close....

More shots, but she didn't hear her father scream and had to believe he was still safe, still running.

The mist was growing thicker. Charlie slammed into a tree so hard she was momentarily stunned. She staggered back and fell, then pushed herself up, trying to rise.

And then she saw them.

It was exactly as it had been when they were filming, except now...

Now it was real.

They rose from the earth, one by one, spectral shapes that slowly populated the high bluff where the church had long held dominion over the landscape. If she blinked, they might have been a part of the mist, they were so ethereal. And then, as she watched with eyes wide open, they became what they really were: ghostly soldiers, rising from their graves, worn, war-weary, dirty, sweaty and exhausted, yet ready to fight for what they believed was right.

Here in this narrow strip of Louisiana between Baton Rouge and Fort Hudson, the Civil War had one day come to a halt, and as a result the men who rose from the earth wore both the tattered butternut and gray of the South, and Union blue. They'd been good men in life, and they rose together now, ready to fight shoulder to shoulder, for at a time when the nation had been torn apart in tragic conflict, they had found, for a few brief moments, peace and friendship.

They were a ghost army, ragged and unearthly, chilling and terrifying in the night, shadows of vengeance marching in the moonlight.

They moved slowly in otherworldly splendor, spectral shapes, faces hardened, joined together to protect the innocent and destroy evil.

Someone flesh and blood burst through the trees. Barry Seymour, wielding his rifle.

He started to aim it at Charlie when one of the ghosts stepped in front of him. It was Captain Anson McKee, Confederate States Cavalry. Barry looked at him and screamed, staggering back. But he still had the gun, and he tried to fire at the apparition before him. Bullets glanced off trees, and he cried out, "I'll kill you, Charlie. So help me God, I'll kill you!"

There was a sudden hard thrashing through the trees, and then another voice rang out—strong, furious.

Ethan.

"Not in this lifetime, you won't, asshole!"

He fired a warning shot over Barry's head and shouted, "Drop the gun!"

Barry fired wildly again.

Ethan fired once more, this time hitting Barry in the arm that held the gun. Barry screeched and fell to the dirt. Ethan strode over to him, ignoring the man's wails, and secured the weapon.

"Ethan, be careful!" Charlie called as he came to her. "Grant Ferguson is still out there, somewhere close. I don't know if it works or not, but he has an old Enfield."

As she spoke, Grant came bursting through the trees, the Enfield aimed at them.

But Ethan turned on a dime and fired, and Grant went down just like Barry had, howling in pain. Ethan went over and claimed that weapon, too. Then he returned to Charlie, giving her a hand and drawing her to her feet. He pulled her into his arms, and for a moment she just stood there, shaking, grateful for his warmth and glad of his strength. Then she pulled away from him and said, "My father—"

"Is fine!" Jude called, walking over to join them, with her father leaning heavily against him.

Charlie let out a glad cry and rushed into her father's arms.

"Charlie, Charlie, Charlie…you shouldn't have come for me."

He stopped speaking and just held her, then suddenly he pulled back, and she realized he was staring over her shoulder. She turned to see what he was looking at.

They were still there.

Tattered, weary soldiers, Union and Confederate, watching. Captain Anson McKee was there, and Ellsworth Derue stood at his cousin's side.

As one, they lifted their hands and saluted.

Ethan and Jude saluted in return. As Charlie watched, her father smiled in wonder and saluted the men, as well.

Then the soldiers drifted away to become part of the mist. Anson and Ellsworth were the last to disappear.

The distant sound of sirens reached them, faint at first but growing louder. Charlie began to shake. It was over.

And yet she felt strangely that her life was just beginning.

Northern Virginia was going to be wonderful.

Working with Alexi and Clara again would be great.

But, most of all, life with Ethan would be everything she wanted.

* * * * *